3314733

5/16

#2

D1306191

I Could

By E.B. Tatby

331H133

This book is a work of fiction. Names, characters, businesses, organizations, places, events, and incidents either are the product of the author's imagination or are used fictitiously. Any resemblance to actual persons, living or dead, events, or locales is entirely coincidental.

Copyright © 2015 E.B. Tatby (Dream Tag)

All rights reserved.

Cover photos by Eric Stoiber.

Cover Design by Christa Holland, Paper & Sage Design

Editing by Susan Reynolds.

ISBN: 978-1-941051-04-7

To my beautiful daughters
who have given me so much joy and inspiration

Chapter 1

As I rocked in the backyard hammock, my tablet resting on my knees, the wings of a hummingbird caught my eye. It hovered near the lilac bushes I'd helped my mom plant last spring. Nothing magical had happened for months—no jinns, specifically, no Jinny Zzaman whisking me away to ancient Morocco, and no Jamila of Diab waiting for me—not since I left camp last summer. So when the deep blue color of the bush's flower pedals and the green of its leaves seemed more vibrant than usual, I shuddered at how they resembled the colors in the wishing stone I'd lost to the Pacific Ocean.

That stone—the Amulet of Omnia—had been the only thing stopping the evil spirit Mazin from haunting me, and keeping everyone I loved in danger. As if designed for that purpose, the stone's perfect size and shape corked his dark spirit, within my boyfriend Ian's hand-carved wooden bottle. Whenever I needed to feel safe, I pictured that bottle bobbing up and down over the choppy ocean waves. At the time, I'd been desperate to banish Mazin, but now I regretted throwing the bottle out over the sea and not keeping it close under my careful watch, as Ian had suggested.

I shook my head to clear my mind. It was the first day all year that the sun over Omaha invited me to bask in it. Most years in March I tried to avoid the outdoors at all costs, only venturing out once I bundled myself in thick insulating layers, and only for a few minutes at a time. I stole another glance at the hummingbird. The sun glinted off its metallic blue body, reminding me of Jinny Zzaman's sparkly dress, particularly when the blur of its wings flapped so fast they seemed to defy convention. Six months ago, when I turned sixteen, so much defied convention. How many teenage girls in Omaha were drawn back to their ancestor's home, 500 years prior, to undo evils that threatened everything she held dear? If I hadn't found allies at the summer camp—particularly Ian—battling Mazin and his evil forces would likely have been futile.

1

"What are you doing out here?" Dad's voice rang out behind me.

I hadn't heard the sliding door open and the sound of his voice made me jump. The hammock swayed dramatically sending my shiny new tablet, which I adored beyond words, tumbling with a crunch onto the cement patio.

"Dad, you scared me." I glared at him, but he didn't seem to notice.

"Kenza Atlas, I told you to be careful with that thing." He bent down to scoop up the tablet.

"You can't just sneak up on me like that," I said. I was still in shock about the tablet, certain the fall had damaged it. Worse, I was afraid my dad was about to flip out.

"Don't put the blame on me," he said. He straightened forcefully, striking the edge of the hammock on his way up. It flipped me sideways and I throttled toward the cement, just like my tablet had.

Dad stood there cradling the tablet in both hands, burning a hole through me with his eyes. He turned, wordless, and walked to the patio table gently setting the tablet on the stone tabletop before returning to help me. When he reached me, he held out his hand and I pushed it away.

"My Kenza," he said in a whisper.

I hoisted myself up, straightened, and stole a glance down at my bare legs (it was the first day warm enough to wear shorts and flips flops). Blood streaked from my knees to my ankles in messy lines.

"You care more about that stupid tablet than you do about me." Deep down, I was just as pissed as my dad. It was my tablet and it was new and I needed it. Who didn't have a laptop or a tablet at my age, anyway? I was the only person I knew of who didn't—until a few months ago, when I got it as a Christmas present.

"Do you have any idea what I had to do to get it?" Dad bellowed.

"Not this again." I threw up my hands and turned away.

"Your tablet was a high-end model, the best available." He talked to the back of my head. "I had to stand in a line that wrapped all the way around Nebraska Furniture Mart. It was Black Friday and I waited, in the

2

cold, from 4:30 in the morning until they opened their doors at 6:30. When I finally walked through those doors, my toes had—"

"Gone numb, Dad." I spun around to face him. "I get it. It was . . . what . . . zero degrees outside?"

He pulled in a long slow breath, exhaled slowly. "Twenty-five degrees. But you try doing that same thing and see if you will last."

Tired of feeling less important than an electronic device, I bolted for the house. Once inside, I sped around the corner ready to thunder up the stairs to my room—and collided with my mom, causing a clumsy tangle of arms and legs, and sending her reeling backward. I quickly regained my balanced and pushed myself up.

Mom had turned to her side and folded into the fetal position, still lying on the carpeted stairs. The signs of pain painted across her pale face ripped me out of my rampage. "Mom. Mom, are you okay?"

Dangerous thoughts ricocheted through my mind: broken bones, internal bleeding, something worse? The color slowly spilled back into her cheeks.

"I'm sorry, Mom," I whispered.

Mom held her hand up signaling for me to wait until she could catch her breath. I couldn't stand waiting, which she well knew.

Finally, she nodded. "I'm okay, Kenza." The breath I didn't realize I was clinging to released slowly. She reached for me, wrapped her hand around my forearm. I half expected her to dig her nails in, but she gave it only a gentle squeeze. "You've got to be more careful, Kenza. You could have seriously hurt me."

Just then, Dad rounded the corner. "Kenza, what did you do?"

I winced. Of course he would assume I'd done it on purpose.

He rushed over, knelt down next to Mom. "My Stars, are you okay? Maybe you should go to the doctor."

"Adam, I'm fine," she said. "Please. You don't need to—"

When she stopped talking abruptly, I followed her eyes to my reddened knees. It looked worse than it was.

3

"What happened to you?" she asked, concern rising in her voice. "Kenza, are you okay?"

I glanced at Dad and he straightened up, his oversized Moroccan eyes opening wide. "She fell out of her hammock. Her tablet—"

Without saying another word, he grabbed my arm and led me toward the kitchen.

"Please, my Moon, let's get you cleaned up." His voice had softened.

As we walked, he eased his hand into the flat of my back, which usually sent twitchy nerves skittering under my skin, but I still wasn't myself after the tornado I just caused. We entered the kitchen and he dragged one of the chairs out from the table. Its legs grated against the wood floor. I sat down while he got disinfectant and gauze, and I removed my blood stained shoes and socks.

He bent down in front of me and patted at the blood. Tears welled up in my eyes.

"I'm sorry, my Moon," he said softly.

I didn't say anything. I didn't have to. I let out an uncontrolled giggle and grabbed for a napkin on the kitchen table to dry my eyes.

"You know, this wouldn't have happened if you were paying attention," he said.

I rolled my eyes. Dad rarely apologized or complimented me, and it was always short-lived. A complaint or criticism closely trailed anything positive that came out of his mouth.

"What were you staring at out there, anyway?" he asked.

"Didn't you see it? The hummingbird?"

"There was no hummingbird, Kenza." Certainty fortified his words.

"It must have flown behind the flowering bush, then," I said.

"Flowering bush? Kenza, did you hit your head when you fell?"

Instinctively, I reached for the back of my head, rubbed. "No, I—"

He crinkled the paper from the bandages in his hands, chucked it in the garbage on his way out of the kitchen, and turned back to see me still sitting in the chair. "Aren't you coming?"

I followed him to the sliding glass doors that led to the patio and pushed my face up to the glass. I had to squint to be sure I was seeing correctly. I shook my head. "No . . . no, no."

I opened the door, walked straight to the Lilac bush. It was still dormant—no trace of azurite blue flowers or malachite green leaves. I reached out to pinch one of the leaves between my fingers; it was one of the few dead ones that still clung to the bush despite the harsh winter. It disintegrated between my fingers.

"Kenza, did you see flowers on this bush today?" I felt Dad's hand rest on my shoulder.

I turned slowly, nodded. "Umm-huh. I mean I thought I did. I must have imagined it when I saw the hummingbird." As fast as this scene was playing out, I realized I'd better cover it up somehow. A fleeting feeling of panic rushed through my veins. Had Mazin escaped? Was Jinny Zzaman about to summon me again? Until I knew whether the mysterious forces were good forces or evil ones, I needed to stay silent.

"Kenza," Dad said, his voice stern. "Hummingbirds don't migrate through Omaha for another four weeks."

If he glimpsed any sign of panic rising inside of me, I couldn't tell. He was, however, using his most gentle voice. "The time has come for me to share something with you, my Moon, something very special."

Chapter 2

"What are you talking about, Dad? Ancient knee healing remedies?" I'd just revealed a magical encounter to the last person on Earth I wanted to know, and I had to cover my tracks fast.

"Better than that." He smiled warmly. He had that look in his eyes—the look he got when he talked about the Tribe of Diab, jinns, or anything from his Moroccan past. Part of me cringed and the other part—the more powerful part, the one who had experienced his magical jinns and met some of his ancient ancestors firsthand—couldn't wait to find out what he was up to.

Mom and I followed Dad up the stairs to the creepy attic door—the one I'd always hurried past when I was little, afraid something ghostly might jump out and snatch me. He opened the door and we followed him up another set of stairs, natural wood stairs that smelled a hundred years old and coughed up visible dust with each step.

We were a tight family, the three of us, even though I didn't like to admit it. A few of my friends had more brothers or sisters than they could keep track of, like Ryan back at camp. A big family would have driven me crazy. Being an only child had its drawbacks, but I knew the benefits outweighed them. I had more privacy than I would ever get if I had little brothers and sisters, and I got more attention than I wanted, like this jaunt to reveal a "very special" surprise.

When we reached the top of the staircase, Dad extended his hands above his head and pushed the attic door, which doubled as a ceiling, up and over. The overwhelming scent of mildew wafted through the opening.

I stuck my head up through the opening in the floor and peered around. I needed time to adjust to the dimly lit attic and the odor protruding from it. Dad took a step forward and the floor creaked under his feet. "Come on you two." He reached his hand out to help us out—me first and then Mom. "Rats are summer animals. You'll never see them in the middle of March," he added just as Mom stepped onto the attic floor.

If he was trying to be funny, it backfired. My nerves were already brittle before I considered rodents skittering among the stacks of bags, and I knew Mom was no fan of the little creatures.

"I'm going back down," Mom said, turning back toward the stairs.

"Right behind you, Mom."

Dad sighed loudly. "Wait, you two. I need you to see something."

"Can't we see it later, Dad?" I asked, already knowing the answer.

"Kenza, you don't understand. I should have shown you months ago." He shook his head, looking disgusted with himself. "I didn't want to admit that you were ready—that you were already sixteen, my sweet sixteen."

I turned to face him. "What do you mean 'already sixteen'?"

"What I mean is . . . what we're about to do is a tradition." He tilted his head to the side, looking at me more like I was six. I recognized that tilt. It was the same one Jinny Zzaman used whenever she wanted the nonsensical words she was speaking to mysteriously make sense to me.

"I'm listening." I made sure my voice sounded flat enough to mask my anxiety, but my heart raced faster and faster.

"Kenza, I'm going back down," Mom warned. "Are you coming or not?"

"Mom, wait." I turned back to Dad. "Tell me about this tradition." It came out sounding like an order, if that was possible with a dad like mine. He looked pleased.

"Happy to." He emphasized the "h" as if he were blowing out a candle, indicating his Moroccan accent had kicked up a notch again—it always did when he was telling me about the legends. "For hundreds of years, it has been the tradition to share a box of heirlooms with the oldest child, son or daughter, on the day they turn sixteen. It is the day when

7

that child—you, in our case—becomes their rightful heir." He dropped his gaze to the floor, searching for the box.

"What's in it?" I asked, intrigued but also suddenly feeling queasy. I wondered if it would shed any light on our ancestor Jamila of Diab—the one I'd met and fought to save last summer—the ruthless Tribe of Diab, or worse, its leader Mazin. I instinctively knew the answer but I dreaded confirmation. Still, I was comforted in knowing that my cruel and inhuman pursuer, Mazin, was still imprisoned somewhere in the Pacific Ocean. I hoped he was seasick.

"It's amazing, my Kenza. You won't believe it," Dad said. The excitement in his voice reminded me of my little cousin Kaleb whenever I took him to the ice cream shop. "Now where is it?" Dad muttered, kicking boxes and pushing piles out of the way.

"Amazing how?" I drew closer to him.

"Ah, here it is," he said, crouching down. "Yes. Kenza, help me move this stuff out of the way so I can get to the box."

"No."

"What?" He turned to look at me, stunned.

"I don't blame you, Kenza," Mom said, her head still poking up through the opening. "The smell is starting to get to me." She covered her mouth with the back of her hand.

"No, Mom, I want to help, but first I want to hear what's so amazing about the box." Even in the dim lighting, I could see Mom frown. She'd never understood my dad's obsession with the legends. I didn't either, until Jinny Zzaman showed up in my bedroom wearing her stunning sparkling blue dress and transported me back in time to ancient Morocco—to when I became a part of the tragedy, but also a force to help heal ancestral wounds. Now, I was as obsessed with the legends as my dad, maybe even more. But my parents had no idea what I'd experienced at camp, no idea of the dangers they'd been in, or how closely we all came to dying.

"Ah," Dad replied in a more understanding tone. "Of course you are interested, Kenza. Do you remember when I told you about the Amulet of Omnia?"

8

My breath caught, and I instinctively reached for the protective necklace that had once hung around my neck—until I chucked it into the ocean. "Yeah, of course I remember," I said, modulating my voice. "Why?"

"In this box, there's a drawing," he explained. "It's old. I don't know how old, but it has to be centuries. There are also details about this energy field called—"

"Nor," I accidentally blurted it out and then nearly clutched my hand over my mouth. Luckily, I managed to stop myself before my hand reached my lips.

He raised an eyebrow at me.

Mom crossed her arms. "I've heard enough."

Dad didn't seem to hear her, but he definitely heard me. He stood quickly, grabbed both of my arms, and looked directly into my eyes. "How do you know about Nor?"

"You've told me about it before," I offered. He shook his head, peered into my eyes. "Okay, I looked it up on the Internet, Dad." I couldn't tell him that the spirit of Jamila of Diab warned me about it last summer.

If the lights had been brighter, my warm cheeks would have given me away.

He scratched his head, shook it. "Yes, of course."

"Here, let me help." I was eager to get to the bottom of the contents in the ancient box and I moved quickly.

"Be careful," Mom warned.

"We will," Dad called impatiently.

He planted himself on one side of the mystical box and I mirrored him on the other side. First, we had to shove a bunch of junk to an opening closer to the slanted attic wall: a pile of dusty boxes and bags, an old set of gloves with a softball tucked inside of one, some Christmas wreaths, and a pair of ice skates. Mom tapped her fingers on the attic door to mark the minutes she must have thought we were wasting. Dad moved a final pile out of the way and I stole a better look at the box. It, like everything else in the attic, was dusty—smaller than a shoe box, but it stood out instantly.

"Camel bone," Dad said, pointing at it.

"What do you mean 'camel bone'?" I muttered.

"The box," he said. "The off-white pieces of the mosaic design are carved camel bone."

"Speed it up you two," Mom urged. "It's starting to rain."

My hopes of enjoying any more blissful sunshine on the hammock washed away with her words.

Dad took a step forward and leaned down to grab the box. As he did, his foot caught on a gap in the floor and he almost face-planted onto a pile of black plastic bags, but caught himself awkwardly. An attic creature, who was probably hoping it wouldn't be disturbed, squeaked and Dad squealed like a girl.

It wasn't a rat. It was a bat with a 12-inch wingspan and eyes that gleamed red in the dim lighting. Mom's head disappeared as she bolted for the bottom of the staircase. Dad and I scampered after her as fast as humanly possible. Mom was a few steps in front of me and when she almost reached the bottom, she tripped.

Everything happened in slow motion and I stood frozen a few stairs up, helpless to do anything to stop it. All the time I'd spent last summer learning to wish proved useless. Within one hour of noticing what might have been a faint sign of Jinny Zzaman's sparkly blue dress in the hummingbird's wing or Jamila of Diab's Amulet of Omnia in the lilac bush, my mom seemed clearly in peril. I flashed back on last summer, when she nearly died, and for the first time in eons, wished their apparitions would flicker and take shape before me, though I knew they would never do so in front of my parents. I, alone, had to bear the responsibility, something I'd learned the hard way last summer.

From behind her on the stairs, all I could see were Mom's flailing arms and legs twisting in directions that would most likely end in a fracture. Her back bent into an awkward it-shouldn't-be-possible position and she thrust her arms out in front of her, but they didn't extend fast enough. From my angle, it looked like she did a belly flop onto the hardwood floor at the base of the stairs.

10

She screamed and Dad shouted, "God bless us."

Tears welled in my eyes. I stood gawking—frozen in fear, unaware I was blocking Dad from reaching her. He gruffly pushed me out of the way and skipped the last two steps all together. My perfect sunny March day had turned dangerously ugly, dangerously fast.

Rain suddenly pattered threateningly against the roof and a heavy surge of thunder rolled in, followed by illuminating flashes and cracks of lightning that lit up every window near the hallway. In an exaggerated panic, I wondered if the storm had taken residence strictly over our house, singling us out while letting the sun shine down on every other house in my neighborhood, or if it was like most storms that simply dished out its fury, in even doses, to everyone.

When the light show was over, I watched Dad fawn over Mom. Thunder exploded again with fury, sounding so close that, for a moment, I thought the noise came from the attic. I crouched right there on the stairs, covering my head on instinct.

"Kenza," Dad said. "Forget the rain."

I shook my head. The rain could be attempting a hostile coup.

"Kenza, listen to me," Dad said.

I stared at him, blinking, trying to rein in careening thoughts.

"Your mother's hurt. I need you to call 9 – 1 – 1!"

"9 – 1 – 1? Are you sure?" I was stunned. I didn't think she'd really gotten hurt that badly. Surprisingly, her legs hadn't twisted as much as I thought and she seemed to be moving them just fine. Another thunderclap rattled the ceiling. "Can't we drive her to the hospital?"

Dad stood and planted his foot on the first stair, leaning on his knee. In a flat, serious voice that reminded me of the one Ian had used last summer, he said, "It may be a matter of life and death."

Chapter 3

Here we go again with the whole life and death bit, I thought. I'd overdosed on that game last summer, and I wasn't remotely ready for round two, but it only took a second for the gravity of the situation to sink in. It ignited a fire within me. I squeezed past my parents and sprinted down the hallway until I reached the stairs. A matter of life and death, Dad's words echoed through my mind, replaying over and over. I thundered down the staircase to the main floor, skipping the last two steps like I used to do when I was little.

I ran into the kitchen, expecting to see my cell phone on the counter and remembered that I'd left it under the hammock. I ran to the sliding glass door, hesitated for a few quick breaths for fear I might get struck by lightning, and—once I found my courage—slipped through the opening, hurrying to the hammock. The rain poured down so hard that water was starting to pool on the patio, but the cover of the hammock seemed to have prevented the phone from getting damaged. My tablet, on the other hand, had a different fate. I glanced over at the table and saw it lying there soaking up rain, since it was now cracked on the screen and had no cover.

I grabbed both devices and rushed back toward the house. As I ran, lightning stabbed down, probably far away, but it felt like it was striking just behind me. Instinctively, I turned back to see a dark shadowy figure standing in front of the now drenched lilac bush. Was it Mazin or simply my imagination playing tricks again? I ran in, slid the door shut and quickly locked it, opened my phone to make the call but it wouldn't turn on. I pushed the power button and held it in but nothing was working. Dad was going to kill me for ruining a tablet and a cell phone in one day. He'd probably even peg Mom's fall on me.

I threw my dripping cell phone and tablet onto the dining room table and ran into the kitchen, my bare feet still wet from the patio. I slid across the wood floor, almost losing my balance but caught myself just in time to grab for the home phone. My fingers stabbed at the numbers 9 – 1 and the lights overhead flickered out with a flash and a boom.

"Hurry Kenza," Dad called.

"I can't see," I called back. The clouds had turned black and it looked like it was well past sunset, even though it wasn't even close—the house was sheathed in complete darkness.

"Do something, Kenza. Every second counts," Dad called.

I tapped the last button on the house phone and the key pad lit up, but I didn't have a dial tone.

"Mom," I called in the direction of the stairs.

Dad answered for her. "What? What are you doing?"

"The phone doesn't work and my cell's dead." I was now leaning against the counter in the dark kitchen.

Mom tried to respond but it came out more like a stifled moan. I could barely hear her over the pounding rain.

"Mom?"

Dad hollered, "Our cell phones are both charging upstairs on the night stand."

"I need a flashlight," I called, even though they couldn't do anything about it.

I fumbled through the junk drawer running my hand through the over-packed piles of miscellaneous papers, safety pins, keys, and pencils. Finally, I grasped a cylindrical object, yanked my hand out of the drawer, fastened the flashlight cord around my wrist, and ran up the stairs, skipping every other one. Just then, the realization that my cell phone battery only needed charging, and wasn't likely broken, hit me and I celebrated the one tiny piece of good news I'd had in the past hour.

"Everything's going to be okay, Jackie. I promise," Dad said, just as I reached the top of the stairs. He didn't usually fawn over people so I realized this was really serious.

I reached my parents' room and scuttled around to the other side of the bed to my mom's night stand. I swiped both phones from the tabletop, accidentally knocking the alarm clock into the garbage can, but I didn't dare stop to fish it out.

"I got it," I called. "I'll be there in a sec." I dialed 9 – 1 – 1 as I ran for the attic door.

"9 – 1 – 1, what's your emergency?" a female voice said.

By the time I reached my parents, I was dictating our address to the woman with the unnaturally calm voice on the phone. It reminded of when Keelam almost drowned last summer. Then I remembered how Jamila of Diab had visited me that same day and wondered if she would show up soon to mitigate this nightmare.

"Stay with me until the ambulance arrives," the woman on the phone ordered. "Can you do that?"

"Yeah okay," I said, pacing up and down the hallway. I tried to abolish all thoughts of the paranormal. "Let me tell my mom and dad what's going on."

I pulled the phone away from my ear and covered the receiver with my hand. "An ambulance is on the way."

Mom's head was resting on Dad's leg; he was stroking her hair. Mom clutched her stomach and I hoped it wasn't a broken rib. Her cheeks were stained with tears.

I ran down the stairs and peered through the window frame of the front door, but saw no one.

"Are you still with me, Kenza?" the woman on the phone said.

"Yeah, but where are they? You should see my mom. She never acts like this. She's afraid."

"Everything's going to be okay," the woman assured me, but how could she know for sure? "The ambulance will be there any minute."

Memories of Mazin torturing my mom last year flashed through my mind. "You don't know what you're talking about," I blurted. "You don't know how powerful he is." What was I saying? I had to cut myself off right then and there.

"How powerful who is? Kenza, is there someone after you?" She raised her voice, concerned. "If there's someone after you, I need to know right now so I can call the police."

Finally, I saw the ambulance pull into the driveway. "No, no it's okay. I was talking about bad luck, that's all."

"Bad luck . . . ?"

She wasn't buying it, so I shut her down. "They're here. The ambulance is here. Thank you, thank you, thank you."

I hung up the phone and opened the door for the two EMTs who were running toward the door in the rain, flashlights darting around. They reminded me of the ERT who had saved Ian after he injured his ankle in Shadow Forest back at camp.

"Where is she?" The blond one said as he crossed the threshold into our living room. His voice sounded deeper than I expected for his short stature.

I lead them up the normal staircase, and then to the attic door. When we reached my parents, Dad immediately ordered me to retrieve my shoes and Mom's purse. I obeyed and the lights flickered back on, which allowed me to move a lot faster than I would have in the dark. By the time I made it back downstairs, the EMTs were pushing Mom on a gurney toward the front door.

"Go ride with your mother in the ambulance," Dad said as he pointed toward the driveway.

"What about you?" It was one of those rare times when I wanted him to come with us.

"I'll see you at the hospital," he reassured me. "I want the car there in case she needs to stay for a while."

I must have looked panicked because that's how I felt inside at hearing his words.

"Kenza," Dad said sternly. "I didn't mean that. I meant that they will probably release her right away. If they do, we'll be able to take her home."

He must have seen that I wasn't buying that.

15

"It's okay," he said softly. "It will be okay. Your mom is going to be fine."

"I'll drive," I said. I'd obtained my license in December, but I had very little driving experience thanks to my overprotective dad and worrisome mom.

"Kenza, you're in no condition to drive—"

"Miss." The tall, balding EMT reached for one of the back doors on the ambulance and closed it. "We have to go." I looked back at Dad one more time and then jumped in. The EMT jumped in behind me and pulled the other door shut, but the sound got swallowed by a thunderclap.

Chapter 4

On the ride to the hospital, I sat next to my mom on the bench in the back of the ambulance. The EMT made me wear an awkward harness whose octopus straps wrapped around me in a hug. It reminded me of something Mazin and the Tribe of Diab would use to torture innocent people, making them powerless to resist. I was glad for the harness, though. The ambulance raced around corners, jolting me back and forth more times than I cared to count.

"You okay, Mom?" I tried to smile. Whenever I got hurt, she always cheered me up.

Mom smiled faintly. "I'll be okay, Kenza, thanks to you."

My smile slipped away. Her gratitude should have eased my worries, but it only multiplied them. It was thanks to me that my tablet was cracked and sopping wet, thanks to me that my mom first got the wind knocked out of her and then nearly fractured every bone in her body. Hell, it was thanks to me that Mazin's dark spirit almost destroyed my family last year, along with so many other innocent people.

That last thought exploded into a volcano of panic erupting in my mind. Why had it been so long since Jinny Zzaman or Jamila of Diab contacted me? Could Mazin have actually escaped and found some way to block my jinn companions, or worse? The only talisman powerful enough to generate that kind of energy was the Amulet of Omnia, and Mazin would have to be free from his prison for its properties to work.

"Kenza," Mom whispered.

"Mom, what? What's wrong?" I leaned as close to her as the straps would allow.

"Your necklace," she seemed to want to point toward my neck, but ended up just lifting a finger. "Remember how you used to grasp it when you felt frightened?"

I reached up and flattened my hand over my chest, remembering what it used to feel like to grasp the amulet whenever I'd felt nervous—or needed to make a wish. It always instantly warmed under my grip, which calmed my nerves. "Yeah," I finally said. "I wish I hadn't left it at camp."

"Maybe it'll still be there where you left it." She smiled warmly. "I want to see it if you do find it," she added. Then she clutched her stomach and turned away so I couldn't see the worried lines on her face.

As we sped along in silence, more than anything, I wanted to lock Mom's pain up in that bottle with Mazin, and send it floating out to sea. I squeezed my eyes shut, repeated Jinny Zzaman's name three times silently in my head, followed by a wish to relieve Mom's pain. I couldn't sniff even a hint of Jinny's foul odor—why she had always been accompanied by the smell of rotten eggs made no sense to me—didn't feel wind against my face, didn't feel a thing, so I opened my eyes and found Mom staring at me.

"Kenza, are you okay?" she asked, looking concerned.

"Mom, yeah, of course? Why?"

"When you closed your eyes, I—"

"You what?" I quipped, purposefully interrupting. "Did you see something?" I added, too eagerly.

"No, I—what do you mean 'did I see something?' All I saw was you with your eyes squeezed shut." She eyed me suspiciously.

"Oh, well, I was praying, Mom." It was partially true. I had been asking for supernatural aid to help someone in need—so yeah, I was praying.

That seemed to pacify her. Her lip curled up on one side and she kept her gaze on me, like she'd just discovered that I'd suddenly grown up before her eyes. I tried to distract myself by looking at the equipment in the ambulance, pretending like the sterile instruments and lifeless tubes fascinated me.

When we finally arrived at the hospital, the EMT, who rode with us in the back, flung the ambulance doors open and pulled Mom's gurney toward them. He, along with two other EMTs hurried to lower

18

her gurney onto the sidewalk. One stood on either side of her and together they rushed her through the large sliding glass doors of the emergency room, then down a hallway until I couldn't see her anymore. It took me that long to get out of the harness.

Just as I readied myself to jump down onto the sidewalk, a female nurse peeped her head in. "They were in such a hurry they must have forgotten about you."

She smiled which did not assuage a knot the size of a basketball in my stomach. Still, I was glad for her outreached hand, which I grabbed to steady myself.

"Here," she said holding out a stick of gum.

I stared at it like I'd never seen one before.

"It helps calm the nerves," she added, and then winked.

I took it from her and we walked through the automatic double doors. "As soon as you get to the end of that hallway, you'll see the waiting room off to your left. I've got to get back to my post. There was a bus accident only a half hour before you arrived, so it's a bit crazy around here." She shook her head and walked away.

"Thanks," I called, heading for the waiting room.

The waiting room was more overcrowded than the other two times I'd visited. The first I'd fallen while rollerblading backwards and landed on my arm, breaking my radius. The second time I'd come with Lacey when she lost her mom to a horrible car accident. I shuddered at the memory. On both occasions, we were practically the only ones here. Today, people were positioned everywhere, mostly elderly, and I instantly assumed a casino bus had crashed. Every single chair was occupied. People were lined up, leaning against the wall, or sitting here and there on the floor. Some were bleeding, or holding their heads, but by the looks of it, the seriously injured had already been wheeled to the back for treatment.

I couldn't find a spot to sit so I paced back and forth until I saw Dad round the corner, his eyes darting around the room. When he saw me, he waved with one hand and gnawed his fingernails with the other, something I'd never seen him do. He'd shown anger and frustration plenty of times, but never signs of fear.

19

Once he saw me, he headed straight for the registration desk where the attendant handed him a pile of papers. He walked toward me, pen dangling from the clipboard, and squatted down to sit on the floor next to where I stood. It took him forever to complete each page, checking his phone every once in a while for information before writing again. By the time he finally finished, two seats had opened up and we sat down next to each other. For a long time, neither one of us spoke. I was busy berating myself for being clumsy and too caught up in my own dramas to notice Mom at the bottom of the stairs.

Dad broke the silence first. "We need luck," he said, peering at my face. "I wish you had your necklace, Kenza."

"Mom asked me about it today, too."

"And?" he urged.

"And nothing, Dad. Why are you both so interested in it today? It wasn't the real amulet . . . it was a replica."

He eyed me suspiciously, one eyebrow raised. "Now I'm not so sure," he said. "I really wanted you to see that drawing today in the camel-bone box. I wish I could compare it with your necklace."

I couldn't repress the gasp that squeezed out of my lungs.

"So it is true," he said. "But how did it get into your hands?" He seemed to be asking himself rather than me.

I fought to stay silent. It would be dangerous for him to know about Jinny Zzaman or that I'd met Jamila of Diab, or that the amulet had granted me access to a tunnel deep inside the Cave of Shadow Forest. Worse, he couldn't know that I'd used it to imprison Mazin.

"If the necklace you had was the Amulet of Omnia, and you're the first born, a descendent of the Tribe of Diab . . . " He rubbed his chin in contemplation, and then buried his head in his hands.

"Dad, what are you talking about? It's just a necklace." I used my best acting skills to pretend it wasn't worth rambling on about. If he knew everything that had happened to me connected to the Amulet of Omnia, I'd never see the light of day again—and I'd never be permitted to go back to camp at Zenith Hill in May. No Zenith Hill, no Ian, no allies, no romance—no anything that mattered to me.

20

Dad lifted his head and laughed. "I'm overreacting."

"Of course you are," I said, nodding vigorously, smiling despite the bead of sweat running down my back.

"Well, at least strange things didn't happen to you once you turned sixteen." He exhaled, laughed. "Did they?"

I searched frantically for a moment and then found my voice. "What? No, Dad. Don't be ridiculous."

"The legend," he began and then stopped short. "The legend says that strange things begin the day the descendant turns sixteen. So did they, Kenza? Did strange things begin happening to you when you turned sixteen?"

"Classify strange, Dad."

"You know, hummingbirds appearing in the middle of winter. Lilac bushes flowering and then shriveling back to their natural dry winter state," he said, with more than a hint of sarcasm.

I gulped hard. I used to be a horrible liar, but ever since my first mystical encounter with Moroccan jinns, I'd honed my skills in the deceptive department. "Ah, I was just joking around with you. I had just been looking at the tablet, at a dragonfly." I gave him one of my flip looks, hoping he'd think I really had been kidding.

Before Dad could continue his interrogation, a nurse burst through the swinging doors and into the waiting room. "Mr. Atlas." Dad jumped to his feet and I did, too. It took her no time to spot us, despite how crowded it was. "The doctor will see you now." She spoke with a thick accent, different from my dad's, probably Mexican.

I trailed my dad as he followed the nurse through swinging doors and down a long stark corridor. As we approached the end of the hallway, she turned to see me swiping tears away from my eyes. "Don't cry, hon. Your mom is going to be fine."

I nodded and then fixated on her slate gray uniform, patterned with skateboards and trick ramps.

"You like?" Her eyes brightened.

I nodded, but Dad raised an eyebrow. I didn't have much experience with skateboards, other than the annoying boy with tight blond curls who lived three houses down from us. He and his friends were always riding the ramps in the driveway in front of their garage. Even though I hadn't looked, they were likely there today. They wouldn't miss out on a beautiful day like this—at least not before the downpour came. Dad frequently complained about the boy and his friends at the dinner table. "One day, one of those damn kids is going to get seriously hurt," he'd say.

If he only knew what kind of danger I'd been in last year—what kind of danger we might all be in if Mazin escaped—he wouldn't be able to live with himself.

The nurse slid her hand under the crook of my arm and led me the rest of the way down a side hallway. This time my dad trailed behind.

"Then you'd like my son," the nurse said. "He's about your age."

Out of the corner of my eye I saw Dad flinch, but the nurse didn't seem to notice.

"You should see what he can do," she continued. "With a skateboard under him, he can fly." She waved her free hand in the air.

"Are we almost there?" Dad asked impatiently.

"You're in luck, Mr. Atlas." We stopped abruptly in front of an oversized brown door. "We are here." She clicked the door handle and swung it open.

Dad and I slipped past her and into Mom's room. Every nerve inside of me relaxed when I saw Mom's smiling face peering past the doctor. As we approached, I noticed mom's wrist in a cast. Dad made his way to the other side of the bed and immediately grasped my mom's good hand in his, wrapping his other hand around it, lifting it gently to his lips. Dad could be such a jerk, but he was the sweetest person when he thought someone he loved was seriously hurt. I stood in his shadow, my hands fumbling awkwardly in front of me. The nurse gave me a reassuring nod and slipped away, letting the door swing shut.

"Your wife will be fine, Mr. Atlas," the doctor said. He was tall, thin, and had short tufts of thinning blond hair.

Dad sighed, inhaled a long breath, and leaned over the rail next to Mom's bed.

"Are you okay?" The doctor asked me, the lines on his face tightening in concern.

I straightened quickly. "Yeah, fine. I'm relieved she's okay." And I was—immensely relieved. I'd been praying that Mom wasn't really hurt, and if she was, that it wasn't really my fault—that it wasn't because Mazin escaped and was menacing us.

"Mr. Atlas," the doctor said. "Your wife is okay. She bruised a rib and broke her wrist, so she won't be able to do any heavy lifting for a while—but I wouldn't recommend it with the baby anyway."

Everything after the word 'baby' sounded like muffled slow-motion murmurs. Baby? " . . . I'd like your permission to let me do an ultrasound. Your wife tells me that the two of you have decided against them as a personal preference, that you didn't have one done when your oldest daughter was in vitro."

"Dad." I grabbed his arm and gave it a hard squeeze.

He looked at me, his expression severe. "Kenza, this is important. Please, not now."

"Dad, this is important. I think she should have the ultrasound." I dug my fingernails into his flesh.

"Kenza," his voice sounded gruff but I didn't care. If there was something—anything—I could do to help protect someone who shared my bloodline, I had to try.

"If she's pregnant you have to make sure the baby is okay," I said in a rush. "She took a major fall. It'd be wrong not to check."

Everyone looked at me. The doctor smiled. "Mr. and Mrs. Atlas, this decision is entirely up to you, but your daughter is right, I would absolutely recommend an ultrasound to make sure everything is okay."

"I appreciate your concern," my dad said. "But Mrs. Atlas and I are not comfortable with ultrasounds. This baby is already a high risk baby because of my wife's age so we don't want to do anything that might disturb it."

"But Dad—"

"I understand and respect your feelings," the doctor said. "The baby's heartbeat is normal and all external signs seem fine. So there is a good chance that the baby is fine."

"What? No—" I began, but my parents both glared at me so hard I instantly shut my mouth. My heart was thundering. I didn't even know this little being existed until now, but I immediately knew that his or her life could be in danger—if Mazin was on the loose.

"That's it then," Mom said. "We've decided to stick with our original plan and not run the extra tests."

The doctor turned toward me on his way out, "Congratulations on becoming a big sister," he said brightly.

"Thanks," I replied, still in shock.

"We wanted to tell you," Mom said, anticipating my fury.

"Then why didn't you?" I asked, my voice rising.

"When we first found out, it was such a surprise and I am a little older so we've been waiting for the pregnancy to get solidly underway," Mom said.

I rolled my eyes.

"Kenza, we wanted it to be the right timing," Dad explained.

"And you think now is the right time? Being surprised in the hospital, by a doctor I don't even know?" I asked, not leaving them time to answer. "When is the baby due, anyway?"

"The end of June," Mom said.

A coil of darkness wove its long thin finger through me and I was sure it showed in my expression. "When I'm at camp? Mom, Dad, how could you? You know what going to camp means for me."

"This wasn't planned," Mom said.

"What am I supposed to do . . . miss camp?"

"Or miss the birth of your little brother or sister," Dad said. "You decide."

I crossed my arms, breathed in and out quickly through my nostrils several times. "I don't want to miss either," I said and stamped my foot hard.

Chapter 5

As soon as we got home I threw my jacket on the kitchen table, ignored Mom when she chastised me for not hanging it in the closet, and ran straight upstairs to my room. I kicked off my shoes, walked over to my bed, and jumped onto it with a twirl—stretching out and staring up at the ceiling. Alone in my quiet room where I was finally free from distraction, the significance of the events that transpired today broke through the self-preserving damns I'd constructed and flooded into the canals of my mind.

As I lay there, I noticed a smattering of flaws in the ceiling and let my eyes wander to a spider web of cracks that spread down the corner to the floor. I'd never noticed them before. Suddenly, my house seemed more fragile, less of a permanent structure than I'd always imagined. Life in general seemed more fragile, replete with potholes and fissures that could suddenly burst wide open at the most unexpected moments.

I dreaded the thought of my parents bringing a little child into this harsh, unpredictable world, unable to protect him or herself from the countless dangers destined to engulf our family. If Mazin escaped, would he harm him or her just to watch me squirm, maybe even to coerce me to agree to one of his diabolical plans? If so, how could I prevent it?

I inhaled a slow breath, closed my eyes on the exhale and kept them shut. For now, I had to trust that Mazin was still locked up. And at least I could rejoice in the fact that my little brother or sister was still safely wrapped in the warmth and comfort of my mom's womb.

Mom probably wanted to tell me about the baby as soon as she found out, and Dad probably thwarted her plans. He could be so secretive about things. I doubted anyone else in our family knew, either.

The bedroom door slowly swung open and I looked up to see Mom standing in the door frame. The lines on her face were tight and her teeth were clenched.

I immediately sat up. "Mom, what's wrong? Do you need to go to the hospital again?"

"Nothing's wrong, Kenza." She grabbed her wrist, even though it was in a cast. "I've never broken a bone before today. I wish they could have given me a more potent pain killer."

I didn't know what to do. Mom was always comforting and fixing things for me, and now that she was the one who was hurt, I felt helpless. I patted the bed for her to come sit and I scooted next to her, wrapping my arm around her. "I love you, Mom," I said softly.

She stayed silent for a moment, and when I looked up I saw tears in her eyes. She patted my leg and said, "Your love helps me heal better than any medicine could."

"Yeah," I said. It was quiet for a while before I spoke again. "Mom, why didn't you tell me you were pregnant?"

"Oh Kenza, I'm so sorry."

"That's not enough, Mom. I want to know why." I reached out and took her 'good' hand in mine. "It was Dad's idea, wasn't it?"

"It wasn't just his idea," she said. "It was mine, too."

"Why?" I searched her eyes.

"I'm not your typical pregnant woman, Kenza. She looked down at her stomach and rubbed it gently. "I'm getting older. There's a lot of risk . . . I wanted to be sure."

"Be sure of what?" I said.

She looked at me and it hit me: She was in a high-risk pregnancy—this baby might not make it.

∞

After Mom left my room, I found my phone and plugged it in to charge it next to my bed so I could lie down while I called Ian. I only had to wait one ring before he answered. The instant I heard his voice, a ball of emotion formed at the base of my throat. I drew in a deep breath, my lip quivering.

"Kenza, are you there?" Ian asked, sounding clearly concerned.

"Yeah, I'm here. I'm glad to hear your voice," I said, my voice nearly a whisper.

"Were you crying?"

"What? No," I said as tears brimmed. "I mean not recently . . . okay, yes."

"My beautiful, strong Kenza, after everything I've seen you do—and that includes saving both of our lives—what is stressing you out so much you're crying?"

I breathed in sharply, sighed slowly, and then quickly described how I'd collaborated with the attic bat to send my mom to the hospital, the ambulance run, the hospital, how relieved I was that she was okay, how I thought I saw the silhouette of a man standing in the rain in my backyard. "What if it was Mazin?" I asked, praying Ian would shoo away my fears . . . but he didn't. Instead, he urged me to be extra vigilant and to call him as often as possible.

"There's one more thing, Ian," I said. "I found out something today that's going to change my life."

"What is it? Are you moving to Rio De Janiero?" he said, teasing me in the way I loved.

"What? No." I laughed out an awkward snort. "It's bigger than that."

"Bigger?"

"Yeah, I'm going to be a sister."

"When?" He sounded more surprised than I did—and why not? It was rather shocking news.

"Late June," I said, crying again.

Ian knew exactly what upset me—that I'd miss camp and my opportunity to spend the summer with him, and with our camp friends. We'd been counting down the days until we returned to Oregon.

"We'll figure something out," he reassured me. "Now, why don't you get some rest. You sound tired."

After everything that had happened recently, I should have felt exhausted but I couldn't sleep. I lay in bed staring, once again, at the flaws in the ceiling, thinking about Ian, the gorgeous guy I'd fallen for last summer. Ian, with his sandy brown hair and mesmerizing cinnamon eyes, had stolen my heart with the perfect mix of charm, intellect and mystery.

He'd put himself in danger—for me. When Mazin showed up in Omaha and things got crazy, he followed me to Zenith Hill and created two epic battles. It was Ian who put his life on the line to protect me. I'd known all along that our ancestors had met and fallen in love some 500 years before—and that we were destined to meet in this lifetime to resolve ancient curses—but Ian didn't know about any of that. He just liked me, the geeky girl from Omaha who'd never been in love. In essence, we'd saved each other's lives, lured Mazin into that bottle and cast him into the ocean.

But thinking about all that also made me think about Mazin and the real possibility that he was behind the bizarre events today: my crunched tablet, the collision with my mom on the stairs, and then her terrible fall. That's how he worked, by creating crises in the lives of people I loved. If he was free, had he been hovering for some time? Had he seen my dad retrieving the camel-bone box?

I kept expecting Jamila of Diab or Jinny Zzaman to appear like they did the last time I ran into trouble, materializing in my bedroom and at school. The first time Jinny came, she totally freaked me out, and whisked me off to Morocco to give me a crash course in family history. Because I saw Jamila first, and was told that she was my ancestor, I found her easier to bear. And then they both came through in the end. The fact that they weren't showing up left me feeling anxious.

When I couldn't stand my own thoughts anymore, I decided to look for the camel-bone box myself.

Chapter 6

My dad would kill me if he found out that I went looking for the box without him, but my curiosity had peaked—and finding out what was in it was just something I needed to know. I tiptoed down the hallway, past my parents' room, hoping to God they wouldn't wake up, and slowly crept to the door that opened to the stairs up to the attic.

Then I stood there—immobilized. Even as a child, I'd always been wary of the attic. Whenever I'd come anywhere near it, I would hug the wall opposite the door and slither by as quickly as I could. It had always emitted an ominous vibe. Now, in the dark solitude of the night, I could almost hear a voice calling for me and hands reaching for me and realized that I'd always felt that succumbing to the door's magnetic pull, would slide me into some other dimension from which I'd never escape.

I suddenly realized that maybe it wasn't the door after all whose allure frightened me. Maybe it was never the door. Maybe it was the camel-bone box that caused my heart to thump and my palms to sweat whenever I set foot in this hallway. What was in that box? I had to know.

I approached the door, wrapped my hand around the knob, and eased it. It creaked and I shuddered, hoping my dad didn't hear. I entered and pulled the door shut behind me, and the blackness swallowed me, making me blind as a bat. The thought of a bat sent shivers from the base of my spine to my neck. About to chicken out, I reached back for the door so I could seek refuge in the safety of my room, but realized I couldn't. The box could contain information that would save me—save us all.

I pulled my cell phone out of my pajama pocket and clicked it so I could see. I didn't dare tug on the cord hanging down from the light bulb in the attic staircase for fear the light shining through the bottom of the door would give me away if Mom or Dad came walking down the hallway. I shone the light on the stairs and took my first step. It creaked

30

and I turned back toward the door, expecting my dad to come flying through it any second. When he didn't, I decided to keep climbing.

When I finally made it to the top of the stairs, I reached for the hatch door above me, made contact and gave it a push. It was heavier than I expected and I had to take another step to use the strength in my legs. The hatch door creaked up and over, landing with a bang.

I knew my dad heard that. How could he not? I had to act fast. I could run back down the stairs as fast as possible, careful not to invite a repeat performance of my mom's fall, and hope I didn't run into Dad in the hallway. Or, I could go for it and open the box to see as much as I could before Dad caught me.

If I were thinking clearly, I would have had the wits to run back down the stairs. Even if I managed to open the box, I couldn't see a thing. I couldn't remember where the light was up here and I didn't have time to look. Besides, if I had any patience left in me, Dad would have brought me up here again himself the next day. The problem was, I didn't want to have to wait that long. Seeing Mom fall down the stairs was too fresh for him to attempt coming up here again this soon.

Since it was the middle of the night, after one of the worst days I'd had in nearly a year, I wasn't thinking clearly. I decided to go for it. I stepped onto the attic floor and crouched down as low as I could, while still being able to walk, for fear the bat might attack. I tried not to think about the advantage the creature had over me. Instead, I slowly slid my feet across the floor, kicking random stuff out of the way as I went. When I reached the area near the sloped wall where I thought I would find the box, I dropped to my knees and scoured the floor with my hands.

I couldn't believe it when I found it so quickly. I flipped open the lid and the instant I did, a bright white light illuminated the entire box, like the Amulet of Omnia used to glow when it was trying to warn me about something. After the box had been open for a few moments, the light began to fade and then disappeared completely. I shined my cell phone light inside and saw a scrap of papyrus reed rolled into a scroll. I grabbed it and unrolled it, my hands trembling. It contained a painting of the Amulet of Omnia, which must have been the source of the light that beamed out when I first opened the box.

"Kenza, is that you?" Dad called up from the bottom of the stairs.

31

I jumped and hit my head on one of the wood panels on the sloped ceiling.

"Ouch," I blurted. My hand instinctively shot up for my head. I searched for my "everything's okay" voice. "Yeah, Dad. I'm up here."

"What are you doing alone in the middle of the night?" I heard his footsteps clamoring up the stairs.

I shut the lid of the box just in time, tucking the papyrus paper into my sock and covering it with my pajama pants. I didn't have time to see if anything else was in the box.

"It's too dangerous to be up here by yourself, Kenza," Dad said, his head peeking up through the opening.

If I moved wrong, he would see the paper glowing through my sock. "Dad, I couldn't sleep and I was curious. What can I say?"

"I don't care, Kenza. This is not the time. Now, get down here." He waved me toward the staircase.

"Dad, I want to know what's in the box." I stood as carefully as I could in case the bat was ready to swoop down. "I thought you wanted me to know."

"Not with a live bat up here, Kenza," he said quickly. "God knows what kind of diseases that thing carries."

That made me laugh. "Dad, are you still afraid of that stupid thing?" I should have known better. He flipped out on me and I knew it was because it had tarnished his manly image.

"Kenza, get over here this moment," he insisted.

"Dad, I'm coming as fast as I can," I replied, but I knew I could have moved faster, if I didn't have to worry about the glowing light in my sock.

Chapter 7

It was the first day back at school after Spring Break and I still couldn't believe my mom was going to have a baby. After I turned ten, I had given up thinking I'd ever have a brother or sister, and now I was used to being an only child. I could lay down a sure bet that I'd get stuck babysitting constantly, like lots of older siblings I knew, and my parents weren't the kind to offer to pay me for it. They'd simply expect me to do it, to cheerfully offer without even being asked. The possibility made me groan. If they'd caught me when I was twelve or thirteen, I'd have been much more cooperative. I had other things than babies on my mind now—like Ian, and camp.

Mrs. Montgomery had yanked me out of math class and we were standing in the hallway outside the classroom door. "Kenza, I need a favor."

"Sure, what do you need?"

"I need your help with a student who's struggling," she said, her voice serious.

"Is that all?" I asked. Like my dad, I didn't mind helping other students with their homework. "Yeah, of course. I'd be happy to help, Mrs. Montgomery, especially after everything you did for me last year."

My principal smiled. "Thank you, Kenza. I knew I could count on you." She patted my arm and then hurried away down the hallway, her heels clicking loudly.

I walked back into my math class and my best friend Lacey eyed me, curiosity washing over her face. I shrugged and slid back into my seat. After only a few minutes, the bell rang. I knew Lacey would want to know what Mrs. Montgomery's appearance was all about, so I waited for her in the hallway.

"So," she said, her bright blue eyes looking eager. "Spill. I'm in a hurry for my next class." She held her hand up, mimicking a stop sign. "Before you do, I already know it's something good because she thinks you're an angel, Kenza."

I shrugged, turned my head away a little embarrassed. "Please . . . "

Lacey rolled her eyes, lifted up onto her toes, and if she hadn't chopped all of her hair off last fall—on a bet with me that she lost during Labor Day weekend—her ponytail would have swished vigorously. "So . . . what'd she say? Did you win some new junior valedictorian award?"

"Not even close," I said. "I won several hours of community service with some poor struggling student."

"I don't know, Kenza," she said. "That sounds like an invitation to a party for you."

"Yeah, whatever." I waved her statement away with a flick of my hand. "It won't be too bad."

"What subject?" she asked.

I shrugged. "I forgot to ask."

"I guess you'll find out soon enough," she said.

A storm of freshman sped past us in their usual stampede. A few of them cut between us and I found myself on the opposite side of the hallway from Lacey. "I have news," I called.

"Does it have anything to do with your lovey-dovey Twin Cities boyfriend?" she asked.

I blushed and a smile spread across my face, despite my desire to remain expressionless. "Actually, no, but I did talk to him about it last night. He's so amazing." I felt myself lift up on my toes and quickly forced myself back to the ground.

"Oh puke!" Lacey called across the hall, as the last of the freshman herd cleared out. She hurried toward me as soon as she saw an opening. "So what's this fabulous news of yours?"

"Not so fabulous," I muttered. "I mean some of it is, but some of it—"

She grabbed my arm, as we walked toward our next class. First, I told her about my broken tablet, and then I told her about when I crashed into my mom head on. I explained that we had some work to do in the attic (I still kept the Tribe of Diab and my dad's mysterious past secret). I managed to share the drama with the bat, my mom's tumble down the stairs, and the baby. Everything. I shared everything I could without giving anything supernatural away.

Lacey sighed, lifted her shoulders and let them drop down in an exaggerated way. "I can't believe it, Kenza. How could life be so boring so much of the time, and then all of sudden your life turns into a soap opera? It doesn't make any sense. It's like a demon suddenly became obsessed with you."

I shuddered, unable to find any intelligent words to respond. I stopped mid-step, turned to face her and blurted, "Gotta' go." I turned and raced down the hall to my next class, which I fortunately did not share with Lacey.

∞

After a few days of what seemed like a return to normalcy (normalcy, minus my paranoia about Mazin's possible return tripling in size), Mrs. Montgomery showed up at the door of Study Hall. Even though I'd experienced so many encounters with her last year, I still wasn't ready to assume that every time she showed up it was because of me. But she looked right at me and held my gaze.

I pointed at my chest and mouthed, "Me?"

She nodded once, cleared her throat and said, "Mr. Snorton, I'll need to take Kenza Atlas out of class for this period."

He bobbed his head quickly and waved his hand, motioning for me to go.

I cursed under my breath. I'd been thinking about going back to Zenith Hill, what it would be like to finally see Ian again—to feel his arms around me, his heart beating against mine. I slowly closed my notebook, snapped shut the decoy book that I had on my desk to make it look like I was studying, and leisurely placed each item into my backpack. If Mrs. Montgomery could interrupt my fiery daydream, I could take my sweet time.

When I finally stepped into the hallway, Mrs. Montgomery said, "Kenza, I thought you were eager to help tutor other students."

I felt my cheeks warm. I'd instinctively assumed something ominous had happened—something that would confirm my suspicions about Mazin and dampen the fire for Ian burning inside me. "Is that what this is about?"

We walked side-by-side about halfway down the long hallway, past the wall of gray lockers that led to the library.

"Yes," Mrs. Montgomery said sharply. "I talked to you about it recently. Don't you remember?" She eyed me curiously.

"Yes, of course," I responded. "I didn't realize that I'd start today. I just assumed we still had to work out the details."

We reached the library and she thrust the door open, holding it for me so I could enter first. "Consider the details worked out."

I said nothing, but thought her behavior odd. What was she hiding? I followed her to the circular reference desk, located in the center of the library.

"Mrs. Montgomery," the librarian said. I couldn't remember her name. She was a short, bubbly woman, probably in her fifties by the conservative way she dressed, but she looked a lot younger. She spoke quickly—as if she'd chugged a full pot of coffee— and that reminded me of my summer camp leader, Mrs. Bartolli. "Are you here for the tutoring? We have a sign-in sheet. The tutors and students being tutored will need to sign in every time they begin their session. It's for tracking purposes."

She shoved a clipboard into my hands. It was already half-full of names. My eyes snagged on Megan Hawk's name, the girl who'd sent her posse to beat the life out of me last year, just before I left for camp the first time. My eyes snapped up at Mrs. Montgomery, searching for reassurance that Megan was not the student I'd been paired with. She held my gaze, but showed no emotion. Lots of names were on the list, surely Mrs. Montgomery would never intentionally pair us up. I dropped my gaze, smiled even. In fact, I felt sorry for the poor soul who had to try and tutor such an unreachable student. I scribbled my name across the page and checked the box for "Tutor", then handed the clipboard back to the librarian.

"Thank you, Ms. Nolan," Mrs. Montgomery said, her voice steady and controlled, contrary to the librarian's fast clip. "Kenza will be here every other day at this time. Can you point us to where her student is waiting?"

Mrs. Nolan propped up a panel of the countertop and slipped through to lead the way. She gently flipped the open panel back down, not making a noise. Even though she had a small stature, she strode quickly through the library, weaving through many rows of bookshelves. Mrs. Montgomery, with her long stride, had no trouble keeping up, but I found it more difficult.

Just as we rounded another corner to more tables, I instantly spotted Megan. She glanced up and frowned, looking as disappointed to see me as I was to see her. As we approached her table, I felt all the blood rush to my face. The room suddenly felt stuffy and suffocating. Megan quickly opened a book and buried her head in it.

"Megan," Mrs. Montgomery said, in the gentlest voice she seemed to be able to find. "Kenza has offered to help you with your studies so that you can successfully complete your class work for the rest of the year."

"Wha...?" I blurted, but stifled my desire to eject more words.

Megan looked up, and slammed her book shut with an audible clap. She lowered her voice to a discreet volume, but I could hear fury brewing in it. "Mrs. Montgomery, I agreed to get help with my studies, but how could you ask her to be the one to help me?"

"Kenza is eager to tutor. She doesn't mind helping others. In fact, she was rather excited about this." Mrs. Montgomery glanced at me, smiled and microscopically narrowed her eyes—conveying her message clearly. Her voice contained an air of pride for my supposed moral willingness to specifically help Megan, which, in fact, I did not and would not have agreed to do.

"I'm going to have to think about this." Megan thrust her chair back, stood quickly. She shoved all of her belongings into her bag, shaking her head the whole time.

"May I remind you, Megan, of your decision?" Mrs. Montgomery paused to let her words sink in. "You will either accept help from Kenza, or throw your chances of a brighter future away."

Megan nodded once. "I will think about it." She left in a hurry, in the opposite direction from where I stood, even though there was no exit on that side of the library. Mrs. Montgomery pulled out a chair and sat down, patting the table with her hand to invite me to join her. Now that Megan was gone, I had no problem approaching the table, but I wasn't ready to sit. Inside, I fumed.

"Mrs. Montgomery, you want me to help Megan? Are you insane?" I asked in raw, unfiltered shock.

"You're the best one for the job and you know it." She patted the chair next to her.

I stood firmly in my place. "How can you even consider this after what happened last year? They beat me to a pulp," I said, straightening my back. "You know Megan was behind it . . . and you know that I didn't do anything to provoke her, don't you?"

The principal smiled warmly and reached for my hand, but I jerked it away. "Kenza, I know what happened last year was horrible, nearly tragic. At this time last year, I would have never considered pairing the two of you up. In fact, I wouldn't even have considered it a month ago. But Megan has become a different person this year. Has she bothered you at all?"

I looked down at the table, shook my head, and drew invisible circles with my finger on the dark wood of the table. She hadn't bothered me this year, but visions of her three best friends pummeling my face and kicking me once I fell to the ground flooded my mind. "Mrs. Montgomery, I was afraid for my life—"

"Two weeks ago, Megan Hawk came to my office with true humility and a desire to seek my help. Something in her has changed. I can't explain it." Mrs. Montgomery shook her head, leaning back in her chair.

I gazed around the circumference of the library. Not a soul was in sight, except us. "Don't you remember what she did to me last year? It was bad enough that she sent her three stooges to attack me. Don't you remember what happened before that? Do you remember her hitting me so hard that she knocked me out?" I spoke those last words slowly, enunciating each one clearly despite my dry, raspy voice.

Mrs. Montgomery shook her head vigorously. "Oh yes, of course I do, Kenza. That's why I so desperately want the two of you to work together. Think of how much healing could take place. Besides, I sense Megan is ready for it. Didn't you see how maturely she left the situation?"

"Didn't you see her refuse to work with me and stalk out of here?" I blurted.

Mrs. Montgomery gave another nod. "Yes, but she did say that she would think about it. Even you have to admit that is a big step for her. I think it would do Megan some good. To be honest, I think it would be for your own good, too, Kenza."

My eyes snapped up.

"I'm listening," I said, shocked at her words. My voice carried with an authority that was inappropriate for a student-to-faculty conversation.

"Good, then please sit down. Don't make me beg you." She patted the seat again and this time I complied. "You know how Megan struggles in school, Kenza. No one knows that better than you."

I nodded once at Mrs. Montgomery's words.

"It's no longer a matter of losing her sports privileges," she explained. "In fact, that has already happened. It's now a matter of failing out completely."

"And that's bad, how?" I asked. I didn't give a crap about Megan, not after the beatings I'd endured last year.

"That's where you come in," Mrs. Montgomery leaned back and crossed her arms over her chest. I could tell she was searching for the right words—words that I could absorb and not instantly reject. "Kenza, let's face it. You've changed. You may not have noticed it like I have. You've had more time . . . to get used to it . . ."

"Change is good, right?" I said. "Isn't that what I'm supposed to do? I'm a junior in high school. Do you know how pathetic it would be if I still acted like a freshman?"

"Let me be blunt," Mrs. Montgomery said, tapping her fingertips together and leaning her lengthy body forward. "You're no longer that kind-hearted, down-to-earth person that won a scholarship to Zenith Hill."

I looked at her, stunned.

"Granted I'm proud of your confidence," she interjected, "but without kindness, it borders on arrogance."

"But Mrs. Montgomery—" I was ready for a fight.

"I've already spoken with Zenith Hill about this," she added.

I narrowed my eyes, glared at her. "What do they have to do with it?"

"Dr. Hendrix agrees," she said.

A heaviness tightened around my throat, grew over my heart.

"He thinks you should start helping Megan right away," she explained.

"He would," I muttered, sarcasm noted.

"It may affect your ability to attend camp again this summer," she said firmly.

"Can you do that?" I asked sharply.

Mrs. Montgomery's tone sharpened, too. "I can and I will." She tapped the side of her fist on the table.

"But . . . but what if Megan doesn't accept the offer to be helped?"

"Then that will be on her and she will face her own consequences. As for you, you can choose to be willing to assist—or not. I can't ask anything more of you."

I stared at Mrs. Montgomery, at her perfect hair wrapped in a tight bun on top of her head, her tailored blazer, and knee-length dress. Suddenly, I hated her.

"You don't have to decide now," she said. "Think about it."

"I will," I replied, knowing I didn't really have a choice in the matter.

"I don't need an answer for a week," she added.

"I'll let you know my decision tomorrow," I declared.

"Well, I—"

I didn't stick around to hear what she had to say. Instead, I stood briskly and strode out of the library with a confidence that surprised even me.

Chapter 8

That night, I sat in the comfort of my room, with my eyes planted not on the ceiling, like the last few nights, but down at the blank page in front of me. I'd promised Mrs. Montgomery that I'd have an answer for her tomorrow morning, but without the advice of Jinny Zzaman or Jamila of Diab, I had no idea what to do.

I grabbed my pen, tugged my notebook up onto my knees and began to scribble: Should I help Megan Hawk?

Without waiting for an answer to pop into my mind, I jumped up and ran to the secret hole in the wall that I'd kept hidden behind furniture ever since I was little. I pushed the desk aside, careful not to let the legs grate across the wood floor, and then squatted down and pulled out the small cork I'd always used as camouflage. White light immediately shone out through the dark hole. I snaked my finger into the opening and pulled out the scroll bearing the image of the Amulet of Omnia.

I resealed the opening, carefully returned the desk to its original position, and reclaimed my still warm spot on the bed. I then grabbed my notebook and flipped back to the page with my question: Should I help Megan Hawk? I unrolled the scroll and peered at the still-glowing amulet. I closed my eyes, inhaled a lung full of air, and opened my eyes, fully expecting to see it turn red, indicating I should definitely not put myself into such a position of danger.

But it didn't.

I decided to ask the question out loud, "Should I help Megan Hawk?"

The amulet on the parchment continued to glow white, and then suddenly radiated light out into the room, like it had when I opened the camel-bone box in the attic. I expected it to turn red any second. I stared until I couldn't stand to look at the light anymore. The light was so bright that it resonated with a low harmonic hum that reminded me of soft wind chimes on a windy summer day.

Then I asked the question again, "Should I help Megan?"

I waited for the bright red glow to appear. Nothing.

I ripped the page out of the notebook, crinkled it into a wad and threw it across my room into the wastebasket. Missed. Rather than get up and jettison it into its proper place, I sank back into my pillow. I could hear the ticking of the hallway clock, the furnace kicking on, a car pulling out of the driveway next door. Not only did I expect the amulet to burn bright red, warning me against helping Megan, I wanted it so badly my stomach ached. Instead, it only seemed to encourage me to do Mrs. Montgomery's bidding.

I couldn't stand to lay waiting for a second longer so I leapt to my feet, squeezed my eyes shut and waved the parchment paper with the drawing of the Amulet of Omnia. "I summon Jinny Zzaman to present herself before me right now," I said.

Moments later, I smelled her familiar rotten egg scent and opened my eyes to see her floating before me, her beautiful black hair waving as if underwater, her blue dress emitting the light of a million tiny stars. She did not hesitate to start beaming words into my mind. "Kenza, we've been waiting for you to find the drawing of the amulet in your father's camel-bone box. Keep it close and do not lose it."

"Does it work like the real amulet?" I asked.

"Its powers are miniscule compared to the power of the real amulet," she explained. "But it does hold some mystical energy, enough to carry us through this crisis."

"Crisis?" I parroted. "It's Mazin, isn't it? He's freed himself."

She nodded slowly.

"What do we do now?" I asked.

"That is what I came here to ask you." She beamed this perplexing statement into my mind.

"Ask me?" I pointed at my chest.

"The moment he escaped," she continued, "he seized the amulet along with all of its powers. While he cannot reduce my abilities in any way, or those of Jamila of Diab, he can block us from helping certain people."

I felt my eyes grow wide. "You can't help me?" I said. "I'm going to need it now more than ever."

"We cannot help without you first requesting our aid, and not without the help of the precious drawing you hold in your hand," she said.

"All right," I said. "I need your help with Megan Hawk, but you know that already, don't you?"

She nodded. "Kenza, our ability to protect you right now is limited. Is Megan really your biggest concern?"

I frowned. "No, my mom's safety, and the safety of my little brother or sister, is ten times more important than Megan Hawk."

Jinny nodded again and started to fade away, but I called her back. "Yes?" she said, her voice calm, unlike mine.

"Where are you going? We're not done yet. What am I supposed to do about Megan? With Mazin on the loose, she's at risk for being controlled by him again."

"With Mazin on the loose, I cannot protect your mother and you at the same time. You must choose," she urged.

"That's no choice," I blurted. "You must protect my mom and the baby."

She held her palms together and smiled warmly, as if commending my decision. Her slight movement caused her dress to ripple and emit bursts of light all around the room. "Take your parchment with the drawing of the amulet with you everywhere you go. If you encounter insurmountable danger, then you must use it. But be cautious of seeking my help. It could be a trap to distract me from your sibling."

"Why would he go after a child when he could come straight after me?" I said. "Now that he's in possession of the Amulet of Omnia, what more does he want?"

44

"What he wants, my dear Kenza, is revenge for being imprisoned." Then she disappeared taking her fowl odor with her, but the word "revenge" repeatedly played through my mind.

∞

The next morning, I walked directly to the office and pushed open the front door, my hands clammy. When I stepped inside the office, I fidgeted with them as I greeted Miss Camden, the secretary.

"No need to sit, Kenza," Miss Camden said in a hurried voice. Her head was down, as usual, buried in her work as she spoke and all I could see was her hair coiled into a bun on top of her hair. What was it with these admin ladies and their buns?

"What?" I asked, my mind in a fog. I'd heard what she said, but I wasn't ready to face Mrs. Montgomery.

"Go on in, Kenza," Miss Camden urged, seemingly oblivious to my stress. "Mrs. Montgomery is eager to see you."

"Okay," I managed as I trudged toward the door.

"Kenza," Mrs. Montgomery said, greeting me warmly. "You are, as always, good to your word."

I smiled meekly, partly kicking myself for that quality. As I sat down, my eyes wandered vaguely around her office. Nothing much changed since my multiple visits there last year: pale white walls, inspirational quotes tacked to a bulletin board, framed photographs of her grandkids hogging one corner of her desk and the shelves behind her.

My eyes snagged on one new addition: a plaque from Zenith Hill with my name etched into the plate: Kenza Atlas, Honorary Zenith Hill Scholar. It gave me the boost of courage that I needed to share my difficult decision about Megan with her.

"So, Kenza. Will you help Megan?" Mrs. Montgomery asked pointedly.

"It looks like it's going to be a beautiful day," I said, trying to make adult small talk to delay the inevitable.

"Yes, it does," she agreed, adding that there was only a small chance for rain.

After that, silence swelled, making me squirm. Mrs. Montgomery relaxed into a quiet patience that I didn't expect. She finally broke the long silence. "Kenza, it is no one's decision but yours to make. As you are aware, there will be positive and negative consequences either way. If it were an easy choice, you would have made it yesterday in the library."

I said nothing.

"You already know the choice I want you to make," she added, "but you may not know that I will respect your wishes, no matter what you decide."

"I know that Mrs. Montgomery. I've always known that," I said. "That's not my problem. My problem is that I know what needs to be done and I know what my decision needs to be. I'm having a hard timing saying it out loud. I guess you could say that I'm a little freaked out here." Even though Megan wasn't there when I got jumped, she'd ordered the pounding, and she could do it again. Then suddenly, a rush of adrenaline shot through me and I blurted out my decision. "I'll do it." After the words left my mouth, I immediately pushed my chair back to stand. "I'll help her," I added. I walked briskly to the door, turning to face her before I left. "Please don't tell my parents."

Mrs. Montgomery raised her eyebrows and I realized my mistake. "Please don't tell them, because I'd like to break it to them gently. They can be super protective, as you know." I knew she knew I was lying. Still, she didn't say anything and I slipped through the door without turning back. I figured most students would get in serious trouble for acting the way I did in Mrs. Montgomery's office, but she didn't treat me like most students.

∞

It must have taken a few days for Mrs. Montgomery to convince Megan to accept her "offer" to have me tutor her, because Mrs. Montgomery didn't show up to study hall again for another week.

When she finally did, Tyler Hamstrom said, "You in trouble again, Kenza?"

Last year, I would have shrugged off his comment and scurried to the door with my head down. Instead I said, "You want a piece of me, tough guy?"

He laughed and three people high-fived me on my way to the door. When I reached it, Mrs. Montgomery frowned. She was wearing one of her typical business suits: gray jacket, knee-length pencil skirt, and heels that she definitely did not need, based on the fact that she towered over me. She crossed her arms to emphasize her disappointment.

"What?" I said.

"That attitude is exactly why I asked you to do this."

I puckered my lips in anger and wore that expression until we reached the library.

"You'll want to lose the attitude before we reach Megan," she said.

"As long as she loses hers," I said, and then purposefully eyed her sharply.

Even though she'd already tugged the library door open, she released it and I watched it close. Mrs. Montgomery stepped in front of it and turned her back to it to face me directly. "Megan's attitude has nothing to do with yours," she reminded me. "You are treading on thin ice, Kenza Atlas. I am shocked that you, of all people, would be so quick to surrender an opportunity like this."

I stood taller and lost the smirk I had been wearing.

"What's worse," she continued, "I thought you'd be one to show more appreciation than this. I am utterly disappointed." She shook her head a few times, turned sideways and pointed at the door. "Megan, on the other hand, is showing a much greater willingness to receive help."

47

"After some prodding, I'm sure," I said, being sure to water down my snarky tone, replacing it with what I hoped would come across as a sense of concern.

"After a lot of prodding, yes," the principal said. "But that doesn't matter now. What matters, Kenza," she paused and looked up and down both ends of the hallway.

I followed her eyes and didn't spot a soul.

" . . . What matters is whether or not you are ready to take on this new challenge."

I nodded, fishing for the right words. Several long seconds passed before I spoke. "I can't say that I am completely ready, honestly. In fact, I'm terrified." I shifted my weight from one foot to the other. "And I'm furious."

"Is there any part in there that is willing to help someone in need? Be honest, Kenza. I don't want this to be about the threat of not going to camp that I've hung over your head. The entire reason I picked you in the first place is because I thought working with Megan offered the real possibility of helping you both."

"To be honest—" I began.

She started to speak, but I held up my hand and she stopped.

"Before I knew Megan was the one who needed the help, I was really looking forward to helping someone. Now that I know it is Megan, a small part of me knows that this will help me face my fears with her."

Mrs. Montgomery relaxed her posture, dropped her crossed arms to her sides.

I went on, "I never told you about this, but I helped rescue a guy who was being bullied at camp last summer. It was horrifying, especially after having gone through it myself. He could have died, Mrs. Montgomery. But the camp leaders forced him to work together with his attackers, and—even though I still can't stand them—Keelam, the guy I'm referring to, gave them all a second chance and was willing to spend a lot of time with them over the rest of the summer. At first, I thought he was crazy—I still do—but I admire him for having the courage and, more importantly, for being so kind."

48

"And how did that turn out for him?" she asked, crossing her arms again.

"His team, he and the people who bullied him, came about this close to winning one of the major camp challenges." I pinched an inch of air between my fingers.

Mrs. Montgomery put her hand on my shoulder and smiled widely. "I think you're ready."

Chapter 9

Mrs. Montgomery swung the library door open and I followed her through it. My feet dragged over the short tan carpeting as we approached the reference desk to sign in. My senses were heightened. The empty silence closed around me, like walls caving in on a small space. The books that lined the shelves all around us seemed more vibrant than usual, and the dark wood stood out more boldly than I'd ever noticed before. I couldn't believe I was actually about to help Megan, but I'd made the choice and now had to follow through.

I expected Mrs. Montgomery to excuse herself any second and leave me to face Megan alone, but she stood by my side as I signed in, and smiled comfortingly at me every time I glanced up at her. As we wove our way through aisles of books to get to the section where Megan awaited us, the knot in my stomach grew tighter. I had no idea what to expect. After facing Mazin last summer while clinging to the edge of a cliff, with only Ian there to help, this encounter in the middle of a bustling school should have seemed like cake. But it didn't. I knew the now free Mazin could easily overtake weak-minded people—like Megan.

When we rounded the last corner, Megan looked up and kept her eyes trained on me until I pulled up a chair and sat next to her. Mrs. Montgomery sat on the other side of her, across from me. I didn't expect her to stay long, but secretly hoped she'd plant herself in that chair during every session.

"Atlas," Megan said in her usual snotty voice.

"Hawk," I answered back in the most apathetic voice I could muster. I looked down to give myself a quick pep talk, reminding myself that I could do this, that I had to do this. I snapped my head back up, looked straight across the table at Mrs. Montgomery and smiled confidently. I turned back toward Megan, forcing myself to continue wearing the smile. "Do you have a test to study for, or just homework?"

She gave me a quizzical look and stuttered a few syllables, but recovered quickly. "I have a chemistry test at the end of the week. None of it makes any sense."

"Okay," I said, nodding reassuringly. "Let's see, may I?" I gestured to the stapled study guide in front of her.

She slid it across the table to me and then lazily reached for her book and dropped it in front of me, too. I scanned the paper and then flipped open her chem book to the chapter on Gas Laws. "Well there's an exciting topic," I declared, laughing.

Megan cracked up and slid her arm under her armpit to demonstrate what gas laws might sound like. I couldn't help laughing. Mrs. Montgomery cleared her throat and shot us both a fierce stare.

"Oh, sorry, Mrs. M.," Megan said.

"I think this is my cue to leave you two to your business," Mrs. Montgomery said, pushing her chair back to stand.

"Wait, what? No," I said, regretting my words the moment they escaped.

"Kenza, we'll be fine," Megan said. "Especially now that we've bonded over gas laws."

I laughed. "Yeah, I guess we have."

"Good," Mrs. Montgomery said, and turned quickly to leave.

As soon as her back was turned, Megan's face became serious and the same darkness I'd seen in her last year crept back in. The look on my face must have reflected my sudden shock because her face lightened and she bent over cackling and slapping her knee. I breathed out a long breath.

"Don't worry, Atlas. I'm playing with you."

But was she?

I decided to focus on the task at hand. Not only was I obligated to assist a complete maniac so that I could be allowed to return to camp this summer, but I knew that truly helping Megan pass science might be the only way to save my hide. And there was no guarantee of that— especially if Mazin returned. Still, these were the only cards I had to play.

51

Surprisingly, shockingly, everything went more smoothly than expected. As soon as the bell rang to indicate our session was over, Megan said, "I'm out of here, Atlas." She offered no "thanks," but she didn't try to bully me either. I let my shoulders relax and even whistled on my way to my next class.

∞

That night, I lay on my bed, looking up at the ceiling, holding the phone to my ear until it ached. I was talking to Ian, sharing what I longed to share with my parents about my first day tutoring Megan, but couldn't tell them for fear it might introduce another roadblock that could stop me from going to camp.

"So it actually went well?" Ian asked.

I pictured him lying on his back, his sandy brown hair resting on his pillow as he stared up at his ceiling, too. I wished I knew what his room looked like, what it would be like to spend time there with him.

"Yes, it did, actually—if you mean I made it out of there unscathed. The girl has a serious mental block to science, though. I mean, I'm not saying it's easy or anything, but I had to explain everything over and over and explain it in a way that was really basic so she could grasp it."

"We can't all be brainiacs like you, Kenza." Ian laughed softly.

"Or you," I added. "Don't pretend you aren't because I know you rock at everything you do."

"But don't assume that Megan's not good at anything, just because school is not her thing," he said.

"Wait, whoa." My voice became stern. "So you're defending her now?"

"What? No, it's not like that. I'm just saying that she's probably good at something. And besides, it doesn't matter so much about her. What I meant was that we need to keep an open mind about people."

52

"You're just saying that," I retorted. I was half playing and half annoyed. "You think Megan deserves some sort of special treatment because I—"

His tone flattened. "I didn't mean that at all, Kenza. In fact, I'm trying to look on the bright side here. I hate that you're forced to help her like this. No good principal in her right mind would allow this, let alone require it."

"Mrs. Montgomery rocks, Ian. So don't go there. Besides, you know Dr. Hendrix is the real mastermind behind this."

"What? No way!"

"Yes way," I snickered. "I told you. Don't you remember?"

Ian sighed loudly and his voice softened. "Kenza, it kills me to be so far away, knowing you could be faced with very real danger at any moment."

"Would it help if I text you after every session to let you know that I am okay?"

"It would. And don't you dare forget, otherwise I'll think you're lying on a bathroom floor somewhere."

"Bathroom, Home Ec room, it could be any floor, really," I teased.

"Not helping," he said, his voice once again a tone deeper. "I can't stand this anymore. I can't stand being apart from you."

"It's only a few more months," I said.

"I honestly don't think I can wait that long. In fact, I'm not going to. I'm coming to see you, Kenza."

"Wait, what? That's crazy."

"Not that crazy. Minneapolis is only a few hours from Omaha."

"But I—"

"You don't want me to come?" he asked.

I envisioned his pleading eyes in my mind and I could never say no to them.

"I do. Of course I do. But my dad—"

53

"I'm not coming to your house, Kenza. I'm not that stupid. I don't want to create another reason for your dad to stop you from coming to camp."

It rubbed me wrong that he said it so brashly, but I let it go. I was relieved that he was willing to let it go, too.

"All right," I said. "When will you be here?"

"How does the last week in April sound?

"Too far away," I answered softly.

"Way too far away," he said, laughing.

Chapter 10

For the next few weeks, I met with Megan every day. I wouldn't say that we bonded, but my comfort level around her increased each time I left unscathed. We almost got into it once when I corrected every single answer she gave, but when I told her that I had gotten a 'D' on the test for this section when I first learned it and had to retake it to improve my score, she mellowed out.

When the last week in April finally arrived, I couldn't wait to see Ian. My fears about Mazin had nearly subsided. My mom was feeling great and all outward signs of her pregnancy pointed to the baby doing well. I still regretted my parents' decision about turning down an ultrasound, but I wasn't the one having a baby. I hadn't heard a whisper from Jinny Zzaman or Jamila of Diab—not since the night I hailed Jinny Zzaman and chose the protection of my mother and little sibling over my own, but everything else was going so well so I figured they wanted to give me a chance to be a teenager again, and not some cross-dimensional superhero.

I nearly walked with a skip to the library to meet Megan, and when I turned the corner, I ran smack into her. "Megan?"

"Kenza, what the hell?"

"Where are you going? We're supposed to meet in the library in about two minutes." I looked directly at her, something I would never have done a year ago, or even a month ago, and noticed she looked pale. "Megan, are you okay? You don't look so good."

"Mind your own business, Atlas." She shoved past me, ramming my shoulder as she passed.

I shrugged, and took my sweet time walking to our table in the library.

Megan nearly always arrived before me, and kept her eyes laser-beamed on me until I sat down. I decided to dish out the same disrespectful tactics to her, but as she entered and I glued my gaze on her, I noticed something I hadn't before. She no longer possessed the spaghetti-thin silhouette that I'd known her to have since the first time we'd met. She'd gained some weight—a lot of weight, and I couldn't hide my surprise.

"Stop staring, you bitch," Megan said. "Damn."

"Megan, I'm sorry. I—"

"Zip it, Atlas. No one cares." She raked the chair out and sat down forcefully. "Besides, I have good news." A crooked smile crept across her lips.

I looked at her quizzically and she held up her finger, encouraging me to wait. Then she fished through her backpack, slapping messy stacks of paper down on the table one after another. "Found it," she finally said. Her smirk grew to a full-fledged smile. She shoved the stapled paper in front of me and pointed repeatedly at the grade at the top.

It was written in red, like every other paper I'd ever seen returned to Megan, but I'd never seen her earn this kind of grade.

"A-," she said. "Can you believe it?"

"No," I said and she shot me a fierce glare. "I mean, yes, of course I do."

Her sharp gaze softened. "Well, it's thanks to you."

"No, it's not me," I protested, feeling genuinely proud of her. "You're the one who was willing to give this a try. It took a lot for you to take this step."

"What the hell is that supposed to mean?" she asked.

"I—"

"Never mind, Atlas." She snatched the paper back and shoved it, along with the other quagmire of papers back into her bag. She pushed her chair back and stood.

"What are you doing?

56

"Don't," she held her hand up. "Just don't."

"But I—"

Like a tea kettle ready to steep, I could see the tension rising in her. Her face turned red and she grabbed haphazardly for her bag, inadvertently knocking her chair over. I released a short burst of laughter, and immediately realized my mistake. Megan's eyes widened and she breathed in and out in short bursts, her nostrils flaring.

She gripped both hands under the table and flipped it up on its side, knocking my backpack, notebook and pen onto the floor. I took a few cautious steps back, glancing around for an escape route should I need one. Not a soul was in sight. Megan took a few steps toward me. A red curtain flashed over her eyes and she reached both arms out for me. I staggered back, held up my hands to calm her down. Before I could speak, her face contorted and morphed into Mazin's. His spirit suddenly shot forward, detaching himself from Megan's body, and she collapsed to the floor.

Mazin went for my throat, wrapped his clammy fingers around it, and squeezed tight. I tried to call out, but could only gasp. I twisted, raked at him, even kicked, but nothing worked. I was starting to feel dizzy and I knew I'd passed out if I didn't do something now. Out of the corner of my eye, I saw my backpack lying next to the overturned table. I stretched my leg as far as I could, pointed my toes until I could reach the strap and then quickly twisted my leg back so I could reach the backpack with my hand. If I hesitated, I'd either pass out or Mazin would stop me. I clumsily unzipped the small pocket on the front with one hand and grasped the ancient parchment with the drawing of the Amulet of Omnia in my hand.

I closed my eyes as Mazin's laughter filled the room. He must have thought I was fading out of consciousness. "As soon as I'm done with you," he said, "I'll go after your precious mother and that poor helpless child she carries."

I silently made a wish for Jinny Zzaman and Jamila of Diab to come to my aid and then everything went black.

When I next opened my eyes, a bright white light nearly blinded me. I blinked a few times and saw the blurry outline of several concerned faces leaning over me. As my vision sharpened, I saw that they were all students kneeling down around me. The bright light that had blinded me was nothing more than a panel of light suspended in the ceiling tile above me. I had no idea why I was lying on the ground, or why so many people surrounded me. All at once, a pounding sensation rushed into my head and my hand snapped up to cover my neck. My eyes darted around and I saw the upturned table.

"Someone get Mrs. Montgomery," I muttered. "Hurry." I closed my eyes again, wanting to disappear into the carpeting, not opening them again until I heard her voice.

"I'm here, Kenza. I'm here." It was Mrs. Montgomery's voice. I opened my eyes and saw her kneeling next to me, tears rolling down her face. She reached out and squeezed my arm. "I'm so sorry I put you through this," she said. "It's all my fault."

"No, it's not," I said. My voice sounded dry and coarse.

Mrs. Montgomery tilted her head and, for a moment, weirdly reminded me of Jinny Zzaman.

"It's Dr. Hendrix's fault," I said.

She grimaced. "Let's get you to the nurse's station. Do you think you can walk?"

"Yeah, of course," I said. When I sat up, all the feeling rushed to my head and I rested my temples in my hands, my elbows propped up on my knees.

"Maybe you should lie down," Mrs. Montgomery warned.

"No, I'm fine." I forced the dizziness out of my mind and carefully stood, instantly feeling wobbly the moment I did. I grabbed the back of the nearest chair, and leaned, resting my forehead between my thumb and forefinger.

"Kenza, maybe you should sit down," Mrs. Montgomery said.

"No, I'm fine," I said, waving away her concern. "Let's go, then."

We walked toward the library exit. She let me do it on my own until I nearly lost my balance, and then she grabbed my arm to steady me. I tried to shake her off, but she was not having it. When we made it to the nurse's station, I was thoroughly examined, and fortunately, there were no serious injuries, but I was warned that I'd have black-and-blue marks outlining where Megan choked me.

My first thought was, great, just in time for Ian to visit. My second thought was that they were wrongly accusing an innocent person: Megan Hawk.

"Wait, no," I said. "It wasn't Megan."

Mrs. Montgomery stopped abruptly and eyed me sharply. "Not Megan? Who was it then?"

I realized there was no trying to explain this. They'd never buy it. So I had to at least do something to soften her punishment. "I mean, yeah, it was her. Who else would it be? But it wasn't entirely her fault."

Mrs. Montgomery grabbed my arm. "Not her fault. Kenza, did you provoke her?"

I had to tread lightly. I didn't want Megan to get in trouble for something she didn't do, but I also needed to go to camp at Zenith Hill. "It all started off really well. Megan shared with me that she got an A- on her Science test. I was so happy for her, but when I opened my mouth, it somehow came out like I couldn't believe she was capable of such a thing."

Mrs. Montgomery's grip loosened.

"I didn't mean to hurt Megan's feelings," I quickly added. "And I don't think she meant for things to escalate."

"Kenza, this is a very serious matter," Mrs. Montgomery said, her voice stern. "Are you saying you won't press charges? If you don't, then this is out of my hands and I have no way to protect you from Megan."

Suddenly, Mrs. Montgomery stood stock still. At first, I thought she was thinking about something, but quickly realized she'd been frozen in time, like everyone else in the hallway—everyone but me. Jamila of Diab materialized next to me, a billion pixels coalescing into the form of a girl two years younger than me with long black hair and the same dark brown eyes.

I would have expected her gaze to be steady, calming. Instead, she looked panic-stricken. "It's your mother," she said.

"What about my mother? Tell me now," I said.

"She's okay now that Mazin is gone."

"Mazin?" I parroted.

She nodded, looking ready to speak but before she could say anything more, I asked about the baby.

"Your mother is at the hospital now confirming that everything is okay," Jamila said.

"What happened?" I said, searching her eyes.

"After you wished him away, Mazin went straight for your loved ones. Jinny Zzaman and I believe it was his plan all along. He knew that if he could entice you to call upon us, we would lose focus on your mother—and lose it we did."

"So this was my fault?" A fury I'd never known shot up like a rocket inside me incinerating every ounce of happiness I had. My whole body ached and I felt trapped, drowning in my own rage. I suddenly wished I could transfer the agony I now felt to Mazin and the moment I had this thought, I felt a disc of energy shoot out from all around me like the shockwave from an atomic bomb.

Jamila of Diab blinked out and Mrs. Montgomery began moving and speaking again. "So will you?" she asked.

"Will I what?" I said.

"Kenza, are you sure you're okay? You don't look so well," she said, the lines in her forehead creased.

I nodded quickly. "I'm fine, Mrs. Montgomery. Believe me. And I'm not pressing charges. Megan's innocent. Now please let me be. I have to go." I hurried down the hallway and as soon as I turned a corner, I pulled out my phone and called Dad.

"Kenza, I was just going to call you," he said.

60

"Is everything okay?" I asked.

"Yes, it is now. It's your mother. She was suddenly having premature labor pains, so I rushed her to the emergency room. I was so worried about the baby. Oh my God, Kenza."

"Dad, get on with it. What did the doctor say?" I asked. I was pacing in the middle of the empty hallway, my phone pressed hard against my ear.

"He urged us to get an ultrasound," he said.

"Please tell me you agreed." My tone was sharp.

"Yes, of course we did," he said.

"And?"

"And there is a tear in the placenta. The doctor can't figure out what caused it. It usually only happens when a pregnant woman is very active and only when there is a family history. Your mother fits neither of these circumstances."

I leaned my back against a locker and slid all the way down to the floor.

"Kenza?" Dad said. "Kenza, don't worry. The doctor assures us that everything will be okay."

"You're sure?" I said.

"Yes, one hundred percent sure," he reassured me.

∞

That night at dinner, I shoveled in my food with a ravaging appetite. I still hadn't breathed a word about the incident in the library with Megan. How could I after what happened to Mom?

"So are you going to tell us what happened to you?" Dad put down his fork and stared at me, that disgusted look I hated on his face. I don't think he had any idea how angry he could look, when mostly he was concerned, or feeling a little more out of control than he preferred.

61

I still hadn't told them I was tutoring Megan. They never would have approved, and if they found out now, I knew I wouldn't be allowed to go to camp.

"We were in the library. No one was around," I said. "Megan flipped out and went for my throat."

We sat at the dinner table. We were eating my favorite food: Moroccan couscous made of small grains of pasta with chicken and vegetables. We hadn't had it in forever, but my mom was craving it, and after the crazy day she had, Dad couldn't refuse her request to make it for her. Personally, I could live on tasty, healthy Mediterranean food. In fact, I could probably never get enough of it.

"I don't believe it," Dad said, shaking his head. "Megan wouldn't be in the library, unless she was forced. Did she follow you in there?"

"What? No." I shook my head, giving myself time for the right explanation to materialize but my mind went blank.

"So what was she doing there?" Mom asked, looking as concerned as Dad. She'd put both of her utensils down and rested her elbows on the table, and her chin on her clasped hands.

"She—" I pushed a piece of carrot around my plate, and then a brilliant idea popped into my head. "She was with a tutor. I'd seen her there before. I think they were forcing her to get tutored."

"A tutor?" Mom said.

"Who in the world would be willing to tutor her?" Dad asked. "That girl is nothing but trouble. She'll always be a walking disaster."

No one said anything. I took the opportunity to shovel fork loads of delicious couscous into my mouth.

"Something's wrong," Mom said. She tilted her head to the side.

I snapped my head up. My mouth was still full, but I opened my mouth to speak anyway. "Wait, what?"

"Kenza, no talking with your mouth full. You should know better," Dad said.

"Oh sorry," I replied, my mouth still full.

"Kenza, I'm serious. Something's not right." Mom got that twinkle of recognition in her eye, and at first I thought she was happy about something and I was off the hook, but then I realized she'd figured it out—as always.

"You're a tutor, Kenza. You have been for weeks."

"Well, yeah," I shrugged.

Dad sat up straighter in his chair. "You never told us who you were tutoring."

I looked at him sharply. "Wait, whoa, where are you going with this?"

"We are getting to the truth," he said. He leaned forward, resting his elbows on the table.

I gazed at him, squinting.

"We need to know, Kenza," Mom said. "Who have you been tutoring for these last few weeks?"

I said nothing and shoveled in another big forkful of food.

"You can tell us, Kenza. It's better if you do. We won't punish you for doing the right thing, even if it led to this," Dad reassured me.

I raised my eyebrow, looked at Dad, then Mom, then back at Dad. "Okay, first, Dad this food is so good. So let's hurry up and get this over with so I can finish my plate. Okay."

Dad smiled.

"So yeah, all right. I have been tutoring Megan for the past few weeks."

"What?" They said it together, their necks craned as far forward as they could.

"Mrs. Montgomery asked me to. How could I say no?"

Dad slapped both hands hard against the table. "How could she? I have never seen such incompetence from a school official."

"I can't believe she would do such a thing, either, Kenza," Mom said. "Why didn't you tell us earlier? Did she ask you to hide it from us?"

63

"What? No way. Of course not," I retorted. "Besides, it wasn't really her doing anyway. I guess it was Dr. Hendrix's idea." The second my words escaped, I wished I could reel them back in.

I saw my dad's eyes widen and braced myself. "Dr. Hendrix from Zenith Hill? That's it." He pushed back and his chair fell to the ground behind him. For a moment, I thought he was going to overturn the table, like Megan had, or throw dishes against the wall, like he did last year, but he didn't. He ignored his fallen chair and began pacing. "How could I ever conceive of you returning to such an awful place?"

"You know, Adam, I'm with you," Mom said. "I am completely confounded. I don't think I can let you go back either, not after he showed such incompetence in his decision. He didn't even consult with us first."

I shoved my plate an arm's length in front of me, clasped my hands together, and pursed my lips. I knew better than to argue, at least now. I'd give them time to cool down, wait until the heat died down. My father hated being blindsided.

"I never should have let you go to that camp in the first place," Dad added.

I puckered my lips, trying to keep them shut, but so wanting to go off on him.

"Adam," Mom said, reaching her hand out for his arm.

"Stop," he said, brushing it away. He looked straight at me. "Kenza, you are not going to camp this summer."

"But Dad—"

"Adam—"

"No, it's simple. I see that now." He shook his head. "You are not going back to camp, and you are not going anywhere out of my sight this weekend."

"Dad, no! I didn't do anything wrong. I was only doing what the adults asked me to do, and Megan had changed so I didn't see the need to make you worry. They did it for the right reasons, Dad." I pleaded with my eyes. "Besides, Dad, I have plans this weekend, important plans."

64

"Not anymore." He shouted, pounding his fist against the table.

I slowly pushed my chair back, stood, and calmly walked away even though I was shaking inside. Would I ever see Ian again?

Chapter 11

When I retreated to my room, I caught a whiff of the awful smell that preceded Jinny Zzaman. "What's wrong now?" I asked the moment she appeared.

"Hello to you, too, my dear Kenza." She smiled and bowed her head as if greeting royalty.

"I'm on edge tonight, Jinny, so can we cut the crap and get right to it. Why are you here?"

Jinny said nothing for a few moments. She just gazed at me, tilting her head this way and that. "You've experienced a very challenging day—one very few humans ever encounter while incarnate on this earth."

"And?" I pressed.

"And I have news that may lift your spirits," she said.

I said nothing, but gestured for her to hurry up and spill.

She inhaled a long, slow breath, released it very slowly. I crossed my arms and tapped my foot as I waited for an explanation. "It seems that you are in the clear with Mazin for some time," she finally said.

I lifted onto my toes. "How can that be? What did you and Jamila of Diab do?"

She shook her head. "I'm afraid we cannot take credit for his dismay."

"Then who?" I asked.

She said nothing and gazed at me until I finally understood. I pointed at my chest. "Me?"

She nodded.

"How? When?"

"We traced the incident to the moment Jamila of Diab visited you at your school today," she explained.

"You mean when my anger took over and I couldn't think straight until I wished I could transfer my suffering to Mazin?" I walked over to my bed and sank into it, staring off into nothing.

Jinny floated over next to me. Her movements caused her blue dress to sparkle and shimmer all over the room. "Why does this news bother you? I thought it would please you," she said.

"I don't know," I said.

"Surely you do," she said. "After all, you are the one feeling it."

I looked up into her eyes. "It scares me that I have that kind of power. It confuses me, too."

I stood and wandered over to the mirror, gazing at the ring of reddened skin around my neck. I noticed how much I resembled Jamila of Diab—in every way, except the freckles and petite nose I'd inherited from my mother. I reached up and ran my finger down the slope of my nose. Jinny Zzaman stood behind me, her dress sparkling in the reflection. She placed her hand on my shoulder and tilted her head. "What else is troubling you?"

"Jinny, why am I capable of debilitating an evil spirit, and yet I cannot control simple things in my life, like whether or not I will get to go to summer camp?"

"Who says you cannot control that?" Her words sank into my mind like quick sand, thrashing around and struggling to fit into my belief system. She smiled warmly, recognizing that she'd struck the intended chord with me.

"So that's it, then?" I asked. "Mazin will stay away from us now?"

"My dear," Jinny responded. "You know him far better than that. You are safe for a time, but he will likely become even more desperate for revenge. Once he regains his strength, he may be willing to do anything to make you suffer." She began to fade away. I reached out to stop her from leaving, but realized I didn't have anything more to say. The rotten egg scent that accompanied her took much longer to disappear and the whole visit left me feeling nauseous.

∞

The next morning, my dad started watching me like a hawk. He insisted on driving me to school, and picking me up afterward. He even walked with me into the school building so he could talk to Mrs. Montgomery. Of course, he didn't let me go with him, afraid I might try to sway his decision about camp.

When I ran into Mrs. Montgomery later that day, she quickly reassured me that she'd continue to do everything she could to change his mind. I proceeded to reassure her that no one would do more to convince him than Mom and me, but I was thankful for her help. I was going to camp again this summer, and no one was stopping me—not my dad, not Mrs. Montgomery, and definitely not Mazin.

Friday night, my parents made me stay up late playing board games with them. On Saturday, Mom cooked eggs and Dad drove me to the library, where we spent hours. I knew there was no way he'd let me out of his sight so I had to act fast. When we got back from the library, I rummaged around in the medicine cabinet. I wasn't sure what I was looking for, but I needed something strong enough to safely detain them for the few hours I needed to go see Ian.

I found exactly what I was looking for: sleeping pills prescribed by Mom's doctor, so I knew they wouldn't harm the baby. I thought it odd that Mom was willing to take sleeping bills while she was pregnant, but reticent to have an ultrasound. In any case, I dumped four pills into my hand, and crushed them into powder. I steeped a pot of tea, filled two cups, and—my hands shaking—sprinkled the white powder into the cups. In no time, the remnants of powder from the pills disappeared into the hot tea. I added a sprig of mint leaves, poured in a smidge of milk, and added a spoonful of honey—just how they liked it.

"Kenza, this is so thoughtful," Mom said.

"It is," Dad said. "What do you want from us?" He smirked.

"Can't a girl do something nice for her parents?"

"Of course," Mom said. "It was very nice."

68

"No, no, no." Dad shook his head. "Kenza wants something from us."

"You got me, Dad," I said. "I want to go to camp, all right." I grabbed the jar of honey and slammed it on the table. "Enjoy your tea."

I turned and left the room, headed up to my bedroom and started getting ready to see Ian. We were meeting at a posh Italian restaurant in midtown at 5:30. I hadn't talked to him all day and was so excited to see him I could barely stand it. It was odd that he didn't call. I promised myself I'd call him the second I stepped out the door. Seeing as how I was grounded from using my phone, calling any sooner would mean risking sending a flare straight up in the air, notifying my parents that I was up to something.

Instead, I applied one last dab of lip gloss, fixed a few loose hairs, and headed for the door. I trotted down the stairs and carefully peeked around the corner. If the sleeping pills hadn't worked, my dad would instantly know that I was going somewhere. At first, I didn't see them anywhere. But when I ventured out into the living room, I found them sprawled out on the couches—Dad on the long one, and Mom on the loveseat, both snoring like lumberjacks.

"Sorry," I whispered as I tiptoed past them and toward the door.

I walked the few blocks over to Lacey's house, where she was waiting to give me a ride. Even though we both had our driver's license, she had a car—albeit an old, clunky one whose breaks screeched when we turned corners too fast. My parents still hadn't even let me drive by myself in one of their cars. Lacey's dad believed that pushing her to experience and learn as many things as early as possible would mean she could gain the real world experience she needed by the time she went off to college. I always wished my dad saw things that way, and was thankful that at least my mom did.

"So how'd you sneak away, Kenza? I honestly didn't think you were going to make it," Lacey said.

"What? Oh, my parents were napping."

"What if they wake up while you're gone?" she asked.

"Oh, don't worry," I said, waving a hand. "They're really tired."

She crossed her arms and stared at me for several uncomfortably long seconds, then snapped herself out of it. "Well, what are we waiting for?"

She drove much like my dad, with a lead foot on starts, and stops. I wasn't complaining, though. I was excited—no, thrilled—to get to see Ian again. Ever since he'd promised to come to Omaha, I imagined the feel of his lips on mine. I shivered at the thought that it would almost certainly happen tonight.

"So he's meeting you at 5:30, right?" Lacey asked.

"I think so."

"Kenza, what do you mean 'I think so?' That doesn't sound very certain." She turned to face me.

"Hey now, new driver, eyes on the road, all right?" I braced myself against the dashboard.

"I am, Kenza. But answer me. Please."

"I—I meant to call him on the way to your house, but got too caught up imagining all the twisted ways my parents will punish me if they wake up."

"I thought you should be more worried about that than you showed." She focused on me again, and I pointed at the road.

"No, it's fine," I said. "I'm fine now. Really." I fumbled for my phone. "I'll call Ian right now."

"Good," Lacey said, nodding her approval.

The phone rang until it went to voice mail, so I hung up.

"Call him again," Lacey ordered.

So I did. Still no answer.

"Maybe he wants to surprise me."

"Yeah," Lacey agreed. "That's probably it. When was the last time you talked to him, though?"

"Yesterday during school. He knows I'm grounded and not supposed to be using my phone except to call my parents, so I bet he's worried about calling at the wrong time and getting me into trouble."

"Kenza, he doesn't know this area very well. He's probably concentrating on navigating traffic and finding the place."

∞

We rode in silence for the rest of the drive. We hit every red light possible, which left me gnawing on my nails. We pulled into a big parking lot, next to a quaint old building surrounded by tall office buildings, new urban bars, and shopping centers. The Italian restaurant's old-fashioned yet posh style stood out like a sore thumb, and a welcome refuge. I jumped out of the car and Lacey did, too. The deal was that she'd accompany me inside until she delivered me safely to Ian. Then she'd hit the nearest bookstore and get lost in books until it was time to pick me up. I owed her big.

"Do you have a reservation?" the hostess asked. I noticed her short skirt and tall heels, and hoped Ian wouldn't.

"I'm not sure," I said. "I'm meeting someone—a guy my age."

"What's his name?"

"Ian. Ian Hampton."

She shook her head. "I don't see that name on our list. And I haven't seen a guy your age yet."

"Can we sit somewhere until he arrives?" Lacey asked.

"Sure. It's such a beautiful evening, I'll seat you outside, if you like. That way you can watch for him."

We both nodded and followed her to a table on a large octagonal-shaped deck outside the door. We were the only ones out there. She brought us two Italian sodas and their meatball appetizers. As we sat and talked, I told Lacey what I could about how much my relationship with Ian had grown over the last summer. I'd already told her so many things before; I had to take care that the stories I told now matched. It proved difficult to leave out all the paranormal experiences we'd had together.

We finished both sodas, and ordered two more. I kept checking the clock on my phone and, after a while, Lacey did hers, too. We finished every last meatball and our second round of Italian Sodas.

"I hate to say it, Kenza, but we should probably get you back before your parents notice you're gone."

I slumped and propped my arm up to rest my chin on my fist. The phone rang and it felt like sunshine poking through the clouds on a rainy day. "Hello," I said eagerly, answering before I checked to see who it was.

"Kenza."

I gulped hard. "Dad?"

Lacey leaned in, reached her hand out and grabbed my arm, pulling me close so she could listen in.

"The oven, Kenza," he said.

"What do you mean, Dad?"

"The oven. Mommy's got a bun in the oven. She's going to have a sweet little baby. Then we'll get to ride the camels and the elephants . . . but not the tigers." His voice sounded groggy.

"Definitely not the tigers," I said, affecting a serious tone, yet unable to stifle a laugh.

"I'm going to go now," he said.

"Yeah, you should hang up and close your eyes," I said softly.

"Hang up and close . . . my . . . eyes." He released a long, slow yawn and hung up.

Lacey and I burst out laughing. "We should go," she said, in between laughs.

I nodded and pushed my chair back to stand.

"Leaving so soon?" It was the sweet sound of Ian's voice calling out behind me. He looked a little taller and very pumped up, like he'd been working out big time. His sandy brown hair swept loosely to one side and his smile was still radiant . . . I'd missed his smile so much.

"Ian!" I turned and gave him a bear hug.

He gave me a quick peck on the lips. Then he said, "Mmm . . . I'd like some more of that." He pulled me close, wrapped his arms around me and kissed me tenderly.

After a few moments, Lacey said, "Okay, okay. Geez, you two. At least wait until you're alone."

Ian pulled away, but not before giving me one last peck on the lips. He turned to Lacey and she reached out her hand to shake his. He ignored it and held his arms open wide to give her a hug.

"Well, aren't you charming," Lacey said.

"You must be Lacey," Ian said, a smile plastered across his lips. She nodded. "Thanks so much for giving Kenza a ride. I don't think I could have gone another day without seeing her."

"That's pretty obvious," she said, smiling back. "Well, why don't I leave you both to it. Kenza, I'll be back in an hour." I flashed her a sad puppy dog face, and she added, "I know it might feel impossible, but you'd better be ready to say good-bye to prince charming by then or your dad will threaten to ground us both for the rest of our lives." I nodded, my smile as wide as Ian's. Lacey turned and headed for her car, shaking her head the whole way, muttering something about young love.

Ian laced his fingers in mine and we followed the hostess to a cozy little round table in a secluded corner. Ian released my hand while I looked at the menu, but reached for it again as soon as we finished ordering. During dinner, he kept leaning way over and gently kissing my cheek. One of the times he leaned over, he whispered softly in my ear, "I can't believe I found you, Kenza. I never thought I'd be this happy."

The entire dinner continued like this, until we were both startled by the sound of my ringtone. It was Lacey chewing me out for making her wait out front, and reminding me that my dad could wake up any second. I assured her we'd be out as soon as the waitress returned the check, even though Ian had already handled the bill a while ago. I needed just a little more time with him.

"Kenza," he said. "I have to tell you something before we leave." His tone had turned serious and he leaned in, his expression stern.

"What is it? Tell me now," I said.

He squeezed my hand harder. "I want to tell you why I was late."

"I meant to ask you about that." I brushed a wisp of his hair to the side.

"I don't know what happened," he said. "I was heading west on interstate 80, day-dreaming about you—about what it would be like to kiss you again, and I suddenly realized I was heading in exactly the opposite direction."

"What do you mean you suddenly realized?" I said, logic kicking in. "You must have exited and got turned around."

"No, Kenza. I mean yes. That's what I must have done. How else would I get turned around? But I don't remember doing. It's like I blacked out. And there's more. I have a vague memory of looking in the rear view mirror and seeing a red curtain over my eyes."

∞

After a seemingly never-ending series of good-bye kisses interspersed with severe warnings from Lacey, I soon thereafter was quietly slipping through the front door. My worry for Ian spiked to an all-time high and, even though it was too risky for him to call me while he was on the road, I made him promise to text me when he arrived safely home.

Both of my parents were still sprawled across the couches, even though they'd been out for over two hours. I wandered into the kitchen to make sure every last bit of evidence had been removed and then decided I needed the aid of Mom's sleeping pills to get my mind off Ian, so I took two for myself and chugged them down with a glass of water.

Before I got too groggy, I quickly changed into what I had been wearing before I dressed to see Ian, retrieved blankets, and draped one over each of my parents. Then I grabbed one for myself and climbed into the recliner. Frightening thoughts pounded through my mind as I dozed off: What if Mazin attacked Ian? Would he be strong enough to protect himself? I closed my eyes, hoping the sleeping pills would kick in fast.

74

Sleep was the only thing that could rescue my addled mind from driving me completely crazy.

Chapter 12

My parents woke up before me and both nagged me to go up to my bedroom, where they assured me I'd be more comfortable. I resisted at first, trying to convince them that I was just as comfortable as they must have been even though they did not retreat to their bedroom. But when I remembered that Ian should have arrived in Minneapolis by now, I sprung to my feet and hurried up the stairs.

"Finally, Kenza," Ian said when he answered my call. "Didn't you get my texts?"

"No, I—"

"I assumed you got caught. You didn't get caught, did you Kenza?" his voice sounded urgent.

"No, my parents were still asleep when I got home, so I lay down on the recliner and fell asleep. When they woke up, they assumed I'd been asleep the whole time right there with them."

"Good strategy," Ian said, laughing as if I'd planned the whole thing.

"How about you?" I asked. "I take it you arrived home safely. Please tell me you did."

"Worried about me, were you?" he said.

"Of course I was."

"Yeah, I made it home with no problems. I placed an ancient Peruvian protective barrier around the car this time before I left. If I thought Mazin might attack me on my way to see you, I would have placed one around my car before I ever left the Twin Cities. I guess I didn't think Mazin had it in him to get to me after what Jinny Zzaman said you did to him."

"I didn't think he had it in him, either. He's more desperate than I thought," I said. I fell back into my bed, still groggy from the sleeping pills. "At least he wasn't able to take over for long yet, or cause any real harm."

"You're right about that, but we should be more cautious than ever. He might be counting on us doubting his abilities. He doesn't play fair, Kenza. You know that better than anyone."

∞

When I returned to school on Monday, I was surprised to see Megan in the hallway. She'd been suspended, and I expected her to be out of school for longer than a day. The moment she saw me, she headed straight for me and I braced myself for another attack. "Why did you help me?" she said.

"What?" I said, stunned at her words.

"Mrs. Montgomery told me you didn't press charges. You should have, Kenza. I don't even remember choking you. What kind of crazy am I if I can't even remember that?" Her strained expression told me she'd probably spent several long, sleepless nights full of angst and regret.

I wished I could tell her the truth, but there was no way I could bring another innocent person into the supernatural mess that was my life. "Megan, please. It wasn't as bad as everyone made it out to be."

"Then how come you still have marks around your neck?" She pointed at the ring of bruises that wrapped all the way around it.

Instinctively, I snapped my hand to my neck. "It's not as bad as it looks," I said. "Besides, you didn't mean to hurt me, and look at you. Clearly, you regret what happened."

"You know, Kenza, you're all right." She patted me on the arm and hurried away down the hallway.

I released a lung full of air and headed toward my next class. Over the next few weeks, Megan and I agreed to secretly meet for more tutoring. She truly had changed and I wanted to help her reconcile her inexplicable act of terror, the one that never would have happened if Mazin wasn't after me. The library was no longer a viable meeting place. We had to get creative and find quiet corners of the school where the staff would not see us together. If they did, they would surely intervene and forbid any further interactions together. I even had to keep our meetings hidden from Lacey, who would not hesitate to go to the office and rat us out if she found out.

Somehow I managed to survive the "not going to camp" threats that came at me from every direction and I was only a few days from flying back to Oregon. For a while I totally believed my dad's threats to thwart my plans would triumph, but I solicited Mrs. Montgomery's help—she owed me, and thus delivered—and worked on softening Mom's resolve at every opportunity. I wheedled and whined and begged and even resorted to guilt to get my way. Yes, I played the "new baby card," acting like I suddenly felt pushed aside, accusing them of not caring as much about me—and my future, i.e. the opportunities attending the stellar Zenith Hill would provide—as they once did. I wasn't particularly proud of myself, but I simply had to go. Destiny called and that destiny depended on me spending the summer in the lush hills overlooking the Pacific Ocean at Zenith Hill—with Ian.

I had my suitcase lying on my bed and piles of clothes and incidentals sprawled all around my room. When my bedroom door flew open, I spun around to see my mom burst into my room. Her eyes were wide and the muscles on her face tense.

She waved her hand and held out the portable home phone. "It's Isabel." She cupped her hand tightly over the speaker. "She's crying."

I jumped up and snatched the phone from her. Isabel always called me on my cell, never the home phone. "Hello, Isabel?" I gnawed on my fingernail, paced. "What's wrong?" I thought that maybe she and Keelam had a fight. Ever since we'd left camp, they talked almost every day. They remained as infatuated with each other as Ian and I were.

Isabel gasped out words. "It's my dad," she said, succumbing to an avalanche of sobs.

Mom crossed her arms, looking even more worried.

"It's okay, Mom," I whispered. "It's her dad. I'll come tell you later." I shooed her away with my hand until she left.

It took a while, but I finally dragged the story out of my camp roommate. Her father, whom she hadn't seen for years, showed up—drunk. The only thing worse than an overprotective dad was an absent one. Apparently the errant father had come in blazing with anger, flashing a gun, threatening them.

"That a-crack!" I said loudly. "Are you okay, Isabel?"

I heard footsteps pattering down the hall. Mom pushed on the door and stuck her head through the narrow opening. I waved my hand furiously, but she refused to go, and insisted I hit the speaker button. Then, we both heard how the Chief of Police had followed Isabel's father from a local bar to their house, worried that he'd do something rash.

My mom's eyes widened and her mouth dropped open. I held my finger to my mouth and shaped my lips into the word "shh." She came and sat next to me on the bed, draped her arm across my back.

"The Chief grew up with my mom and dad, so he hauled Dad off to jail," Isabel explained. "Mom is going to get a restraining order." Just then Isabel's mother called for her and she quickly hung up, but only after promising to call later.

"Kenza, I'm so sorry," Mom said, wrapping her arms around me like I was a little kid again, my head on her shoulder. "I can't believe the Chief of Police would swing by and check on her," Mom observed. "That would never happen here. Omaha is too big. By the way," she added, "don't tell your father about this or he might change his mind about letting you go to camp."

"Why?" I asked.

"He'll think Isabel's dad will follow her there," she said.

I felt myself tense, wondering—no, certain that Mazin had overtaken him.

"But that will never happen," she continued. "Not after they incarcerated him."

Chapter 13

I did harbor some guilty feelings—and delivered a little self-bashing because I was leaving my mom when she was seven-and-a-half months pregnant. I definitely felt guilty about that, but she'd been fine, the doctor had said everything seemed to be progressing fine, and I could always fly home when the time came—or at least that's what I kept telling myself.

To save Mom and Dad the trouble of driving me to the airport—and me the guilt-inducing task of actually seeing their faces as I boarded the plane—I called a cab. They protested, of course, but I convinced them it would be best for Mom to avoid the stress, and that Dad shouldn't leave her alone that long. How could he? How could I?

I expected everything to be normal back at camp—like it was last year with our tiny dorm rooms and time to settle in followed by a series of outdoor survival challenges, but there was nothing normal about it. I arrived around noon and met Isabel, who had arrived minutes before me. Seeing her smiling face made me happier than I'd felt in a long time. Her dreadlocks were gone and her blond hair was now short and streaked with pink highlights. I wondered if her spunk was still intact after what happened with her father.

The sophomores hadn't arrived yet—only juniors and college bounders. Nobody knew where Seniors were. Sophomores were not expected for another few days. Isabel didn't know if Mrs. Bartolli would once again be our faction leader, or if she'd been replaced. Even when we reached camp, no one reported seeing her. I really hoped she'd be back, but I also wondered what it would be like to have a more lenient faction leader. Having an FBI agent bossing you around, giving you impossible tasks, and watching your every move had distinct drawbacks. She piled on the pressure—and limited our fun, or at least that's the way we mostly felt.

No one had seen Ian, either, and that news caused every muscle in my body to tense. I'd spoken with him just before I left; he was already changing planes in Colorado, so he should have arrived before me. Still, he didn't answer any of my texts or calls since my plane landed here in Oregon. I couldn't stop thinking about Ian: obsessing, really. What if Mazin had gotten to him again?

Isabel and I made a beeline to our room to drop off our stuff. We were no longer staying in the "Costa Rica" wing. This summer, we were housed in "Guatemala," and it wasn't a wing—it occupied the entire top three floors of the "Central America" dormitory.

"No way," I said, as the doors swung open.

They'd replaced the cram-packed dorm room concept from last summer with a spacious apartment. We had a living room, kitchenette, and even a balcony. Better still, Isabel and I each had our own rooms. That was the best part; I tended to cherish my privacy, but I never expected it here.

I'd almost finished unpacking when I heard a knock at the door and rushed into the living room, praying it would be Ian, but instead I found Ryan, his curly head bobbing as he peered into the opened fridge. He'd grown about a foot, and was even skinnier than last year. Ryan was always about food. He'd nearly fainted with hunger when we lost a challenge last year and barely ate anything.

"Yours is full, too," he said.

The thought of checking out what might be in the fridge hadn't even crossed my mind.

"What? No hug?" Isabel asked, laughing at his predictability.

I heard an audible thump as Ryan bumped his head against the roof of the fridge as he backed out.

"Always for you." He smiled, stretching his arms out wide for Isabel, who rushed into them. They looked too eager to hug, and if I didn't know any better I would have guessed they were crushing on each other, but I did know better. These two were like brother and sister.

"Where's Naomi?" I asked before they separated. She and Ryan got pretty close last year and I wondered if their relationship developed over the winter like mine had with Ian.

"She's still unpacking." He gave me a squeeze, too, his glasses flattening against his face as he pushed his cheek against mine. "Good to see you, Kenza," he said, releasing me quickly. "Get your swimsuits on and we'll head to her apartment before heading to the lake."

"Swimming suits?" I asked, not liking the sound of that. Over the past year, my curves really took shape. Being short like my mom, they stood out and I only wanted one pair of eyes on me: Ian's. "Yeah," Ryan said. "The leaders are doing some big reveal at the lake, and they told us to wear swimming suits or trunks."

We slipped on our swimsuits and were soon closing the apartment door behind us.

"We have to stop by Keelam's first," Isabel said, as she jiggled the door to make sure it was locked. I was anxious to see Keelam, too. A memory flashed through my mind of Isabel and me dragging his unconscious body out of Atlantic Ocean Lake. I wished I could erase that memory, but keep the one of him throwing a water balloon and hitting Mrs. Bartolli squarely in the chest. It was the first time he'd met everyone on our Gandhi collaboration team and he won them over instantly.

"Of course," Ryan said.

My jealousy felt like fiery red ants racing around inside me. Isabel and Ryan had already connected with their other half. Suddenly I couldn't wait anymore: "Have you seen Ian?"

"Nope. He won't answer my calls or texts or anything. I think he wants to break up with me," Ryan said, giving me sad puppy dog eyes.

His joke landed with a thud in my gut. Isabel shot Ryan a sharp look and he retreated, appearing to realize his mistake. Anger and worry wrestled in my mind, two alligators splashing and rolling in murky water, ever since I arrived in Oregon.

Isabel quickly changed the subject. "What's at the lake anyway?"

Ryan shrugged. "No one knows. Mrs. Bartolli just said everyone has to meet there. No details, but that shouldn't surprise us. Remember

82

last year when they tossed us into boats and then forced us to rescue our drowning leaders, just to see how we'd react?"

"So Mrs. Bartolli is here," I said, not sure that was a good thing. She'd put us through the ropes last year, kept such a tight grip on what we did and where we were that we'd constantly been sneaking around, terrified that we'd get caught and suffer the consequences.

"Of course she's here," he answered. "Where else would she be?"

∞

By the time we reached the lake, it was almost 2 p.m. Ryan, and his big mouth, had done a bang up job of spreading the word for all the juniors to meet there, and we'd helped. We stood, scattered across the eastern shore of Atlantic Ocean Lake, along the side that led to "Africa's" exercise facility. I could see a clear shot of our tree house from where we stood and powerful memories continued to flood in: memories of our Collaboration Team building our tree house, of my first kiss with Ian, and of nearly getting raked over the edge of a bridge by Mazin.

Access and the view to Atlantic Ocean Lake had been blocked off with red curtains all the way around it. Camp director Dr. Hendrix stood in front of a podium, on a makeshift stage next to it. His hair looked grayer against his mocha skin than it had the previous year and, while he didn't wear a formal robe like he had at most events, he still looked rather proper in his khakis and white button-down shirt. "Welcome back juniors!" he bellowed.

Last year on the first day, we would have kept our mouths shut— this year we were obnoxiously loud, whistling, hollering, and clapping. A few of the guys even ripped their T-shirts off and swung them wildly like lassoes above their heads.

Dr. Hendrix waited a few minutes for the crowd to quiet down. "Last year was a very significant summer. Many of you spent more time away from home than you had ever previously done. Each one of you was a stranger when you first arrived, and yet you made friendships that are likely to last a lifetime. Together, you managed to escape the

83

underground on your first day, you met a collaboration team leader who made a significant impact on your time here, and at home, and every single one of you survived the Sycamore challenge—building tree houses more impressive than we've seen in years. Last summer, your sophomore class also overcame many unexpected conflicts and injuries by reaching out to help one another, even when it was scary, and even when offering help personally put you in a position of risk.

"For those aforementioned reasons, it is with great pleasure that the camp staff would like to dedicate a new structure in honor of your commitment to leadership, discovery, achievement, and philanthropy. Please join me in welcoming an honorary student from your class, who will introduce this structure to you. Juniors, please welcome Ian Hampton to the stage."

My heart leapt and color poured into my cheeks. Isabel reached over and squeezed my hand. "He's here," she said, her voice amped up.

My eyes snagged on hers and I smiled widely, but at the back of my mind I wondered why he hadn't told me about this. When Ian made his way to the front of the makeshift stage, Dr. Hendrix and the camp staff stood. He looked more sun-kissed than when I saw him at the Italian restaurant in the spring. Ian cleared his throat and scanned the crowd—looking for me, I hoped. Unfortunately, I was lost in a sea of people. If everyone at camp were there, we would have come close to four hundred people instead of the hundred or so juniors present.

"Junior campers," Ian began, and the crowd cheered—even louder than Isabel, Ryan, and me. Naomi, her red hair pulled back in a ponytail, whistled loud enough to drown out the crowd.

"What many of you do not know," Ian explained, "is that I owe my collaboration team, the Gandhi's, for their honor—and I owe them dearly. You see, even when I broke the rules during the tree house challenge last summer, they literally saved my life."

A murmur erupted throughout the crowd and many eyes focused on me.

Ian paced back and forth on the stage. "Determined to debunk a myth I'd heard about Shadow Forest, I struck out by myself—long after everyone sane was in bed. The act was even more reckless than I'd realized, as I was soon lost in the middle of the forest, in a downpour.

Just as I realized I'd done the wrong thing, I tripped over my own feet and fell into a cold stream. At the time, I didn't realize I'd broken my ankle, but I couldn't walk on it. Thanks to our training, I knew I was susceptible to shock and worried that I'd pass out. The pain became excruciating and early signs of hyperthermia began. At first, I started shivering uncontrollably. Then I started hallucinating."

"As you might imagine, I was not in my right state of mind. I should have activated the red button on my Datadrix," he cuffed his hand around the spot where our implants had been installed last summer, "but I didn't. I was afraid to get my collaboration team in trouble. So instead, I called Kenza and Isabel and asked them to risk their safety by coming to retrieve me."

Naomi and I locked eyes. She leaned over and whispered, "He's an amazing liar."

I shushed her and she didn't say anything more.

"When Kenza and Isabel realized how badly hurt I was," Ian combed his fingers through his hair, "they called on Naomi and Ryan for help. Naomi and Ryan had the courage to contact the ERT, something I should have done immediately. Thanks to them, my ankle healed more quickly than the ERT—or any doctors who treated me— expected. I don't know where you are right now, but you guys rock! I love you guys."

While many cheered, Ian's eyes scanned the crowd until he finally spotted us. When his eyes engaged with mine, he smiled warmly and crossed his hands over his heart. The crowd roared, pumping their fists into the air and bouncing up and down in a chaotic dance.

"So," Ian called and the volume in the crowd dropped a notch. "I bet you want to know about the structure Dr. Hendrix mentioned." The volume spiked, but silenced when Ian pointed to the endless stretch of red fabric that blocked our view of the lake. "The structure is visible just beyond that curtain. Atlantic Ocean Lake is still there; it hasn't disappeared. But now it looks much more like a real ocean than a mere lake. Last year, a group of campers from the college freshman team collaborated with SeaWorld, the Omaha Henry Doorly Zoo, Schlitterban, and Infinity Pools Construction to create the world's very first lake— made up of one-part fresh water and one-part salt water. The fresh water portion on the top is now a giant clear-water swimming pool and, while we are swimming in it, we will be able to see silver schools of fish passing beneath us as they glide through the coral reefs. We will also see sting rays, sea turtles, and even tiger and zebra sharks."

When a hand shot up, I lifted onto the tips of my toes to see who it belonged to, but the person's face was shielded by the swarm of people. "How do we know those sharks won't bust through and eat us?" Keelam! He must have wandered off to find his own collaboration team.

Ian laughed and nodded. "I wondered that same thing, my friend. The glass is reinforced and has been thoroughly tested to withstand the pressure. You know, we could stand here all day and talk about it, but if you're anything like me, you're ready to pull down this barrier and dive in."

Fists shot up into the air and the crowd erupted into clapping and cheering.

"That's what I thought," Ian yelled, pumping his fist at the crowd. "I need the help of every single junior to line up along the wall of fabric. We've measured and there should be plenty of space for everyone."

We obeyed and, within a few minutes, we stood facing the fabric—all except the camp staff and Ian, who remained standing at the podium back on the stage.

"On my 'go'," Ian called, "reach your hand out, grab a piece of the curtain, and pull it down. Are you ready?"

The crowd shouted, "Yeah!"

"Ready?" Ian called. "Three . . . two . . . one, go!"

We yanked at the fabric and it fluttered to the ground, looking like a ribbon rippling in the wind. It revealed the sparse outline of wooden scaffolding that had served to hold the curtain in place. It also revealed the largest crystal clear swimming pool I'd ever seen, with a collage of underwater color from the center of the pool all the way to the sandy beach where the swimmable part of the lake was the most shallow. Like a flock of birds all taking flight at the same time, the crowd of one hundred junior campers ripped off their shorts and shirts, exposing bikinis, one-pieces, and swim shorts, and kicked their shoes into the sand. We ran, uninhibited, toward the water and splashed right in.

The water felt warmer than I expected, and my observation was confirmed when Ian announced that the salt water below had to be kept at 77 degrees for the survival of the sea creatures, so the water on the top needed to mirror it within a few degrees. He explained that all the sea creatures had been rescued from a life-threatening injury, as evidenced by the malformed shark that swam below me. At such close proximity, I couldn't help shrieking and running to shore. When I looked up to see if Ian had seen my cowardly escape, I caught him staring straight at me, laughing. I waved him down to join me from the stage. He smiled even bigger, ripped off his shirt and came running.

Everyone else had already reached the water—everyone except the camp staff, who had a perfect view of us embracing on the beach, a few feet from the water line. I didn't care, though. Our embrace wouldn't disqualify either of us from participating in camp activities, not even with Ian's screw up last year. And from the looks of it, Ian's involvement with the reveal of sea creatures under the lake may have helped make up for some of his forfeited points from last summer.

We wrapped our arms around each other and I didn't want to let go—not ever. After a moment, he eased his hand up my back to stroke my hair, kissed my forehead, and then leaned back to look down into my eyes. I'd forgotten how beautiful his eyes were—cinnamon colored with little flecks of yellow.

"I've missed you." His voice was a deep whisper.

"I've missed you, too." My response was light years from the fiery one I'd rehearsed in my mind before I knew he had arrived safety at camp. "But where were you? How come you didn't—"

He lifted his finger to my lips. "Shh. We're together now. Let's just be happy about that, okay?"

When he pulled his hand away, the magnetism between our lips burned to the core of my being. I squeezed my eyes shut, trembling as I waited for his mouth to reach mine. As if playing with my soul, as if intending to torture me, he slowly inched his face down, stopping milliseconds from our lips touching. When I sensed the warmth of his mouth so close, I opened my eyes only to see that his eyes were still closed. He looked so happy, as if this was the moment he'd been waiting for, too.

I wanted to smash my lips against him, to kiss him with power and fury, but I didn't allow myself to move. I held my breath until I finally felt his skin on mine—a soft feathery touch that deepened as we pressed our lips and our hearts together. He opened my mouth with his tongue, and whatever anger I'd been clinging to transformed into dancing smoke and stars swirling around me. Our embrace lasted longer than I expected, but not long enough. After all the threats from Mrs. Montgomery and my parents, and the baby being due this summer, I feared we'd never be allowed this moment at camp again.

When at last I stepped away, we looked at each other and smiled like two little kids who'd succeeded at invading the candy jar. He reached out his hand and I laced my fingers in his. We turned toward the water, he kicked off his shoes, and we ran in. The beveled glass under my feet felt like soft sand, and it even slowly sloped down, just like the shore.

We ran hand-in-hand, fighting the resistance of the water, until we were neck-deep in it. Ian pointed toward something moving under us. I drew in a deep breath and dove in, keeping my eyes wide open. Underneath me, a gray shark at least twice my size swam past, his tail waving to propel him forward. I came back up for air and instinctively lifted my knees to my chest, waving my arms to keep myself afloat.

"What's wrong?" Ian asked.

"It freaks me out to see a shark swimming under my feet."

"Don't worry." He reached his hand out to my shoulder. "The glass they used is reinforced and there is no way it will break. It's a prototype for an underwater city experiment."

The word "prototype" made me shiver. My dad had explained to me how they made them in his engineering program. Prototypes were just like they sounded: not fully tested.

"Come on," Ian said and then dove beneath the surface.

Despite my fear, I followed him but hesitated to open my eyes this time. The moment I did, I saw scores of color heading toward me. A four-foot sea turtle floated past, its feet paddling slowly. I noticed a long scratch scored into its back, and remembered that these creatures had all been rescued. Despite the fact that my scars were all invisible, I understood the painful memories that came with each. Once the sea turtle passed, a school of silver fish, about ten feet below, swam in one direction, and then turned to swim in another, as if performing a carefully choreographed dance. Way below them, the sea floor was spotted with giant gray and brown boulders, sea anemones swaying this way and that, and a few sea horses bopping up and down in the current.

Longing for another breath, I pushed my feet off the fresh water's glass bottom and emerged to fill my lungs with air. I wiped the excess water off my face and slicked my hair back. Ian emerged right after me, shaking his head like a dog and dotting my face with water.

"Thanks." I laughed.

"Isn't it amazing?" he said.

"This whole thing is amazing." I stretched my arms out wide above my head. "With the fact that a jinn brought us together, that we'd been lovers centuries before who met again at this weird camp in Oregon, that we fought off an evil spirit together, and now we're swimming above dangerous and amazing sea creatures swimming below us, I still sometimes think I'm dreaming."

Ian reached out for my arm and pulled me toward him. I wrapped my legs around his body and we embraced again, kissing without coming up for air for a long time.

Chapter 14

Mrs. Bartolli allowed us the luxury of an entire day to swim and enjoy ourselves before forcing us back into the usual rigid camp routine. Still, we had to meet at 8:00 a.m. sharp the next morning, and instead of meeting in the France Room of the Europe building, like last year, she called a meeting in our Gandhi tree house. Ian, Isabel, and I met for breakfast and walked together to The Sticks. I didn't see Naomi or Ryan at breakfast, so I assumed they'd had an early breakfast and wanted to be prompt to our first team meeting.

When we reached the clearing on the path where our tree house came into view, we all began to sprint toward it. As soon as we approached the staircase, Isabel and Ian bounded up to the tree house and disappeared through the door. I, on the other hand, stopped at the bottom of the wooden stairs and craned my neck back. Images from last year's drama flooded into my mind, a torrent of bliss sprinkled with fear and regret: getting to spend a solid week in our tree house with Ian, Isabel's arm nearly being sliced in half by a falling window, and me nearly being flung by an evil spirit over the railing of one of the tree houses on the edge of the cliff. Before I had time to clear my thoughts, Ian peeked his head through the tree house door and frowned when he saw me still standing in front of the staircase.

He bounded back down the stairs and headed straight for me. "Kenza," he said softly, reaching out for both of my hands. "What's wrong?"

I shook my head and pasted on a fake smile.

He tilted his head, bent his knees enough to gaze level into my eyes. "It's okay," he whispered. And then a little more loudly, "Mazin can't get to you. Remember? Not directly, anyway." He released one of my hands and squeezed my bicep. "Wow! Somebody's got a killer arm. I wouldn't be surprised if you threw Mazin all the way to the Atlantic

Ocean. You probably threw him all the way to Morocco, where he had allies that helped him escape."

I cracked a real smile.

"There," he said, drawing out the word. "I knew that was in there somewhere."

"When I say 8:00 a.m., I mean 8:00 a.m." It was a boisterous voice, one that I recognized instantly.

I turned to see Mrs. Bartolli approaching behind me.

"You both best have your feet planted in that tree house before mine are or you'll seriously regret it." Her voice sounded as scratchy and antagonizing as ever.

Ian released my hand and we raced up the stairs. He pushed the door open and I followed him in. It felt good to see the tree house again—a home away from home. I looked around and breathed in the rustic scents, and then made a sweeping glance at the couch and the beanbag chair, the kitchenette, and the wood—so much wood. That thought led me to Ian's missing Bottle Full of Wishes, the Peruvian good luck charm that the villagers where Ian was first abandoned— and later adopted—gave him. I shivered, wondering what kind of havoc Mazin might bring this summer—if he brought any.

Ian interrupted my thoughts. "Where the hell are Naomi and Ryan?"

Isabel was already sprawled out on the couch—the Gandhi motto hanging above her head: Live not for you alone but for the greater good. She shrugged sharply, as if she thought Ian was accusing her of hiding them.

"Mrs. Bartolli's on her way up," I said.

Isabel's blue eyes widened, and before we could say another word, Mrs. Bartolli walked through the tree house doorway. "Tell Ryan and Naomi to get out of the bathroom or wherever they're hiding. We've got business to attend to," she instructed.

We exchanged glances.

Mrs. Bartolli appeared to catch on immediately. "They're not here yet? What the devil?"

91

Her words conjured an image of Mazin in my mind, nearly identical in looks to Ian except stiff and cold-hearted. Ian, the reincarnation of Mazin's twin brother Amal, would never be completely free of his psychopathic relation, but neither would I. How could two people look exactly alike and have diametrically opposed personalities?

"Time stops for no one," Mrs. Bartolli said, clicking her heels together and beginning her usual routine of pacing. I squeezed into a spot on the couch between Isabel and the now seated Ian.

In the cramped space, Mrs. Bartolli's pacing made me dizzy. She stepped quickly and did an about face every few seconds. "This summer will be different from the last, Gandhis. There will be no more light challenges like building a tree house."

The three of us exchanged another glance.

"This year, you must earn your keep."

"What do you mean earn our keep?" A voice called from the door.

Mrs. Bartolli spun in that direction, just as Naomi and Ryan entered hand-in-hand. Naomi's hair looked disheveled and a twig was sticking up out of it. I assumed they'd been rolling around in the grass together. I expected Mrs. Bartolli to immediately bark orders at them, but instead her lips creased into a long flat line and she stood stock still, her hands welcoming them into the room like royalty. They both looked at their feet as they scurried to a spot on the floor next to the couch.

"Thank you for gracing us with your presence," Mrs. Bartolli said, bowing to them, her voice laced with arsenic. "Do I have your permission to get to business or perhaps you'd like me to make you some bacon and eggs first?"

"No, please," Ryan said, coughing nervously.

Mrs. Bartolli's eyes widened in shock at Ryan's gall to speak, and Naomi socked him in the arm. "Ow." He grimaced, but shut his mouth.

Mrs. Bartolli clicked her heels together again and resumed pacing. "It seems that Kenza, Isabel, and Ian have lucked out." She crossed her arms and kept moving. "You see, this summer, you will be responsible for paying your way through camp. I bet you all love your

92

new apartments, don't you? Spacious and equipped with the latest in sound and TV entertainment, including your very own bedroom."

We nodded in unison.

"Bet you thought that was a perk. Bet you thought it was going to be free, cost you nothing. You were wrong. This summer, you must earn your keep. You'll need to make enough points to pay for your room and board, plus an extra 1,000 points each toward your Gandhi faction fund."

"Where are you going with this?" Naomi asked.

Mrs. Bartolli drew in a long, slow breath, and then exhaled forcefully. "Naomi, you still need to work on your patience. I shall be sure to provide this skill development as another requirement that must be met for you, in particular, to hold a new job."

A job? Many of my friends back home—Lacey, Zack, and Hannah—sought jobs this summer. I always thought I was exempt from that—that I'd spend my summers here at camp and be entitled to a free ride at college, again foregoing the need to work. Now that I knew I had to work, I wasn't worried. I was attending one of the most intriguing camps in the US. The jobs here had to be equally intriguing.

"Why do we need a Gandhi faction fund?" Naomi asked as she leaned back, her arms propping her up behind her.

"That is not your concern right now, Naomi. Think of it as a savings account. Surely, you understand why everyone needs one of them."

Naomi's expression went blank.

"How do you expect us to earn our keep? Where are we going to find jobs around here?" Ryan said.

"First," Mrs. Bartolli said holding up one finger. "You and Naomi will be working much harder than Kenza, Isabel, and Ian. I just changed the rules. You will each need to make 2,300 points toward the fund and they will only need to earn 1,800 each."

"But—" Naomi blurted.

"I can make it worse if you'd like," Mrs. Bartolli warned. Naomi and Ryan remained silent. "Good choice. A better choice will be to arrive on time to your duties. Now, let me explain how it works. Last year, you may have thought that adults were waiting on you hand and foot, but that was not the case. You see, behind the scenes, the juniors were really the ones keeping this place afloat. In the cafe, junior chefs cooked your food, and they composed the cleaning staff, pet care attendees, you name it. Sure, each had a supervisor. For example, Mr. Rylan supervised the pet care barns, but the juniors were the ones who kept the stables clean and the horses and dogs fed."

"Is that why Carter and Lisa served as tour guides?" I asked.

Ian eyed me sharply, likely due to my mention of Carter. He'd been jealous of the attention Carter paid to me, said he'd never trusted him.

"Precisely," Mrs. Bartolli said.

Isabel meekly raised her hand.

"Isabel, if you have something to say, speak," Mrs. Bartolli barked.

"It's a bit off topic, but is Carter's dad okay?"

"Oh yes." Mrs. Bartolli clapped her hands together and lifted onto her toes, dropping back down quickly. "He had a long, slow recovery, but he's fine now. In fact, he was able to leave the hospital right before Christmas."

Ian jumped up and raced for the door.

"What is with you people today?" Mrs. Bartolli said. "Anyway, thank you for your concern, Isabel, very thoughtful . . . very, very thoughtful. Now, back to the available job opportunities—"

Ian returned, pointing at his throat. "Sorry, bug in my mouth."

I knew better. He looked queasy and I knew it was because I'd told him how Mazin had possessed him last year and used him to place a curse on Carter's family. Even though Ian was in no way to blame, he felt full responsibility for Carter's father spending half of last year in the hospital.

"You will spend the next week completing a series of tests," Mrs. Bartolli continued. "They will serve two purposes: 1) they will help us match you to potential colleges that will support your unique talents and interests, and 2) they will narrow down your options to jobs at camp that will help develop skills you will need to complement those talents and interests. Now, do not underestimate the value of menial tasks, such as cleaning toilets. Hard work, humility, and perseverance can all be gained from such an important responsibility."

We all groaned and the creases around Mrs. Bartolli's mouth deepened. "At 9:00 a.m. today, you are expected at the United Nations cafe, where your Datadrix imprints will be reinstalled. After that, your tests begin at 10:00. Oh, and Naomi and Ryan?"

They raised their eyebrows.

"Be prompt." She clicked her heels one final time and turned abruptly to leave. I felt the tension seep out of me the moment she was gone.

"Let's go then," Ian said. He jumped up from the couch and reached his hand back for me to follow. I grasped it, warm and strong, and he pulled me to my feet. He held my hand, so securely I felt invincible, like nothing could ever go wrong again.

"Kenza, look," Isabel called from across the room in front of the door.

I'd been focused solely on Ian and didn't see what was happening in the center of the room, but as soon as I took one look, the blood pumping through my veins turned to ice and I felt the connection between Ian and me grow cold, steely. Jamila of Diab, my ancient ancestor brought back to life for the first time since the incident with Megan in the library, as a sort of hologram, stood before us in the middle of the tree house, her usually crisp signal so fuzzy and jittery, I feared she would blink out any second.

"Jamila," I called, happy to see her beautiful face again. I let my hand slip away from Ian's and reached for her. When my fingers approached her skittering image, a current jolted through me, causing me to yank my hand back.

"Please," Jamila said. "I don't have much time or energy. Do not try that again. It depletes my energy, and I have something I must tell you."

"I won't," I said, a bit gruffly. I looked down at my hand and shook it out to ease the pain. Ian approached and stood next to me, his arm pressed against mine.

Jamila held up her hand slowly and tried to speak, but static mangled her words. Somehow I heard the next ones very clearly. "It's Mazin . . . blocked your access to us again. Find the amulet . . . " Her image blinked out completely and didn't return.

Even though I wanted to purge myself of every last insecurity, even though I wanted to pull Ian and Isabel aside and talk for hours about the dire news we just discovered, I had to eat my words. I had to gulp down hard, twisted knots of fear and fury. Mazin, a psychopathic spirit was on the loose again with nothing to get in his way—and it was all my fault.

Ian looked into my eyes, reached for my hand, and gave it a squeeze. I nodded quickly, acknowledging his concern, acknowledging his support. He should have been pissed. I was the one who'd captured Mazin. I'd outwitted him, and the moment I did, I threw away all hope of keeping him trapped. Out of fear and hatred and the desire to send him hurtling as far away from me as possible, I'd chucked the bottle—him corked securely in it, thanks to the Amulet of Omnia I'd sacrificed—out over the cliff, near the Teresa's tree house and into the Pacific Ocean below. But there was no undoing it now. The bottle, the Amulet of Omnia, and clear communications with Jinny Zzaman and Jamila of Diab had become a faded figment of my memory, like Mazin had been. If I'd only had the foresight to keep the bottle with me, he'd probably still be my prisoner.

"So you guys coming or what?" Ryan suddenly said. It was an innocent question—an obvious one. Ryan had missed the lapse in time we'd just had, completely unaware that it happened.

My head snapped toward his direction. His sudden reanimation startled me and I must have looked like I was ready for a fight.

"Whoa, Atlas." He stepped back a few feet, chuckling. Then he cocked his head toward Ian. "What did you do, man?"

Ian shook his head. "Come on, Kenza. We'd better leave now or we'll be late."

I followed Ian, my hand gripping tightly to his. I didn't allow myself another glance at Ryan on my way out, but I could feel his eyes—and Naomi's—following me suspiciously until I cleared the door and headed down the tree house staircase.

Isabel, Ian, and I tried to distance ourselves from them several times on the way to the UN cafe, but to no avail. Even though they were incapable of seeing Jamila of Diab materialize in the middle of the tree house, they weren't idiots. I could tell that they knew something was up.

Chapter 15

When we reached the UN, we were directed to a room off the main cafeteria to get our Datadrix imprints reinstalled. Then we were directed to our first exams. I'd hoped that I'd be able to stay with my collaboration team during the exams, but of course—like in school, friends were separated into different rooms. On the bright side, I somehow lucked out and ended up sitting in front of Keelam. He looked exactly like he did last year: same towering height, thin but not gangly, and medium-length, curly black hair. I decided to tease him, so sat down without acknowledging him. Of course, he was having none of that. I instantly felt a quick sharp tug on a strand of hair at the very back of my neck, right where it hurts.

"Ouch," I called, catching the attention of Dr. Dunbar—correction, Astronaut Dunbar—at the front of the room.

She looked like the type who preferred spending month-after-month in isolation, out in the open skies, over supervising a full class of rowdy teens. She hurried over to where I was sitting. "Everything okay, Kenza?"

I had to crane my neck back to look up at her; she towered over me. I bobbed my head a few quick times and said, "I'm fine. Sorry about that." I didn't have it in me to cook up a lie, and I was relieved when she smiled and walked away.

The moment I felt comfortable that she was gone long enough, I turned back toward Keelam and raised the tablet in front of me, pretending like I intended to smack Keelam with it.

"Easy, easy," he said softly. "Besides, I was just trying to get your attention. I can't believe you didn't recognize me."

"Keelam, I could never forget you. I was playing with you to get a reaction, but I wasn't expecting it to hurt so badly. It made my eyes water."

"Kenza, my girl, I'm sorry about that. Sometimes I don't know my own strength."

I let out a short laugh and turned back to face the front, but immediately felt a tap on my shoulder. I turned, prepared to retaliate against Keelam, until he motioned for me to get closer. "What now?" I whispered.

"How does Dr. Dunbar know your name?"

"I'm sure she knows everyone's name," I snapped.

He shook his head. "She didn't even know mine, and I'm kind of popular with the staff, after what happened at the lake last year." I suddenly tensed at the memory of Keelam lying unconscious under the surface of Atlantic Ocean Lake, Isabel and I pulling him out and me contacting the ERT to cart him off to the mini camp hospital the staff referred to as the North Pole.

I squinted my eyes, turned and faced front in time for Dr. Dunbar to explain the tests we were about to take. "These aren't actual tests," she said. "Today, we are simply gathering data on your preferences—things like: are you better solving theoretical problems, teaching others, or working with your hands."

Several people laughed at that last statement. She cleared her throat and started swaying front to back from toe to heel. "As I was saying, we want to find out what you are really interested in—find out what intrigues you. Studies show that when you pursue a field you love, even if it doesn't come naturally at first, you are far more likely to excel and even make breakthroughs than if you pursue a career based on external factors, such as family pressure or a desire to make money. Often, those reasons end up backfiring, negatively affecting the quality of your work and even your health."

She began to pace at the front of the room, from one end to the other, and back. Her pace crawled compared to Mrs. Bartolli's, and I found myself tapping my foot nervously. She finally spoke again, "Please answer honestly. Answer what you think and feel, not what you expect we, or anyone else, would want to hear. Ready? Go!"

It took all day, with two short breaks and one hour for lunch. By the end of the day, my wrists felt stiff and my butt ached. I couldn't wait to exit the room and never return, but that wasn't happening. "Be here again tomorrow morning at 9:00 a.m. sharp. We'll have you complete tests all week. ACTs are next, followed by SATs and then a few college essays to help you become better prepared. You should all be used to this sort of thing." And we were, but it was the last thing any of us wanted to do on our summer break.

All week, they released each section at different times providing the perfect opportunity to eat lunch with Keelam and catch up on how he was doing. During one of the mid-morning breaks, he told me that he and Isabel talked almost every day from the time camp let out last summer to the time we'd returned. I'd heard Isabel drone on about their connection all year, and now I was hearing it directly from him. He was enamored with Isabel, and she was enamored with him. From what I could tell, she had good reason—he was so real, so easy to talk to and be with that I confided in him about how Ian visited me at the Italian restaurant in the spring.

"He's a hopeless romantic, just like someone else I know." Keelam said, smirking as we walked back into the test room from break.

My eyes snapped up. "Who, you?" I said.

He laughed. "You may be right about that. Isabel put some kind of magic spell on me and I can't resist."

"Yeah," I replied. "I kind of know the feeling."

"Kind of?" he parroted.

I let out a nervous laugh. "It's like you can read my mind sometimes," I said.

"Hey now." He held up both hands. "I never read minds. I just hear stuff . . . "

"What stuff?" I asked as I slid into my desk, my heart pumping a beat faster.

"Why did I have to go and open my mouth?" He sank onto his chair, looking deflated.

"Keelam, what are you not telling me?" I'd twisted myself to face him directly, resting my elbows on the front edge of his desk.

100

He gave me a furtive look. "Grab something for lunch and meet me outside, behind the hedges that line the walkway around the lake, but don't let anyone see us. They might get suspicious."

My eyes widened. "I—"

Keelam snapped his head up and eyed someone approaching. I assumed it was Dr. Dunbar, so I slid around toward the front and buried my head in my work, not bothering to look up. We worked all morning on our ACTs and, while it was one of the most important exams I'd ever taken, I struggled to concentrate. I barely finished the math section before they called "time."

When we were excused for lunch, Keelam whispered in my ear, "Hurry and meet me by the hedges." His shoulder brushed mine as he sped past.

I raced for the cafeteria, where I grabbed a protein bar and an apple. I was almost out the door when I heard Ian call my name and ground to a halt, weighing options in my mind. I wanted to take off in a sprint and hope Ian would assume he'd mistaken me for someone else, but my rational self knew with one hundred percent certainty that he'd follow me. So I decided to turn around, my mind scanning for reasonable escape options. Sadly, nothing came to mind.

"Kenza, finally our schedules match up," Ian said, huffing to catch his breath. "My lunch break is almost over, but I'm guessing yours is just starting." He nodded to the protein bar and apple in my hand.

"Hmm, yeah. We don't have long, though. I have to . . . go—"

"Where?" He asked, looking annoyed.

"Nowhere," I quipped.

"Kenza, what's going on? Has something else happened?"

"No . . . no, it's nothing like that. I mean I am worried about Mazin being on the loose, but right now I'm more worried about the tests we've got coming up. Keelam was going to help me, so I was—"

"Why Keelam?" he said, the lines on his forehead showing concern.

"Oh come on, Ian. You aren't jealous of Keelam are you?" I said, in a teasing way.

101

"No, I—of course not." He waved his hand to blow the suggestion away. "No, please."

Part of me longed for him to be jealous, to show his jealousy outwardly like he had last year with Carter . . . but he shrugged, smiled sweetly, and turned to walk away.

I ran out the side door and headed straight for the hedges Keelam had mentioned.

"What took you so long?" he said.

"I ran into Ian." I pointed back at the door.

Keelam quickly stole a glance behind me, scanning the area to make sure we were alone. "We don't have much time." He raked my protein bar and apple out of my hands and tossed them into the hedges. "We'll pick them up on the way back."

"Keelam, I'm starving."

He ignored my protests and grabbed my arm, leading me toward the trail that wound around Atlantic Ocean Lake.

"Where are we going? I don't want either one of us to be late for our ACTs."

"That's why we need to hurry. Are you okay to run?"

I nodded and we broke into a steady gallop until we passed Australia on the far end of camp. Next to his long legs, and the fact that I detested running, I had a hard time keeping up. "Stop, please," I finally said, holding up one hand and leaning with the other on my knee.

Already several strides ahead of me, he turned to face me. He barely sounded winded and I wouldn't have guessed that he'd been running if I hadn't just witnessed it. "Let's at least keep walking."

"Where are we going?" I demanded, straightening up, stretching my spine. "I'm not taking one more step until you tell me."

He examined me, squinted his eyes. "I really wanted to show you. If you find out how much I know, you might flip out. Lord knows we don't have time for that."

"How much you know?" My voice rose. "What the hell do you know?"

He held his hands out in front of him, lowering them slowly as if his gesture could release all the tension in my muscles. When he spoke again, in the gentlest voice, his efforts to calm me were successful. "I know that we need to look for something along the beach," he said. "I know it could be a matter of life and death. If finding it could help Isabel, if finding it could help you, then that is what I need to dedicate myself to doing."

"First," I said, pointing at him sharply. "Do you have any idea how long it would take to get down to the beach? There's no way either one of us is missing our ACTs. Second, what exactly do you think we're looking for on the beach? Seashells?"

He inhaled a long slow breath, his shoulders rising and falling as he did. "Kenza, I know a short-cut."

"A short-cut?" Despite my desire to stop it, a stubborn smile crept onto my face.

He nodded and smiled. "Come on. I'll explain as we walk. The trail is right behind these bushes."

We ducked past the bushes and headed down a steep, sandy path that led straight to the beach. "A promise is a promise." He said, shrugging. "I said I'd tell you what I know so are you ready to hear it?" I nodded. He drew another deep breath. "I know about Mazin. I know about Jinny Zzaman, and I even know about Jamila of Diab. At first I thought Isabel had a very active imagination, but when I found the Bottle Full of Wishes lying in the sand down here—"

"You found what?" I said, digging my shoe into the soft sand.

"The Bottle Full of Wishes," he repeated. "I found it empty near—"

"Empty?"

"Empty," he parroted. "It's right over here."

"You left it down here?" I spun around, my finger instinctively pointing at him.

He nodded, didn't say anything.

"If you know about how dangerous Mazin is, how could you do that?" I said, poking my finger into his chest.

He laughed and I could feel tension boil up within me. Without thinking, I raised both arms above my head and waved like a wild ape. "Stop laughing. This is serious," I barked. He doubled over laughing even harder, which transformed my anger into laughter, too.

When we regained control, he said, "I thought it would be safer here, looking only like just another throwaway. I also thought it'd be best if you were the one to pick it up. I didn't want to risk disrupting whatever vibe it might have. So now that we're here, let's stop wasting time and find it." He turned and started kicking at the sand.

"Where did you leave it?"

"I could swear it was right over here." He kicked at the sand a few more times, then knelt down to sift it between his fingers.

"Let me help." I rushed over to where he searched.

Keelam stood swiftly and turned to face me, fire in his eyes, as if a red curtain of anger had closed over them.

I took a few steps back, tripped over a long, thin, tree root partially buried in the sand, and landed flat on my behind. When Keelam rushed toward me, I skittered back like a crab on all fours, until I felt something unexpected: the wooden lip of a bottle. Keelam stood over me now, his eyes still glazed over, reflecting the fiery red signature of Mazin's dark spirit.

"Keelam, you're not yourself right now," I said, trying to buy time as my fingers dug furiously to unearth the bottle that was deeply wedged into the sand.

"You're going to drown in this ocean, Kenza, and no one will know what happened," Keelam said, his voice raspy, another sign that Mazin had overtaken his physical body.

Trying not to attract his attention to what I was doing, I gently wiggled the bottle, but couldn't free it from the sand.

"Keelam, tell me about Isabel," I said, hoping deflection would work.

He hesitated for a moment, and I could tell that the real Keelam was struggling for control of his mind. I finally managed to free the bottle from its grave and quickly aimed the opening at Keelam's face, sand flying at his eyes.

He yelled and covered his face with his hands. I turned, scampered to my feet, and bolted for the trail that led back to the UN, gripping the bottle as tightly as I could. With every gasping breath, I felt like my entire body could collapse—not from exhaustion, but from sheer panic.

As I rounded the path along The Sticks, halfway between Australia and the Africa fitness building, I heard footsteps pattering behind me and turned to see Keelam, his long gangly legs closing the gap between us. I ran harder, faster.

"Kenza," he called, not once but several times.

I tuned him out, ran with every ounce of energy I could muster. We were about thirty feet from the UN when I felt his hand on my arm.

"Kenza, please," he said. "It's me. I'm back."

I turned quickly, afraid I'd still see the red curtain over his eyes, but his beautiful chestnut-colored eyes had returned to their normal color.

"Keelam, what happened to you?"

"I don't know. It's like I was on autopilot." He shook his head, trying to clear any residue left behind from Mazin's energy.

I clicked my Datadrix and glanced at the time. "Come on. We're late." I yanked at his sleeve, dragging him toward the building. We jogged through the double doors to the UN, down the long haul, and into the classroom.

Dr. Dunbar greeted us with silence, but her face reflected a twisted ball of confusion. I followed her eyes to the Bottle Full of Wishes, with bits of sand still clinging to it, and shoved it behind my back, even though I was already busted. I'd never heard Dr. Dunbar raise her voice, until she belted out one boisterous, pointed word: "Atlas!"

I slowly walked toward her, wishing I could make the bottle disappear behind my back. Keelam scurried to his desk.

"You're not off the hook, Keelam Sky," Dr. Dunbar added, her eyes darting at and scalding him. They only lingered for a moment before returning to scald me. "Hand it over, Kenza."

"What? No, I—"

"What is it anyway?" she asked. "It looks very old."

I still had it hidden behind my back and had been hoping she didn't get a good look, but realized she had eagle eyes. "It is very old, actually. It was a gift."

"Is that the reason you are late to the test?" She crossed her arms.

"Not exactly." I looked down at my feet. "Someone gave me the bottle last year, but I lost it and Keelam told me he'd seen one like it down on the beach, so we—"

"I see." Dr. Dunbar uncrossed her arms and softened her face into a smile. "It was such an important gift that you had to look for it the minute Keelam offered to help you find it."

"That's right," I said, and then lifted an eyebrow, sensing she was up to something.

"You didn't think I was going to let you off the hook that easily, did you?" she asked. "Kenza, these tests have strict rules about start and stop times. I shouldn't allow you or Keelam back in."

"But you will, won't you?" I gave her my best puppy-dog eyes.

"I will," she said, "if you will give me your bottle."

"What are you going to do with it?"

"I'm going to keep it."

"You mean while I take the test, right?" Nerves danced up my spine. Ian would never speak to me again if he knew I'd recovered the Bottle Full of Wishes, only to lose it so quickly.

"That's debatable," she said.

"But I—"

"Kenza, you're about to miss out on ever being able to take this test here," she said, "let alone being able to get your precious bottle back."

106

I nodded, handed the bottle over and inhaled a long, slow breath. My lungs filled with air, but it wasn't nearly enough to steady my nerves. I made my way to my desk, and slid in, a wave of dizziness washing over me. Everything went black, so I gripped the edges of my desk and fought to clear my mind. The blackness slowly faded away and the world, with all its colors and movements, painted its way back into view. I stole a glance at Keelam, who crossed his eyes and stuck out his tongue at me. I had to cover my mouth so I wouldn't laugh out loud, and, as I turned back around, felt the presence of someone standing over me.

Dr. Dunbar had pushed her face up against mine, so close I could feel her hot stinky breath against my face. "You have a lot of lost time to make up," she hissed. "The test ends when it ends, and there'll be no exceptions for you, or your friend Keelam Sky."

I nodded, but didn't give her the satisfaction of another glance. After several minutes of breathing down my neck, she finally stood and walked away. I blocked all thoughts of Mazin and forced myself to focus on the exam. All my life, I'd done everything I could to secure my chances of going to college and acing this test was something I had to do. When I finally reached the last question, sweat had pooled on my forehead. Seconds after I filled in the answer, Dr. Dunbar called time and instructed us to put our pencils down.

Everyone flooded out of the room—even Keelam, but I fought the current. I made my way to the front of the class and approached Dr. Dunbar.

"Yes?" she said curtly.

I cleared my throat. "May I please have my bottle back?"

"What makes you think you're ever getting it back?" A red curtain slid over her eyes.

"Sorry, I—" I turned and ran out the door as fast as I could, straight into Keelam's arms.

"What the—"

"She wouldn't give it back. She . . . her eyes—" My breath caught.

"Slow down," Keelam said. He released me, but kept his hand on my back and rubbed it gently. "So Mazin got to her, too?"

I nodded vigorously.

"What the hell is going on?" I heard Ian's voice, floating through the air from down the long hallway.

Keelam's hand dropped away.

"What the hell is right?" I said. "Mazin is on the prowl, here at Zenith Hill."

"Already," Ian said, shaking his head.

"Mazin just overtook Dr. Dunbar. Her eyes. . ." I said.

Silence sat between us for several long seconds.

"How do you know?" Ian finally asked.

I looked around to make sure no one would follow us and then grabbed Ian and Keelam by the sleeve and led them toward the door. "Not here," I said.

Chapter 16

We rushed back to my apartment, but Keelam had a collaboration team meeting and scurried away. The minute we were safely inside, Ian turned to me, his face contorted in anger. "How could you brush me off to go tromping down to the beach with him?" he asked.

I held my hands open in front of me in a questioning gesture, but said nothing. How could he ask me such a ridiculous question?

"Did you think it was okay to go to the beach? With him? Alone?"

"Jesus," I muttered, "what century are you from?" And then I realized how idiotic that sounded and busted out laughing. Some core part of Ian's being, particularly in relation to me and our relationship, was, in fact, from the past, the distant past . . . around 500 years back.

He didn't even crack a smile. "Why did you go with him there? What were you doing?"

"He had something to show me. It couldn't wait, Ian. I promise. You know I wouldn't risk being late for a college entrance exam unless it was something extremely important."

"Did he try anything on you?" Ian asked, eyeing me suspiciously.

The door swung open and Isabel came bounding through. "Did who try anything on who?"

"Good, you can help me," Ian said. He stood and hurried to Isabel's side, jabbing his finger pointedly in my direction. "Kenza went to the beach today, alone, with Keelam."

"And?" Isabel asked, her disposition as cheery as it was before he told her.

"And, don't you think that's odd?" he asked, quite earnestly.

"Odd, how?" She plopped down onto the loveseat, flicking off her flip-flops and lying down, her bare feet dangling over the armrest.

Ian turned away from her, let out a frustrated grunt, and shook both his hands. He swiveled back in a hurried motion and said, "Do I have to spell everything out for you? They were together—alone. Don't you get it?"

She sat up on the couch and shook her head, her face blank. I had to give her some credit. She obviously trusted me—and her boyfriend—as much as she trusted her lungs to breathe. Her already high rating with me skyrocketed.

Ian began pacing, his arms shooting off in different directions as he muttered something incoherent. I'd never seen him act like this, ever. Sure, he'd occasionally played the jealous boyfriend, but—not since cursing Carter last year, causing Mazin to overtake Carter's dad and send him to the hospital—he'd never acted so aggressively.

A shiver zigzagged through me and I jumped up from the couch sending my cat Jazz running for cover, little wisps of fur dancing into the air behind her. I stood in front of Ian and reached out for both his hands.

"Look at me, Ian," I said, using a gentle voice.

We gazed into each other's eyes. Thankfully, no sign of Mazin's red curtain overshadowed his eyes. All I could see were the yellow flecks in his light brown eyes that I loved so well.

"Kiss me," I said.

The tension on his face melted and he leaned forward until his lips met mine. I squeezed my eyes shut. Time stopped and I felt magic coursing through us, real magic, magnified by two ancient powerful beings connecting through us. Then something soft, but dense, hit me in the back of the head and Isabel started laughing hysterically. Ian and I separated, opened our eyes, and saw couch pillows all around our feet. Isabel lay sprawled out on the loveseat again, her legs kicking wildly at the air to the tune of her laughter. She looked like she was five years old again, wearing the widest smile.

"See Ian, she loves you," Isabel said.

"I see," he admitted. Then in a more intimate voice, he said, "I'm sorry for doubting you, Kenza." He gave me a quick peck on the lips.

"It's not me you should worry about offending," I said, narrowing my eyes.

"Shit, Keelam," he said.

I nodded vigorously and Isabel jumped to her feet to approach. "Wait, did you two find the Bottle Full of Wishes on the beach?"

I nodded.

"That's what this was about?" Ian asked.

Isabel held her hand up in front of his face to silence him.

"What about the Amulet of Omnia? Was the bottle still corked?" Her words were now racing.

"And where is the bottle?" Ian asked. "You did bring it back with you, right?"

"Whoa!" I held up both hands, signaling for them to put on the brakes. I hurried to the couch and plopped down so I could explain everything. They both remained standing, seemingly too shocked to move. I gave them the rundown of events.

"So Dr. Dunbar still has the Bottle Full of Wishes?" Isabel asked. "That doesn't sound like something she would do."

"I know," I said. "Even though Mazin had escaped, his vibes clung to the bottle like bits of earth clung to sea shells. Only this 'dust' could possess enough potency to poison someone, if they got too close to it."

"We have to get it back, Kenza," Ian said, sounding frantic. "The Peruvian villagers where I grew up during my first few years of life designed it to hold good energy, but in the wrong hands it could be manipulated to increase someone's negative energy. Think of it like a magnifying glass."

"If the Bottle Full of Wishes works like a magnifying glass for energy," I said, "then the Amulet of Omnia works like a transmitter that could jettison energy into space."

"Finding the bottle may help us find the amulet," Isabel suggested.

111

"What we need is a plan," I said, "some way to get the bottle back, without arousing any suspicion."

∞

Unfortunately, in addition to all of the SATs, ACTs, and personality tests designed to help narrow down the best fit for careers and colleges, we were expected to prepare and submit at least five college applications. We didn't have the time or energy to immediately hatch a scheme to retrieve the Bottle Full of Wishes. And the very next morning, Mrs. Bartolli called an 8:00 a.m. meeting in our old tree house in The Sticks. This summer was proving far more mentally draining than the previous year, albeit less physically draining — so far, at least.

Based on the previous meeting, we knew well enough to arrive early, so everyone on our collaboration team showed up at least fifteen minutes ahead of schedule. We also arrived looking like a haggard bunch — the girls' had wound their hair into loose pony tails, except for Isabel whose hair was now too short, and the guys hadn't taken the time to shave. We had time to joke and laugh and reminisce, and just when I let myself forget the real purpose for our meeting, Mrs. Bartolli barged into the room holding a box of donuts. Ryan practically raked the box away from her and within moments, there was nothing but crumbs.

"Mongrels," Mrs. Bartolli muttered under her breath. She cleared her throat. "On to more important matters. Last year, you were challenged to escape the underground after first rescuing your new team leader — me. Then you were asked to find your way home after being led deep into the woods. For your final challenge, you constructed this tree house."

Isabel and I exchanged glances. I knew a shoe was about to drop.

"This year, we granted you much more sophisticated living quarters and all we've asked you to do so far is take tests and complete standard college entrance requirements. Most collaboration team leaders haven't said a word to their teams about getting a job, but luckily you have me as your leader, and I thought you would benefit from receiving advance notice."

She'd been standing in the same spot near the door—so unlike her. She clasped her hands behind her back and began pacing, her heels clicking against the natural wood floor. Naomi chewed her nails. Isabel raked her hand through her now short pink-streaked hair. Ryan crossed his arms in front of him and tapped his foot. Even I alternated between bending and straightening my legs, shifting my weight from front to back. Ian was the only one who stood relaxed—a curious look on his face, both arms resting at his sides.

Mrs. Bartolli abruptly stopped pacing, turned to face us, and clicked her heels together, as if to offer an exclamation point to her tension-building behavior. "You have matured a great deal since the first day you set foot on these grounds. You have matured, and yet you have a significant amount of maturing left to do to fully tap into your skills and capabilities."

"What kinds of jobs are available?" Isabel asked.

Mrs. Bartolli's mouth shifted to a long thin crease. "Who do you think cleaned your toilets and your showers last year, cooked your food, maintained the grounds, and helped organize events?"

"You want us to be the cleaning crew?" Naomi asked.

"Not all of you," Mrs. Bartolli said, "just you."

Naomi balled her hands into fists, straightened her arms to both sides, and stomped out of the tree house, just like Tinker Bell in Peter Pan.

"Of course, she can always deny her destiny," Mrs. Bartolli said, glancing toward the door.

"Are there other options for her if she does?" Ryan asked.

"Of course," Mrs. Bartolli replied, "one always has options. In this case, she can choose to leave camp."

Ryan abruptly turned and ran after Naomi. Mrs. Bartolli reached into her pocket and handed each of us a piece of paper that had been folded over and sealed. "On these notices, you will find job requirements based on the unique skills the camp staff has concluded you most need to

113

develop. The requirements are based on your test results, coupled with our observations of you."

She handed me the papers for Ryan and Naomi. "Will you be so kind as to make sure these get delivered to their intended targets?" she asked.

I nodded quickly.

"Good," she confirmed. "Remember, in addition to these requirements, you must earn enough money to cover your living expenses, which includes room and board, plus savings for your collaboration team. For the three of you, that equates to 1,800 points each—the equivalent to $1,800 dollars."

"Remind me, what about Ryan and Naomi?" I asked.

"The world does not tolerate latecomers or people who run out at the slightest sign of stress," Mrs. Bartolli explained. "For them, the price is steeper: they will each owe 2,300 points."

Isabel's eyes widened and she craned her head forward. "But—"

"I assure you," Mrs. Bartolli said, "we are being generous. It would likely cost you a lot more in the real world. Now, you must work at least ten hours a week at your recommended jobs. In order to earn enough money, you may supplement your income with additional hours, or by finding different jobs. You may also offer to help each other, so that each of you successfully achieves this goal. You are allowed that option, if you want to help Ryan and Naomi. Remember, if one of you fails, you all fail."

Chapter 17

In typical camp fashion, the staff kept us so busy that Ian and I barely got a moment alone together. So at our first opportunity, we snuck off together. "We have to find the Amulet of Omnia," I said. Ian and I were sitting on the cliff overlooking the spot where Keelam turned all psycho on me—the spot where I dug up the Bottle Full of Wishes. The salty air from the ocean assaulted my senses. I glanced over at Ian through errant strands of my hair whipping my face. He reached out and swept my hair to the side.

"Kenza, you're right to be concerned," he said, his voice soothing. "But Mazin's not here right now. I am, and I want to enjoy this moment— just you, me, and the sound of crashing waves below."

I smiled and let his charm wash away my worries like the waves pulling back from shore, knowing full well they'd eventually— inevitably—regain momentum and pound against my resolve even harder when they returned. He gently stroked my cheek with his thumb and gazed into my eyes, finally saying, "You're so beautiful."

I smiled and looked down, still not used to hearing compliments like that. I felt his hand on my chin, lifting my head gently. He leaned in slowly until his lips pressed against mine. I suddenly was able to tune everything out: the rhythm of crashing waves below, the smell of salt in the air, the sun beaming light into my closed eyes, and most of all, my worries. For a few priceless moments, I lost myself in that kiss until suddenly, as clear as if my eyes were wide open, I saw the faded image of Jamila of Diab, her brown eyes wide, frantic, as she mouthed the words, "Find the amulet".

I gasped and pulled back from Ian. "We need to hatch a plan," I said.

"Mmm-hmm," he said, a smile plastered across him lips. He stared out over the water and picked at the grass next to him.

"Ian, snap out of it. You seem like you're a million miles away." I placed my hand on his forearm, just long enough to get his attention.

He turned his attention back my way. "I'm trying to savor that kiss."

"It was a amazing, I'll admit it," I said. He reached out and tucked a stray strand of hair behind my ear and I nearly lost my focus. But I pictured Jamila of Diab again and instinctively, I pulled away, stood, and began pacing.

Ian jumped to his feet, his eyes trailing me.

Suddenly the words came out in a rush. "It's Mazin, Ian. Do I have to remind you that he's escaped, is on the loose, and has instant access to everyone here and, worse, to my family bloodline? I'm about to become a big sister, Ian. Last year, I basically placed a powerful weapon, the Amulet of Omnia, in his hands. Jamila of Diab just visited me again to warn me to find it."

"Wait, I didn't see her. Did she freeze me out this time?" he said, crossing his arms.

"Not exactly," I said, my cheeks burning. "I saw her while we were kissing. She warned me to find the amulet."

"That's just great," Ian said. He kicked at the ground and a clod of dirt flew out over the ocean, then he mumbled something about our ancestors needing to learn some boundaries.

"Who knows what Mazin will do with the amulet if we don't get it back. Maybe he'll use it against me, you, Ian, my sweet little sibling yet to be born, and anyone and everyone else I know . . . probably even people I don't know. And why? For the sick joy of harming and even killing completely innocent victims." A loud noise that sounded like a growl escaped from my mouth and spiked in volume until I ran out of breath.

"Kenza," Ian said, his voice calm and steady, "freaking out isn't helping."

I spun around to face him. "How can you be so relaxed? Who do you think turned you around on the highway when you came to visit me without you even being aware of it? This is serious!"

116

"Kenza, you're right, all right? You said we need to hatch a plan so that's what we're going to do." He reached both hands out, grabbed my shoulders, and locked me in his gaze. "Just tell me what to do and I'll do it."

I resisted pulling away, and kept my voice stern. "You know Jamila was barely able to reach us in the tree house last time, and I've tried to hale Jinny Zzaman, but to no avail. I've tried and tried so many times." Despite my resolve, my voice cracked.

"You've tried," he said, a smile creeping across his lips, "but you didn't have your friends around you to help."

I narrowed my eyes. "I have an idea," I said. "We're going to create and perform a ritual—you, Isabel, me, and Keelam will all participate. Can you perform a circle ritual like you did last year?"

"Not without the Bottle Full of Wishes. It's useless," he admitted.

"I'll handle everything."

Finally, I felt the heavy weight on my shoulders lift and a light sense of hope creep in, allowing the hint of a smile to form on my lips. I hugged him with everything I had. Then, we both turned and sprinted toward the apartments.

∞

Even though Mazin occupied most of my thoughts, over the next several days, I was forced to pour my focus into finding a job. We all were. Isabel and Keelam were both challenged to find a job working with people, while also challenging the status quo to be successful. They decided to be camp tour guides, just like Carter and Lisa had the previous summer. They had to lobby Dr. Hendrix, the camp director, since no one from two different collaboration teams had ever attempted to work together. It allowed them to take a double shift and bring in more income than what they needed, enabling them to contribute back to their respective collaboration teams and help anyone who didn't have enough to cover his or her own expenses.

117

As expected, Naomi got cleaning duty for the sophomore bathrooms, a job designed to humble her and force her to be successful in areas she never thought possible. Her meticulous nature made her pretty good at it, after she got past the fear of dealing with other people's filth.

Apparently, the camp staff had noticed that Ryan was always bouncing off the walls *and* needed to slow down. He needed to exercise patience and observation skills. After applying for several jobs—a dishwasher at the cafe, a cashier at the camp store, and a mail delivery person—none of which appeased the camp staff, he applied for a job researching why many of the plants, patches of grass, and trees on the camp grounds showed signs of a rare disease that was spreading and killing them. When I found out that this was happening, I instantly knew why: Mazin was leaving a trail of destruction in his wake. I made a mental note to hound Ryan for information on areas that suffered from the disease, especially those rapidly decaying.

Ian continued his efforts on the amazing aquarium under Atlantic Ocean Lake, but in a different capacity than the creative role he'd played prior to camp convening. Now he'd guard a top-secret underground entrance. Apparently, the camp staff thought his protector skills needed to be exercised—if only they knew how good he was at this.

As for me, the camp staff completely surprised me by requiring an entrepreneurial position. What I was going to do and how I was going to pull it off, I had no clue. I tried unsuccessfully to pick everyone's brain about what to do, but they were all so busy with their jobs and devoting most of their waking hours to them, that very little energy was left over for creative thinking.

Soon, I would owe my share of the rent and wouldn't have money to pay it. Even though Isabel's and Ian's jobs earned more than they needed to cover the bills, their extra income didn't stretch far enough to cover mine. What stunk about not being able to pay the rent was not that I might soon become homeless, but that my roommate Isabel would be dragged along in the destructive current of my unemployment.

Despite the squeeze on everyone's time, I worked behind the scenes to organize a ritual gathering. On Friday night, we all snuck out of the apartment complex well after curfew and met in The Sticks under the deck of the Gandhi tree house, out of sight of campus security cameras. I

118

still hadn't found a way to diplomatically wrestle the Bottle Full of Wishes from Dr. Dunbar, so I snuck into the room where we'd had our tests and used a heat sensor scanner on my Datadrix to spot it in one of the locked drawers. Fortunately, it only took a little jimmying with one of my bobby pins to get the drawer loose. As a result, I was the last one to arrive at the gathering. Everyone gave me grief—as we passed the various tree houses along the trail from ours to the clearing near the cliff overlooking the ocean, where Ian had performed the protective rituals last year to guard us again a weather attack from Mazin.

We soon arrived at the clearing, and Ian hurried to etch a circle in the grass and dirt, overlooking the cliff. We all took our places around the forming circle and helped to shape it. It was a lot easier than last summer—diseased vegetation had left the ground virtually barren.

As soon as the circle was fully formed, Ian urged us to step inside the "lines," thereby doubling our level of protection. Once we were in, I pulled something out of a small purse I'd been carrying—a towel that I carefully unfolded to reveal the Bottle Full of Wishes.

Keelam stepped back a few paces, outside the circle.

Ian's head snapped up. "Keelam, get back in here."

"No way, not with that thing," he said, holding up his hands. "How did you get it back, anyway?"

Ian eyed me and I smiled mischievously. "Before we do anything else, we'll cleanse the bottle, Keelam. That will return it back to its original pure, positive state," he said.

"How do you know?" Keelam took another step back and I followed him, my protective instincts kicking in. The moment I did, I felt a cold rush of what felt like a dinosaur-sized snake brush past my back. I turned abruptly to reveal the source, but nothing was there—probably just the wind. Keelam leapt back into the circle, but I just stood there, staring.

"Kenza." Ian stepped out of the circle, his hand reached out to urge me back into it . "What was that?"

I shook my head. "I don't know."

"Come into the circle. Please?" he pleaded.

I obeyed.

Ian moved to the center of the circle and continued to cleanse the bottle and strengthen the protection of the circle. He raised his arms above him, while clutching the Bottle Full of Wishes in his right hand. He closed his eyes and muttered words I didn't understand, in a language that sounded long expired. Given his Peruvian heritage, it was probably Ketchua, a language spoken by Peruvian natives. As he spoke, the feeling in my hands numbed, my heart warmed, and I felt some sort of energy field pulsate outward from me, connecting with the others in the circle, until we were all united by some inexplicable, undeniable force.

Ian turned to face us, his eyes glinting in the moonlight, his hair sticking up on all ends like a mad scientist. "It's time," he said. "Everyone join hands."

Ian tucked the Bottle Full of Wishes upside down in his pocket so that the base was still sticking out. He joined the circle and, one-by-one, we clasped hands, making the circle even more impenetrable. After standing in silence for several long moments, Ian nodded to me and I stepped forward toward the center of the circle, releasing my grip on Isabel's and Keelam's hands. They immediately closed the gap I left behind.

I stepped into the center of the circle and raised my hands above my head, closed my eyes, and waved my arms. "I call upon the good spirits of my family's past to come forth and show your presence. We need you now, more than ever. We all need you—Isabel, Keelam, Ian, and me . . . and not just us, but everyone here at camp, our families, our friends, and anyone else who might end up in the wrong place at the wrong time. Make your presence known now, so that we can seek your guidance. We need your wisdom. We need to know how to capture Mazin and lock him away in permanent shackles."

After I'd said everything urgent I could think of, I kept my eyes shut for several more seconds. I knew that what we were doing would work—there was no doubt in my mind, but I didn't know how long it would take to summon the powerful jinns that I so longed to see. Suddenly, I felt a shift in the wind. My hair danced straight up around my head, blowing this way and that. Stubbornly, I refused to open my eyes until I was sure I would see a familiar face standing before me.

When I smelled Jinny's familiar putrid odor, I opened my eyes to see a being that was certainly supernatural, but it wasn't either of the jinns I expected. In fact, it wasn't even female. For a moment, I recoiled, afraid I'd accidentally summoned some dark form of Mazin, but it was just as likely that the only common threads they shared were their supernatural existence and male presence. I stepped back into the circle and rejoined hands with my friends.

The being was tall and his feet hovered above the ground, floating in a faded mist, just like Jinny Zzaman had. His skin reflected an iridescent rainbow of light that glinted every time he moved, as if bouncing off shiny metal. His eyes glowed yellow and his shoulder-length, black hair, much like Jinny Zzaman's, waved as if submerged in water.

"Who are you?" Isabel asked.

The being slowly bowed his head and closed his eyes to acknowledge her. When he spoke, his voice was deep and projected an echo. "Ayam," he said. "My name is Ayam."

He approached Isabel and then toured the circle, looking everyone in the eye, which made everyone jump, their eyes opening wide, as if a deep secret had been revealed to each. Once Ayam had made his way around the circle, he returned to his place in the center, directly in front of Ian and me. "I am here to warn you of a devastating fate that could be yours, if you do not heed my warning," he said. "I am here on behalf of Jinny Zzaman and Jamila of Diab—"

"Where are they?" I asked, desperation straining my vocal chords. "I've tried so many times to reach them."

Ayam held up his hand, offered a consoling smile. His warm gesture silenced me—and momentarily calmed me. "They are in grave danger," he said, "as are you. Mazin, as you are aware, has escaped his meager prison and has used the Amulet of Omnia to lock them both away."

"Lock them away, where?" Ian asked. "If we know where they are, we can rescue them."

Ayam tapped his fingers together to form a steeple and lifted an eyebrow. "Can you?" His gaze silenced Ian. "You do not understand the

121

danger you are in." His voice deepened, adding to the air of mystery. "Mazin could be lurking nearby—is lurking nearby—and we must use this time we have together wisely, or the streams will cease to flow and the wind will cease to blow."

A shiver ran up my spine. I glanced around my close circle of friends—Ian, Isabel, and Keelam—suddenly realizing a downpour of bad luck was accumulating in the skies just beyond our line of sight. The others had no idea what fury Mazin could ignite. They'd only seen glimpses, but me, I'd nearly lost my mother, my school, Keelam, and my long-lost soul mate Ian. Isabel had nearly lost her arm. Worse than all of that, in the struggle to capture Mazin last summer, I'd almost fallen to my death on the cliffs towering over the Pacific Ocean, twenty feet away from where we now stood.

"Listen true and listen well," Ayam said, his black hair waving gently behind him. "You will find what you seek in the tropical zone, which is littered with sharks and other dangerous sea creatures. It's near the biggest boulder."

"I know where that is," Ian said. He turned to me, "I can show you."

"Can we go now?" I asked, a seed of hope germinating within me.

Ayam shook his head as he spoke. "There is no way for you to free them, for you are susceptible to the sharks' jaws."

I tossed up my hands and stormed out of the circle. "Then, what the hell are we supposed to do?" I cried as I walked several steps away from the circle, toward the cliff.

"Kenza!" Isabel screamed like no one I'd ever heard before.

I spun around just in time to dodge the attack of a dark shadowy cloud, which barreled toward me, its mouth wide open and its teeth sharp as a wolf's fangs. I fought to regain my balance and then watched as the shadow circled back to face me. Despite the fact that I recognized the power behind this dark entity, despite the fact that I knew with certainty that my life hung in the balance, I was frozen in place, unable to take a single step or even move.

Suddenly, arms wrapped around my chest and before I could think or react, someone or something began dragging me backwards. My

122

heels raking through the sand. I twisted and rotated as much as I could to resist, afraid the energy would hurl me out over the cliff. I finally found my voice and yelled from the depths of my being, "No!" The grip didn't loosen so I bit down on the hand of my perpetrator.

"Stop! Kenza, it's me," Ian yelled, without letting go, not even a little.

We must have been close to the circle because he tugged hard against my chest, thrusting my feet up into the air, and we both fell backward, me on top of him.

"Get your legs in." Isabel's scream pierced the air once again.

We both scrambled to get all of our limbs into the safety of the circle, and just in time. The shadowy entity slammed into an invisible wall that lined the perimeter and a gritty, screeching, fingernails-on-chalkboard sound ripped through the air. I covered my hands with my ears—everyone did, and everyone, but Ayam, dropped to our knees, doubling over. Ayam continued to hover in the center of the circle, his hands pressed together, as if in prayer, his eyes closed, smiling a peaceful smile.

In moments, a translucent wave of energy shot out from Ayam's body like rays escaping from the sun. Ringlets of rainbow light rippled outward for several seconds. When the rainbow light struck the dark cloud, the dark entity ignited like embers on burning wood. Patches of fire blazed through it, burning pathways of light that connected to other pathways of light, until the entire creature was ablaze with connecting veins of smoldering fire. Smoke filled the air and clouded what I now saw was an invisible dome that wrapped protectively around us and over our heads. The orange fire completely consumed the dark creature, and the earth began to rumble, and trees we could barely see through the growing smoke shook, dropping their leaves like rain. The leaves stuck to the dome, creating a roof and we could no longer see out.

Ayam's eyes abruptly snapped open. "Rise, young army," he bellowed. "Rise and join forces to destroy this evil." He held his palms upward and lifted them repeatedly, using his hands as conductors, lifting us upward until we stood once again in a complete circle. "Clasp your hands together, each of you, now," he urged.

Once we did as he instructed, Ayam began whirling his arms, stirring the air, creating random patterns and waves. A humming noise emitted from inside the circle, soft at first, and then more and more pronounced. When he thrust both his hands straight out to his sides, what sounded like a bomb exploded outside the dome, and Ayam pixilated, slowly fading into nothingness before our eyes.

"Dude," Keelam said.

I suddenly remembered that Keelam hadn't seen anything like this before. He was the only one in my small circle of camp friends who hadn't yet witnessed a jinn. Unfortunately, his fate was now sealed. Keelam was irrevocably one of us and would never be blissfully unaware again.

"How the hell are we going to get out of this dome?" Ian asked.

I glared at him for a moment, squinting my eyes. I wanted just a little more time to celebrate the fact that we were all still alive, all still standing. I longed to revel in the explosion that likely incinerated the beast—and maybe even Mazin—but I didn't have the luxury of time. Instead, it was up to me to find a way for all of us to escape. For me, that meant also returning to an unwanted reality that pressed forcibly down on both of my shoulders. I'd brought this mess to Zenith Hill. I'd hurled Mazin's dark spirit over the cliff into the Pacific Ocean, opening the gate for him to flee. Me. I did it. And now my friends were forever changed because of it.

Suddenly Ayam's voice bellowed, just as deep and mysterious as it had been when he floated before us. "The darkness is fading and the light will return." The debris of leaves lifted from the dome and flew away, the smoke clearing moments later.

"Woo-hoo!" Keelam yelled, punching a victorious fist into the air.

His victory call triggered an outpouring of celebration and hugs. We jumped, hugged, and laughed uncontrollably.

"I'm afraid I must clear something up for you," Ayam's voice quickly returned. "The danger remains. The shadow beast is gone for good, but its source flows endlessly from the one you call Mazin. As I departed, I placed a protective barrier around the dwellings of your nearby encampment, but its bounds are limited and do not reach beyond them. When I say 'run,' you must run like the wind to your dwellings and stay within the bounds of the camp dwellings or you will be inviting more sorrow into your meager existence than you ever thought possible."

"Wait," I called, my voice firm, my hand stretched out in front of me like a stop sign.

"You are just as bold as the others predicted," Ayam said, chuckling. He flattened his hands together and bowed his head in my direction, closed his eyes. "As you know, I am bound to respond to your wishes."

"You must tell me how to fix this," I said, planting my feet and looking up. "I implore you."

"Ahhh," Ayam said, dragging out the word. "There is only one way, and we jinns are helpless to assist you in this matter."

"Tell us," I said firmly.

"Find the Amulet of Omnia, the great wishing stone, and all your wishes will come true," he said.

"But—"

Ayam's energy began to dissipate. "Get ready, now run!" he shouted.

Everyone bolted for our tree house—except me. I saw a soft, opaque image of Ayam's face coming back into view and paused to thank him. But before I could speak, a hand—likely the hand of Mazin himself—snaked around Ayam's throat and yanked his head forcefully backward. Ayam's eyes opened wide and he mouthed the word "run!"

I turned and ran like the wind.

Chapter 18

It was broad daylight—not the smartest time to sneak into the top-secret underwater aquarium—the very one Ian was responsible for guarding, but compared to other risks we faced, it seemed like a calculated one. Ian stole a few quick glances in both directions. "Just in case someone is in the wrong place at the wrong time," he explained.

Not likely, I thought. If anyone reared their heads, it would no doubt be because Mazin found a way to remotely control them, outside the parameters of the protective spell Ayam had placed before he was so ruthlessly attacked.

Ian reached out for a nearby hedge, taller than all of us, and sunk his hand into a gap between the branches. He wrinkled his face, as if concentrating hard on something until a look of relief washed over him. He reached for a branch and pushed it to the side, exposing a door behind it. Keelam laughed and rubbed his hands together mischievously. "This is going to be fun."

Ian pushed the door open and held it open while we all passed through. As soon as we were safely inside, he let the door swing shut behind us. A light automatically switched on overhead, illuminating a spiral staircase in front of us. Ian pushed his way past us and trotted down them, waving for us to follow.

Keelam went first; Isabel and I headed up the rear. When I first reached the bottom, I didn't see Ian until he stepped out from the shadows and reached for my hand. He led me into a large room, shimmering with watery light reflecting all around us through the aquarium walls and glass ceiling, out onto the floor. Being down here with Ian—where no one could find us or even know where we were here—made it all feel so magical. No thought entered my mind—not of home and the little sibling growing inside my mom, or of dark spirits or missing jinns . . . Nothing . . . just Ian and I—holding hands, together in this moment.

As if sensing the same, Ian reached for a strand of my hair and twirled it in his fingers. His smile grew, and his eyes reflected the sparkling light from the dancing water. He leaned in for a kiss, his hand warming my cheek, sliding down to cuff my neck. When our lips met, it felt as if time ground to a halt, gifting us the pause we needed for our souls to commune, exchange knowledge, and share a mutual sense that our love was eternal. Before we parted, his lips met mine one more time, and when he eased away slowly, he kept his eyes closed, as if lingering in the moment. When he opened them again, we both smiled like two, very happy school children on a playground.

I looked around, suddenly realizing we weren't actually alone—suddenly remembering that Isabel and Keelam could be in danger. I jerked toward the opening that likely led to another room, but Ian drew me back into his arms.

His voice was soft and gentle. "Let them be." I gave him a sharp glance and he looked at me, surprised. "If I know Keelam, they're doing the same thing we are."

"Or worse," I muttered.

He laughed. "Or worse."

Ian stood right in front of me, still facing me, and clasped both my hands, his fingers laced in mine. Overhead, a sea turtle floated past stealing both our attention, its flippers paddling slowly as if nothing in the world could go wrong.

"You have to see this," Isabel said, rushing over, shaking her head.

"Now," Keelam added from a short distance away.

Ian and I exchanged glances and followed Isabel into the next room, which was equally beautiful except this area had more coral, whose vibrant colors captured my attention.

"This is beautiful," I said, feeling an even deeper sense of peace.

"No, Kenza, look," Isabel said. Her unusually serious tone caught me off guard.

Ian and I walked hand-in-hand to the aquarium wall and peered in toward the spot where she pointed. A speckled boulder the size of a small hatchback car sat directly in front of us.

"Look," Ian said, pointing at a piece of coral next to the boulder. "I see it." The blue and green colors of the crystal shimmered, looking even more mysterious in the water.

"We have to get it," I said, pressing both hands up against the aquarium glass.

"How?" Isabel asked.

"I know a way," Ian said. Behind him, a shark floated past, its tail moving menacingly back and forth. His answer iced my veins. Just as Ayam had warned, we were truly on our own, the usual jinns blocked from helping us, leaving no one but us to figure out how to retrieve the Amulet of Omnia.

Ian turned and walked straight toward a faux stone wall at the end of the aquarium. He pushed on a waist-high spot on the wall and a door opened. We followed him through it and up a staircase into a small room with air tanks and scuba gear. "Come on, guys, help me into one of these," Ian said.

"What? No," I said, stepping forward.

"Kenza, this isn't the time." He held his hand out, signaling for me to stop trying.

"Ian—"

Keelam stepped forward. "Kenza, he's right. You have to let him do this."

I eyed Isabel, looking for an advocate but all I got was another enemy. "All Ian has to do is reach the amulet, then he can summon its magic if he needs it to escape."

"That's actually not true," Ian said, as he reached for a wet suit. "No one knows how to invoke the amulet's powers except Kenza."

Everyone turned and stared at me, and that's when it hit me. I had to be the one to retrieve it. After much resistance from Ian, he finally stormed out. As soon as he was gone, Isabel and Keelam helped me into the wet suit. Once I was zipped up in it, they took their spot on either side of me and helped me to the next room, which opened up to a huge area with water pooling like a lagoon.

From my vantage point, standing on the edge and looking down into the water, I could literally see sharks, fish and turtles swimming from above the water. All around us, there were pipes, ladders reaching up to platforms stretching ten feet over the water, green tanks labeled 'green algae' and yellow tanks labeled 'baby brine shrimp'. I lifted both legs over the stone edge of the tank, my flippers splashing clumsily. Then I sank in up to my neck in the warm water.

Keelam turned and ran to the ladder and climbed to get a vantage point from one of the platforms above the water. "Hurry Kenza," he called, once he was sitting on it.

I stuck the regulator in my mouth and breathed in and out a few times to make sure I had it in correctly. Then I gestured the okay sign and sank under the water, glancing around to make sure the shark was nowhere near me. I pushed off the edge of the aquarium with my feet and swam full speed ahead toward the giant boulder. It was actually a lot farther than it appeared from my vantage point with my head above the water before I sank in, but I finally reached it and saw Ian peering in through the glass, watching me like a hawk. I blew him a kiss and he pretended to catch it. I floated in that same spot gazing at him, and he signaled for me to hurry it up.

I had to dive down to reach the amulet draped around a piece of coral. I grabbed it, but immediately dropped it. I had to reach way down in between the boulder and the coral to get a hold of it again. I pulled, but it wouldn't come loose. I yanked harder, but quickly stopped myself, afraid I might damage the amulet. The ebb and flow of the water kept lifting me upward so I had to wedge my foot between a rock next to the boulder and a clump of coral. Once secure, I crouched down to get a good look at what was stopping me from retrieving the amulet. Every so often, I glanced over at Ian, who stood in the same exact spot, gnawing his nails nervously. Every time I looked up, I nodded my reassurance or gave a thumbs up that everything was going to be okay, even though I didn't fully believe it myself.

As soon as I got close enough to the amulet, I could see that its chain was tangled on the coral. I spent what felt like an eternity trying to free the chain. After picking and twisting and easing the chain this way and that, I nearly had it. I figured I'd have it free in a minute or two, but an echoey banging sound suddenly rang out from the direction of the glass. I looked up to see Ian's eyes wide and frantic. He was pointing behind me, mouthing something I couldn't decipher. I rotated around, my foot still firm in its foothold and saw the shark swimming right toward me about twenty feet away.

I instantly tugged as hard as I could on the amulet, but the chain didn't break so I dropped it and tried to yank my foot free. It didn't budge either. The shark was within seconds from taking a chunk out of me. I raked myself between the boulder and the front of the glass—barely fitting—squeezing my eyes shut hoping the shark couldn't reach me here. It swam close, its mouth inches from my leg, but turned and swam away.

I had to bend myself into a pretzel to reach the amulet again, tugging with all my strength. This time the chain gave way and broke free. I glanced quickly at Ian, who was tapping hard against the glass. I turned and saw the shark coming straight for me again. I twisted and pulled my foot. It still wouldn't budge, so I wedged myself as far into the crevice between the boulder and the glass as possible. Again, the shark came within inches, but turned and swam away.

I wriggled my way back out into the open water as quickly as I could, completely exposing myself. Now that I was free, I was able to get my foot free, just in time for the shark to turn around and head straight for me. Ian pounded frantically on the glass and I heard his muffled screams. I squeezed my eyes shut, gripped the amulet tightly in my hand, and made the most important wish I've ever made: to send the great white shark as far away from me as possible.

I opened my eyes just as a sea turtle swam right between us. The shark suddenly lost interest in me and pursued the turtle as it swam toward the opposite end of the lake. I had no idea if the shark's interest in the turtle would waiver, but I knew this was my only chance to make a break for it. I pushed both legs off the aquarium wall as hard as I could and swam with everything I had toward the opening at the top, not slowing to glance back.

The moment I surfaced, Ian—who must have raced here—and Keelam raked me out of the water and I landed with a slippery thud on

130

the floor. I looked up to see Isabel now perched on top of the platform. She stood quickly and scurried down the ladder. I still had a clear vantage point of the shark heading straight for me. He rammed into the side of the aquarium, looking dazed, and swam around the rim of the aquarium.

"Let's get you out of this suit and get the heck out of here," Ian said, his voice shaky.

"Wait," Isabel said, sounding only slightly more rational. "Did you get the amulet?"

I opened my hand to reveal the dripping amulet and its broken chain. "This is what saved me, again," I said.

∞

When Isabel and I returned to our apartment, all I wanted was to crawl into bed and forget the nightmare I'd just experienced. When we walked in, we found an envelope lying on the floor. Isabel swooped it up, and her bubbly expression flattened as soon as she opened it. Capitalized letters were stamped across the paper with these words: EVICTION NOTICE.

"What the—?" Isabel looked stunned.

I, of course, was not stunned. I still hadn't started my entrepreneurial business and wasn't earning an income. I thought that I'd have more time to figure this all out. "Isabel, I'm so sorry." Tears welled up in my eyes. It was bad enough that I was being kicked out of my apartment, but Isabel, too? It didn't seem fair.

"What are we going to do?" she asked.

Not having an answer left me feeling small, angry, and afraid. After nearly getting eaten by a shark, this shouldn't have bothered me, but it landed like one more blow to an already-out-of-control situation. "I don't know, but I'm not going to sit around here to wait and find out," I said.

"Where are you going?" she asked. She'd wandered over to the couch and forcibly plopped down. Jazz immediately leapt onto her lap, curling into the adorable gray fur ball we've loved so well.

"I'm going to find Mrs. Bartolli," I announced, and then followed Isabel's eyes to the window and the soft evening light spilling into the room. "If I can't find her, then I'll find Dr. Hendrix. And if he isn't around, I'll keep looking until I find someone who can help." I turned toward the door, my hand on the knob.

"Kenza," Isabel said softly.

I turned back to find her smiling.

"We're in this together, you and me. Where you go, I go. We'll figure something out. I know we will." She gave a wide sweeping glance around the room. "Besides, this old apartment was getting dull anyway."

I knew she was lying. She loved this place. Still, I ran over to her, smooshed her with a quick hug, and then ran out the door.

Chapter 19

There was no convincing Mrs. Bartolli, Dr. Hendrix or any of the other thirty staff members at camp to let us stay at our apartment. I knew this because I talked to every single one of them. The last one I spoke to, Mr. Rylan, the pet care leader, told me I was wasting my time and energy when I should be out starting my dream business. "You have an idea in you, Kenza. I know you do, and so do the rest of the camp staff members, or they would never have made this a requirement for your job."

He was right; I knew he was. I had been avoiding the inevitable, which landed Isabel and me in the Gandhi tree house. At least we weren't tossed out of camp entirely. Plus, we had a shower, a bathroom, and a kitchen. It was actually kind of cool—way better than being crammed in the Owens tree house like we were last summer, where we'd spent a miserable week with limited space, blankets, and food. Besides, Jazz was able to stay with us in the tree house.

I liked Isabel even more for going along with it, and for not blaming me. "I blame myself, really," she shrugged. "I should have been helping you come up with an idea, but instead I whined and complained about my own job."

Everyone on our collaboration team—Ian, Ryan, and Naomi— had come by to commiserate. Even Keelam found time to take a break from his collaboration team, the Owens, to come and cheer us up with his cheesy jokes.

"We all should have helped you, Kenza," Ryan said. "We are a team, after all."

"Yeah, well, even I think it's cool that you guys are willing to stay in a god-awful tree house again," Naomi said. She was sprawled out on the couch, with Jazz lying on her stomach. She let her arm drape over the side of the couch, her knuckles resting on the wood floor. "But I cannot understand how you can stand being here all the time, with no air conditioning. It's ridiculously hot."

"It's not bad at night," Isabel said.

"But it's been so hot these last few days," I admitted. "Ever since we moved in, it seems like we've had a heat wave. I wish I had an ice-cold glass of watermelon juice."

"Watermelon juice?" Naomi parroted. "I've never heard of that."

"Then you've been deprived, even more than I realized," I said, jabbing her.

Naomi abruptly swung her legs onto the floor and bolted upright. She looked like she was about to rush at me and maybe even take me down, but Ryan jumped up holding his arms out to block her. "Wait, can you make us some?"

"What? Watermelon juice?" I asked.

"Yeah." He looked a shade too eager.

"Um, yeah, I guess I can make you some. Does it sound that good?"

"Heck yeah," he said, never passing up on an offer for food.

"You know," I said. "It sounds better than good. It sounds like a business."

Ian came and stood next to me, a smile spreading across his lips. "Kenza, you're a genius."

"You are a genius," Isabel chimed in. Then she added, "Way to get us out of being homeless." I shot her a sharp look and she shrugged. "Just saying."

An hour later, everyone, except me, was perched around Ian and Ryan's kitchen table at their apartment. I stood over a blender, a bowl of cut watermelon pieces next to me, a cup of ice, and a bottle of local honey that I purchased at the camp store. I blended up a batch and gave everyone a cup. It went over a lot better than I expected.

"Hey," Ryan said. "Can you add other flavors besides honey?"

"Like what?"

"I don't know. Like raspberries, peaches, strawberries, maybe even mango."

134

"Yeah, I guess I could," I said.

"Looks like you're in business," Isabel said, "and we'll soon be back in our own beds."

∞

We spent the next day figuring out the best location for my stand and decided on a spot close to where Keelam had fallen into the lake last summer, ignoring its bad karma, and celebrating its great location. It was about halfway between The Sticks and the Africa fitness facility—perfect for campers who were completely worn out, either from exercising or from building their tree houses, and just far enough from the United Nations cafe where there were more options available. We scrambled to gather supplies from the used supply center, and we pieced them together to create a stand.

We paid Mr. Rylan to go into town to pick up a case of inexpensive local honey, and enough fruit to last at least a week. Not only had the team provided their only free time outside of work to help build the place, but they gave up any spare money they'd earned, too. Our Gandhi faction motto rolled like a sonata through my mind, "Live not for you alone, but for the greater good."

On the first day the stand opened, everyone on our faction took shifts to pass out coupons and samples. Since I didn't have anywhere else to be, I stayed the entire day, coordinating shifts and helping customers. We sold each cup for $2, a profit margin of $1, and on the first day alone we made a mint.

At the end of the day, when closing time finally came, Ian showed up with a dozen red roses and the promise of a surprise, if I'd accompany him to the beach. I was so tired after my first day of work that I wanted to just go home and watch a movie, but Ian started kissing my neck up to my ear until I caved.

We walked hand-in-hand to the embankment where Keelam first found the empty Bottle Full of Wishes. After the recent events with Ayam, I was hesitant to go to the beach for fear it wasn't protected like

135

the rest of camp, but now that I had the Amulet of Omnia back in my possession, my fears morphed to mere worries. Ian led the way down the sandy path to the beach, turning back the entire way to make sure I didn't fall. When we reached the beach, he led me to a log that had been placed where the waves broke. It looked like it had been there for years, its circumference too big for me to wrap my arms around it.

Ian kicked off his shoes and started removing his socks, nodding to me to do the same. I followed his lead, stealing a seat next to him on the log. We sat hip-to-hip, gazing out over the water—both of us digging our toes into the sand.

Ian turned and knelt down on the sand to face me. "Do you know how much I adore you, Kenza?" I nodded.

Ian looked as though he wanted to devour me—as if he might not let me return to camp, not ever. He reached out to gently touch my face and I soon tasted his lips on mine. When he moaned softly, my heart raced faster and faster. This felt different than other times we'd kissed. Every other time, we'd been limited—limited by people lingering in the vicinity, limited by our own fear of being vulnerable, limited by time itself.

Now, we faced no limitations. His mouth slipped away from my lips and the moment they did, I longed for them to return. He kissed the edge of my lips, my cheek, my ear, and then my neck. He gently lowered me to the ground, dropped to his knees, and then gently lowered himself onto me. His hands began to roam, but respectfully remained outside of my clothes, even though I yearned for him to stop holding back. As he kissed me and gently caressed my body, the repetition of the waves rolling in and falling back serenaded us, our bodies moving in concert with the rhythmic sound.

After a while, Ian pulled away and propped himself up on one elbow. The yellow flecks in his eyes glinted in the reflection of the sun and he smiled, looking so happy.

"Where's your amulet, anyway?" he asked out of the blue.

I reached into my pocket and pulled it out.

"Turn around," he commanded. "Let me help you with that."

"The clasp is broken, remember?"

136

"I think I can fix that," he said.

He motioned to put it on. I lifted my hair, and he clasped the necklace around my neck. I let my hair fall back down over my shoulders, but his hand swept it away again. He kissed the back of my neck, in the same spot he had a tattoo of a wolf on his neck. I shivered. I felt his hand on my arm, then running down to my wrist slowly, as he circled to face me. He reached out for the amulet, loosely grasped it in his hand, and then kissed me. Suddenly we were catapulting through space, riding in a fast-moving elevator. The darkness of a night sky fell over us as we ascended, still lost in our kiss.

We suddenly came speeding back down to earth, moving faster than the speed of light as if we were in a simulation at a theme park. We landed with a thud, but managed to stay on our feet. We were now standing inside the Cave of Shadow Forest, the amulet still around my neck, our shoes and socks mysteriously back on our feet.

"What the—?"

"Use the amulet," he said. "You remember how."

Of course I remembered how to insert the amulet into the small slot in the back wall of the cave, just like we had last summer when Isabel and I were trying to find out what was hidden behind the cave wall. The wall cranked slowly open and I heard the sound that always accompanied it when it moved: the echoey thumping noise of a beating heart. I walked along the wall as it slid open, this time knowing that it would stop before crushing me. When it finally did stop, I jiggled the amulet free and followed Ian through the entrance to the rest of the cave.

We approached the pair of bridges that forked off in different directions, and we each activated the flashlight on our Datadrixes, which were always on our wrists. A shiny new bridge had replaced the one that collapsed into dust last summer. Ian ran to it, calling, "Come on."

"No," I ordered, reaching out to grab his arm. "Stop, now!" He looked startled. "That's the bridge that collapsed last year. It's not the right one." Ian nodded and more cautiously approached the rickety bridge on the right. Sensing his hesitation, I stepped in front of him. "Let me go first."

When I reached the halfway point across the bridge, I turned to make sure Ian was following, but I shivered and lost my balance, causing the bridge to sway. I grabbed for the ropes that served as a meager railing, and Ian grabbed for me, cupping both hands on my hips. I turned and said, "Really?"

He smiled wide. "It makes me feel more relaxed."

I nodded and started to turn, but he stopped me. "Wait," he said. "Before we go further, why did you get so afraid a second ago. It seemed like it happened before the bridge swayed."

I sighed. "When I turned and saw you right behind me, I flashed back to last summer, when Mazin pretended to be you and tried to throw me off this same bridge."

Ian reached over and kissed me, and I was immediately lost in the thrill, the intensity of his lips on mine, even for the danger of being on such an unstable surface, so high above the sightless bottom below.

"See, I'm not Mazin. It's me, Ian," he said, pulling away to look into my eyes.

I smiled, exhaled a long breath and whispered, "Yeah, you're definitely not Mazin."

We traversed the rest of the bridge, enduring more sway. At least Ian's hands remained planted on my hips the whole way, as I meticulously moved my hands along the rope.

When we reached the other side, Ian fell to his knees and kissed the ground. "You'll kiss anything, won't you?" I said.

"Jealous?"

Instead of responding, I headed for the purple high-tech elevator door that I remembered seeing last summer. When I reached my hand out to it, Ian mimicked my motion, and then sharply jerked his hand back, clearly not expecting to feel the electric vibration pulsing through the door. I held my hand steady and felt the hum flowing through, watching it shake my fingers.

"Where do you think this leads?" Ian asked.

"That's what we need to find out," I answered. Then I added, "Let me try something." I placed both hands on the door and my whole body was soon shaking. The hum grew to a rumble.

"Step away from there," Ian said, wrapping his hands around my shoulders to pull me back. But a jolt of energy sent him flying backward. I held my hands firm and turned to make sure Ian was okay.

"How can you stand touching that?" he said.

"I don't think we feel it in the same way," I said. "Maybe it's the amulet." Suddenly a small tablet-sized screen materialized at eye level. "Ian, a picture," I said, turning toward him, nodding toward the screen.

Ian jumped to his feet, fumbled with his Datadrix, and finally snapped a picture. "I got it," he said.

"Does it show up on your Drix?"

"Yeah, what do you think? It's not going to show up, like a ghost or something?"

I shrugged and pulled away from the wall. My head spun and an echo rang in my ears until I collapsed into Ian's arms. I woke up lying at the entrance of the cave, no clue how I got there or how long I'd been out. Ian was nowhere to be seen. I reached up and felt for the amulet, panicking when I couldn't find it. I ran my hand along my neck to be sure—it was gone.

I slowly pulled myself to my feet, still a little dizzy. I ducked through the entrance into the full sunlight. About twenty feet away, I saw Ian holding out the amulet, talking to himself.

"Who are you talking to?"

He turned and smiled, running over to me, the amulet in his hand.

"No one. I was just looking at the shadows and trying to decide the best way to return to camp." He held the amulet out to me. "Here."

"Why do you have this?"

He looked down at it, pointing. "It kept pulsating, blinking in and out in fits of different colors. I thought it was going to explode. I thought it might hurt you."

Chapter 20

The next day I returned to the watermelon stand for another full shift. We decided to call it Jizzammee Dibs, named after my favorite two jinns, and had stayed up late the night before to paint and hang a sign. Since the sophomores had already started building their tree houses, my juices were a big hit. Customers lined up from 2 p.m. until dinnertime, and everyone on our team, even Naomi, stopped by to help, in between their own work shifts.

"It's weird that neither of us has any siblings," Naomi said.

"Yeah," I said. "It is weird that we have that in common, especially because we're so different."

Naomi shot me a sharp look, her green eyes piercing through me—reminding me of Megan Hawk and her bullying ways, if only for a fleeting moment. "What, so you think you're better than me?" she asked.

I felt the color drain from my face, unsure if she was serious or if Mazin had slipped in to overtake her.

"Just kidding, Atlas," she said, laughing. "Jesus, you are sensitive, aren't you."

My hands were wet from just being washed and I flicked water on her face before drying them.

"Really?" she said, grabbing a handful of cherries from a bin, cocking her arm back to pummel me with them.

"Whoa, whoa, whoa, not the cherries," I said. "They're the most expensive ingredient we have."

She stared at me for a moment, conflict written all over her face. Finally, she dropped the cherries from her gloved hand into the empty bowl she was holding.

"You're no fun, Kenza."

"Me?" I paused for a long moment, leaning with both arms on the counter. "You know, we're not going to have that much in common for long."

"What do you mean?" Naomi asked, her voice taking on a more serious tone.

"I'm going to be a big sister sometime this summer."

Naomi squealed and leapt onto her toes—something I would expect Isabel to do, but never Naomi. "I've always wanted to have a little brother or sister," she said. "When I was little, my parents promised I would, but then they got divorced and it never happened."

"Sucks that I won't be there for the birth, though," I said.

The bowl of cherries Naomi was holding fell to the ground with a clatter and cherries scattered everywhere. A squeal escaped her lips. I could have reacted like my dad, who would always freak out when I dropped something, making the situation worse in the end. He would have grabbed another bowl of fruit in his anger and haste—or worse, a can of powder enriched with vitamins and minerals—and thrown it as hard as he could onto the floor. Instead, I reacted much like my mom would. Whenever I broke things growing up, she'd always say, "It's just a thing, not a person."

"Are you okay, Naomi?" I asked, kneeling down to help her scoop up the fallen cherries.

"Why are you helping me, Kenza? You just got done telling me cherries are the most expensive."

"They can be replaced," I said.

"Hmm," was all she could muster as a response.

When we finished picking up the cherries, I couldn't resist the temptation to grab a handful and throw some at her. She, of course, retaliated in true Naomi fashion, with no ounce of prodding from me, and the supply of soiled cherries dwindled in no time.

Naomi then sucked in a slow breath and leaned her back against the counter. "So why can't you go home for the birth?"

"I just can't. I'm here and my parents don't have the funds to fly me back and forth."

Naomi bounced her back against the counter, a nervous habit I'd seen her do a few times before. "Since they can't use the camp's free plane tickets for immediate family members to come here, why don't you ask the camp to give you a free ticket home?"

I grabbed a piece of ice from the tray I planned to put back in the fridge before the cherry incident happened and tossed it in my mouth. I crunched down loudly, and then shook my head, crossed my arms. "Can't."

"But why not—"

"God, Naomi." I turned away and leaned on the counter. "This is exactly why I didn't say anything to anyone else. It's useless."

I felt her hand on my shoulder and turned, still frowning.

When Naomi spoke next, her voice softer and gentler than I knew possible for her. "When my mom was pregnant—"

"I thought you were an only child."

"Listen, please." She shot me a dirty look. "Anyway, I was seven when my parents sent me away to stay with my grandma for the summer. I wanted to be there for the birth, but they said I'd be in the way. They had my little sister that July." A smile spread across her lips. "Her birth was normal, and everything was going great. I would call just to listen to her breathe." Naomi stared off into nothing. "She used to make these sweet cooing sounds. They named her Nellie, which sounds so old fashioned. I'm embarrassed to admit that I picked the name. Still, my parents fell in love with it."

She looked back up, laughed nervously. "I got to see Nellie on video chat a few times, all bundled up in these adorable onesies—her head all bobbly, as if a cantaloupe was trying to balance on a twig. The technology wasn't the greatest back then, but it felt like I knew her and I couldn't wait to see her." Naomi looked down at her feet. "The night before I flew back home with Gran, Nellie died in her sleep. It was SIDS, which made no sense at the time. Still doesn't."

Naomi stared off into the distance. I expected her eyes to water, but they hardened instead. After a moment, she snapped back into focus and raked her fingers through her hair—something I'd never seen her do before.

"Anyway," she said. "You have to go home for the birth, Kenza. At least promise me you'll ask Mrs. Bartolli or, better, Dr. Hendrix."

"Can't," I said, tugging at my pony-tail holder.

"Why not?" She looked offended.

"Naomi, I already asked them and they both refused."

"Then explain it to them," she said, her voice forceful.

"I did, and they said no, again."

"You're going home, Kenza. I promise you that. And I'm going to help you." She reached out and pulled me into a bear hug.

Ian poked his head around from the back of the stand. "Did I interrupt something? I mean you two seemed to be sharing a moment together. Do you need more time to yourselves? Maybe a key to my apartment?" He laughed.

I spotted a lone cherry on the counter, clearly covered in bits of dirt, and lobbed it at him. He caught it and ate it.

"Ew!" Naomi and I said in unison.

"Anyway," Ian said. "Naomi, good that you're here."

"What's that supposed to mean?" she asked.

"It's supposed to mean that we need you."

Naomi looked at him quizzically. "I'm already here. I'm already helping."

"Cover for Kenza, would you?" Ian pushed his way into the small space, yanking the ties on the back of my apron and lifting it over my head.

"What's going on?" I asked. "Is everything okay?"

"Everything is not okay," he said. "I need you to come with me right now."

"I know what this is," Naomi said, crossing her arms. "You're just looking for another excuse to rake her off to some secluded place, probably the beach, so you can kiss her face off."

143

"You know about that?" he asked, cocking his head in my direction.

I shrugged, struggling to wipe away any possible traces of guilt lingering on my face.

Ian led me to the South America library, talking twice his usual speed the whole way. I could barely get a word in. Apparently, he found something that matched the words that we'd found etched on the high-tech purple door deep within the Cave of Shadow Forest. He didn't tell me anything about what he discovered, which is what I was trying to ask each time I opened my mouth, but he did tell me how long it took him to find it, where he found it, the age of the book it was in (very old), and the fact that he ran into Dr. Dunbar while he was there.

We climbed the stairs to the top floor where the antique books resided. I panted trying to keep up, falling further and further behind. "Remind me again why we didn't take the elevator?"

He stopped abruptly, and then turned to face me. "Trust me, you wouldn't have wanted to wait for that ridiculously slow contraption to find this out."

He held out his hand for me and helped me find the strength to climb the last few steps. He continued holding my hand as we walked as fast as we could to the table, and then released it to pull out a chair, which I thought was for me. Just as I started to sit down, I saw an ancient, dusty brown book on the seat. I reached for the book and the moment I touched it, I saw images flashing through my mind, as if I were seeing scenes in which my ancestors in ancient Morocco fluttered about. I suddenly felt dizzy and grabbed for the back of the chair.

Ian caught me in his arms and helped me to the chair next to the book. "Let me get you some water," he said.

"No," I said abruptly, grabbing his forearm. "I'll be all right. Just please don't leave me alone."

"All right," he said, reaching for the book, placing it on the table in front of us. He sat in the seat next to me and scooted his chair toward me so that our thighs were touching. He leaned over and gave me a peck on the lips, smiling blissfully. "It's just you and me up here, Kenza."

"You, me, and this 500-year-old book," I reminded him.

He laughed. "Always the realist."

He flipped open the book and leafed through the tattered pages. It took him a while, so long that he started to wear his frustration in the lines of his forehead. Finally he pointed at a page and said, "There it is."

"Let me see it." I pulled the book closer to me.

"Wait, we have to be sure." Ian activated his Datadrix and located the picture he'd taken back at the purple door in the cave. He projected it so that I could see it, too.

"They're an exact match," I said. "Wait, what does that say underneath?" I leaned in. The letters were written in Arabic, and I couldn't make out what they said. "I'll be right back." I jumped up to find an Arabic-to-English dictionary and my dizziness returned. I braced myself against the chair back with my arms, until I felt confident I could make it across the room without collapsing.

"You okay, Kenza?"

I nodded, even though I wasn't sure of myself, and went in search of a dictionary. I returned with one a few minutes later and flipped it open to the section with the letter of the first word.

"How do you know what you're looking for?" Ian asked. "I mean, I know we were both there and both spoke Moroccan Arabic, but I don't remember anything." He seemed pleased with his joke—referring to the fact that we were long lost soul mates torn apart some 500 years ago in Morocco, which was when this odyssey began.

"That's not how I know." I shook my head but kept my eyes and finger glued to the page, continuing to scan as I spoke. "My dad taught me the alphabet. I know a few words, too, but not enough to speak it or understand much—unless, of course, I'm traveling back in time. Then I can somehow magically speak and understand everything."

Ian looked at me differently than he ever had before. "You never told me that." He laughed, but it sounded more like a grunt. "So if you can't figure out what these words mean, at least we can send you back in time to figure it out."

"Very funny," I said. "That's not happening again, if I have anything to do with it." I scanned through the words silently, flipping through a few more pages. "There it is," I finally said.

"What does it mean?" He leaned in closer, resting his chin on my shoulder.

Shivers ran up and down my spine. "It means 'gift'," I said.

"What about the other word?"

This time I found it more quickly, now more familiar with how the Arabic alphabet worked. "What the—?"

"What?" He moved away and stared straight at me, his eyes burning a hole in the side of my head, but I refused to look away from the book.

"It says 'twam' . . . that means 'twins.'"

Chapter 21

I spent the next several days working in the watermelon stand by myself. Everyone agreed to work double their normal shift in each of their jobs to make extra cash, in case having it would help with a surprise challenge. Based on everything we knew about Zenith Hill, going above and beyond their minimum requirements was not just smart it was essential.

Our Blue Melody drink—a mix of blueberries, watermelon, crushed ice, and honey—was the most in demand drink. People lined up fifty deep on the hottest afternoons just to get a taste of it. In one week alone, we cleared $500 dollars, which meant that Isabel and I were able to move back into our apartment. We'd been trading off sleeping space between the floor and the couch in the tree house, and my back and neck thanked me for sleeping in a comfortable bed again.

"Why'd you call it that?" One of the patrons at the stand asked. It was 95 degrees that day, which almost never happened in Oregon, and the line snaked all the way into The Sticks.

"Call what that?" I asked. Sweat poured down my back; I swiped across my forehead with the crook of my elbow.

"Jizzammee Dibs," he said, pointing at the sign for my watermelon stand. He reminded me of Ryan, younger than most of the rest of us, wearing glasses and possessing a sharp eye for detail.

I laughed. It was impossible to explain that the name originated from two magnificent jinns: one who shared her spirit with me in a past life—Jamila of Diab, and another with the power to float and time travel, among other things—Jinny Zzaman. "It just sounded cool," I finally said.

"It does sound cool," he said, smiling broadly as he reached for his drink.

Suddenly, his eyes hardened and he stood perfectly still. The buzz that only moments ago hummed loudly from the impatient patrons of Jizzammee Dibs instantly silenced. Nobody moved, not even the branches on nearby trees, or the blender that I'd left running. Nothing.

I nearly doubled over when I smelled Jinny Zzaman's foul odor, somehow more magnified on a sweltering day like this one. Despite the fact that I wanted to wretch, my spirit danced in anticipation of her presence. When the nausea finally eased and I straightened back up, I saw not one but two jinns. I'd seen them together when Jamila of Diab lived in Morocco 500 years ago, but I'd never seen them together in my present time. There, above the grass a few feet from the long, winding line of patrons, Jinny Zzaman floated in her midnight-sky dress next to Jamila of Diab, whose holographic image projected itself next to her. This time her image came through crystal clear, like the crisp image of one of the real people standing in line.

I let go of the cup of Blue Melody I'd been in the process of handing to the Ryan look-alike, thankful that it didn't crash to the ground, and I ran out of the stand to greet them.

"Jamila of Diab, Jinny Zzaman, I'm so happy to see you. I wish I could hug you."

They exchanged glances, smiling.

"We wish you could, too, but you know that's not possible," Jamila said.

"What are you doing here? I thought I'd have to summon you with the amulet. I'm so sorry I didn't get around to it yet—"

Jinny Zzaman held up her hand to silence me and I suddenly realized that I'd had diarrhea of the mouth, which was so unlike me. I was too excited to contain myself.

"There is much to discuss, but we will be brief. We do not want to alert Mazin of our presence." Jinny communicated those words telepathically to me.

"But I—"

"Please Kenza," Jamila warned. "We need you to listen." She nodded to Jinny Zzaman to continue.

"Kenza, there are many who love you here at camp and that is one of your gifts, but trust no one. Keep the Amulet of Omnia over your

148

heart. Give it to no one, not even Ian, at least until you find the Gift of Twam."

"The Gift of Twam?" I parroted. "Does that mean my mom is having twins?"

"It is not time for us to answer that question," Jinny said.

"Kenza," Jamila interjected. "You must return home for the birth."

"But I can't. There's no way."

"Find a way," they said in unison. Then they both faded into nothing.

∞

Out of the corner of my eye, the video of life that had frozen in time all around me suddenly reanimated, bursting with sounds and movement. The guy I'd just served a Blue Melody dropped his drink and I cursed myself for not setting it down on the counter before walking away. I ran at full speed for the door at the back of the watermelon stand, hoping no one noticed I was out of place.

"How'd you get so far away?" The guy, now covered in Blue Melody splatter, asked.

"I—" I glimpsed up at the long line, and suddenly felt completely overwhelmed. I glanced down at the blueberry watermelon juice spilled all over the counter and my throat began to burn. The last thing I wanted to do was cry in front of all those people waiting in line. It could ruin all future business if I did.

"Do you have an extra apron back there?" he asked.

"What?" I said, impatiently.

"Another apron." He trailed around to the back of Jizzammee Dibs and opened the door, letting himself in.

"What are you doing?" I asked.

"I'm helping you. What does it look like?"

I'd just been warned by Jinny Zzaman and Jamila of Diab not to trust a soul, not even Ian, and now some wimpy Ryan look-alike that I'd never met suddenly wanted to help me. Still, I didn't have a better alternative so I grabbed an apron from the hook near the door and tossed it to him.

"Fine," I said. "But you better keep up."

He raised an eyebrow, just like Ryan always did. "I guess we should at least know each others' names, if we're going to be working together."

"Fine, I'm Kenza," I said quickly, tapping a finger on the laminated sheet of recipes on the counter. "Here's everything you need to know. Fruit is in the refrigerator behind us. There's a blender for you to use on your side." I pointed at it. "You do know how to use a cash register, right?"

He nodded and I took the next person's order. Now that there were two of us, the customers formed two lines. After serving a few customers, I glanced over and noticed my helper was cranking out smoothies nearly as quickly as I was.

"How'd you get so fast?" I asked.

"My parents own a frozen yogurt shop in a little tourist town. I've worked there every summer for as long as I can remember. It's not the same as this, but it's the same idea."

"Hmm." With the line still snaking beyond where I could see, I couldn't think of anything intelligent to say, but I was smiling ear-to-ear that he was helping. "So what's your name, anyway?"

"Dexter," he said, after he handed a Strawmelicious to a short-haired Asian girl.

"You looking for a job, Dexter?"

"Um, not really." He laughed. "I kind of don't think I'd be able to work very often."

"Oh, you mean because you're a sophomore and don't have to hold a job like juniors?"

"Something like that," he agreed.

150

We worked side-by-side, just Dexter and me, until all the people who'd been waiting in line were served. It would have been impossible to tell how many we'd served because the line still stretched back into The Sticks with new customers, but I distinctly remembered seeing a guy in a fluorescent green shirt at the back of the line, and he just walked away with a Lemony Slush in his hand and a look of satisfaction after waiting in such a long line.

Dexter held up his hand to high five me. I slapped his hand and he jumped in a way that reminded exactly of Ryan.

"Why are you looking at me like that?" he asked, taking a step back.

"Oh, sorry. Am I staring?"

"Yeah, you kind of are." He hiked his glasses up on his nose.

"It's just . . . you look exactly like someone I know, only younger. It's kind of eerie."

He didn't say anything, just turned to greet the next customer. "What can I get you?"

Just then Ryan came running around the corner. His eyes instantly lasered on Dexter. "What the—"

Dexter opened his eyes wide and ripped off his apron. "Gotta go," he said, then ran out the back door without even saying good-bye.

I stood in the doorway and called, "Thank you."

When I turned back toward the counter, Ryan was gone. Moments later, he returned out of breath. "Who the hell was that?"

"His name is Dexter. He was a customer. I spilled his drink and the line was so long that I was freaking out . . . Ryan, are you okay? You look pale."

Ryan concentrated hard on the counter that separated us, like he was trying to solve a puzzle. He finally looked up. "Don't worry about it," he said. "It's nothing. Anyway, I have news for you."

"Are you going to serve us, or what?" The next customer in line asked.

Ryan turned to her and held up his hand. "Please, give us a minute. This is really important." He looked back in my direction and spoke slowly. "Kenza, I need you to see Dr. Hendrix. He has a message for you."

"Ryan, I can't do that right now. Look at this line." I pointed toward all the people still waiting. "You know how important this business is to our collaboration team."

"I'll help you." He slapped both hands down on the counter.

"Come on," the customer at the front of the line said. "When are you guys going to be done?"

The guy behind her stepped forward, too. "Seriously. This is ridiculous. You call this a business?"

Two people behind him left the line and started walking back toward The Sticks, and a buzz erupted among the crowd, followed by several more individuals and pairs ditching the line. Ryan immediately exited the stand and headed for the patch of grass alongside the middle of the line, holding both hands up to signal for the deserters to rethink their decision.

"Come back, please," he urged. "You have to know that this is only temporary." A few of the people who'd been walking away stopped and turned to listen. "You see," he said, "this girl, right here, is Kenza and she's one of my best friends. I know you are all busy building your tree houses for the Sycamore Challenge, but I'm begging you, please, to have patience. Kenza here is about to leave and I'm going to take her place as server, as soon as I can convince her to go."

"Why should she get to leave?" The tall guy, who was one of the first to leave the line, shouted.

Ryan turned to me and smiled. "Because she is an only child and her mom is in labor. She's about to have her baby."

Chapter 22

I yanked off my apron and threw it on the counter, not bothering to pick it up when it slid onto the floor. I sped for the door and pushed on it so hard that it flew open and banged against the outer wall. I took off in a sprint toward the North America office building, but stopped mid-step, turned back, and ran straight for Ryan. I gave him one of the biggest hugs I could and, without saying a word, I turned and ran as fast as I could to see Dr. Hendrix.

When I reached his office, I found Naomi sitting next to him. Both were smiling from ear to ear. "So how's my mom?" I asked, still panting from the long run. "Is she at the hospital? Is everything okay?"

Dr. Hendrix nodded. "Your mother is indeed on her way to the hospital right now." His voice remained calm. "Everything seems to be okay, Kenza, no need to worry yourself."

"But the baby's not due for another week, or more," I said.

"It's very common for babies to be born a few weeks early, or late," Dr. Hendrix explained. "Babies who are born only a week early suffer none of the risks that premature babies often have, because early arrivers tend to be fully developed."

I sighed and sank into the comfortably cushioned black leather chair next to Naomi. "Wait, so why are you here?" I asked her.

"I'm here, Kenza, because I made you a promise."

I looked at her quizzically.

"I know the rules state that you are not allowed to use your scholarship money this year for anything but your college fund, so the Gandhi team—with permission from Dr. Hendrix—" she nodded his way, "took up a collection from all the juniors. Everyone pitched in $5 dollars, which was more than enough to cover your plane tickets home and back, and a bag full of adorable gifts for the baby." Naomi turned in her chair to face the door and cupped her hands around her mouth, "Isabel, come in here."

Isabel slinked around the corner, a sweeping smile on her lips, and walked straight to me. I jumped up and hugged her. Tears surfaced and I wasn't strong enough to stifle them.

"Don't thank me," she said, leaning back and placing both of her hands on my shoulders. "Thank Naomi. It was all her idea and she's the one who pulled off the whole thing."

I glanced over at Naomi, who was smiling, but looking very humble, as if what she managed to do wasn't a big deal. But it was a huge deal to me. Being there for my mom, being there to support my dad and help him feel like he didn't have to do it all by himself, and meeting the baby—or babies—for the first time meant everything to me. I couldn't think of anything more important in the world.

I reached out for Naomi's hand and pulled her to her feet. She stood reluctantly. "Don't get all sappy on me, Atlas," she warned.

"Oh please." Isabel rolled her eyes. "Kenza is the last person to get sappy."

I gave Naomi a tight squeeze. "Isabel's right, Naomi," I said. "It's not usually in my nature, but what you did deserves a truckload of love sap."

"Great," she said. "So are you guys going or what?"

"What, now?" I asked.

"Of course, now," Naomi said.

"I'll drive you," Dr. Hendrix said.

Naomi glanced at Isabel and then at the door. Isabel nodded, slipped out and quickly returned with my luggage and a carry-on. "This should do it." She rolled the suitcase next to me.

"You packed my stuff?" My throat tightened and tears threatened to resurface.

"Why wouldn't we?" Isabel said. "What kind of friends do you think we are?"

"The best kind," I said.

154

Naomi rolled her eyes and said, "Ugh! Enough with the sap."

Dr. Hendrix pushed back in his chair and stood quickly, shutting his laptop lid until it clicked. He walked to the door and grabbed his raincoat from the coat tree next to it.

"There isn't a cloud in the sky," Naomi said, eying him curiously.

"Not yet," he said, winking at her.

I followed him to the door and turned suddenly. "Wait, I should let Ian know what's going on."

"I already did," Isabel said.

"Well why isn't he here, then?" I asked.

Isabel glanced at Naomi, with a look of concern. Her words did nothing to comfort me. "He had to work."

∞

Aside from a sudden downpour on the way to the airport in Portland, the flight to Denver was uneventful. With only a thirty-minute layover, luck was on my side when I discovered my connecting flight would board next to the gate I'd just departed. The first flight had been packed, but the second one wasn't. Despite the fact that I usually dreaded chatty passengers next to me, this time I longed for the company. Instead, I settled for an empty row at the back of the plane, so I at least had the luxury of stretching out across three seats.

The minute I closed my eyes, images began to flash through my mind, as if I were dreaming, but I knew I was awake. I saw two people's arms holding up identical twin babies—both screaming at the top of their lungs, their faces red. The high-tech purple door deep in the cave of Shadow Forest flitted through my mind. At first, I saw it from far away, then nearer and nearer. Thoughts of Ian assaulted my senses—him embracing me, and then pushing me away with erratic unpredictability. When an image of Mazin's face suddenly appeared directly before me, his fiery red eyes burning through me, I jumped.

The plane rumbled and the pilot's voice sounded over the intercom, too calm for the nerves flitting through me. "This is your captain speaking. We are experiencing minor turbulence. Please fasten your seat—"

The plane suddenly dropped several feet in altitude and an evil cackle echoed through my mind. Several passengers gasped and looked around suspiciously, as if looking for the source of the noise. Could they have heard it too?

I squeezed my eyes shut and began muttering the closest thing to prayer I knew. "Forces of good, please protect us right now. Please keep us safe and allow us to arrive safely in Omaha. Protect all these innocent people from the danger that haunts me." I kept my eyes shut, afraid the world, as I knew it, would crumble in a dramatic plane crash if I didn't. The plane continued to bounce and rumble, reminding me of long drives on the endless dirt roads in the countryside, just outside Omaha.

The plane lurched forward and my stomach dropped, but despite the fear that should have been coursing through me, I felt a warm wave of peace. It started in my mind then rippled down my back until I felt it all the way to my toes. I opened my eyes and heard the distant echo of Mazin's voice one last time.

The plane suddenly smoothed out and the intercom beeped. The captain spoke once again. "It appears we are out of the turbulence and have nothing but clear skies ahead. You are free to move about the cabin." The intercom beeped one more time and the fasten seatbelt sign blinked off.

Forty-five minutes later, we landed in Omaha and the moment the wheels touched down, what felt like the flutter of hummingbird wings overtook my stomach. I thought I might be sick. I didn't sense Mazin's presence anywhere nearby and thus ascribed my upset stomach to pure adrenaline and overprotective feelings flooding in—all because I was about to meet my little brother or sister, or both.

I sat in the back row, bouncing my heels impatiently. When the rows finally cleared out and I was able to reach the wide hallway that lead to the terminal, I tried to zip around as many passengers as I could.

I hadn't checked a bag, so was able to race to the escalator and down the moving stairs, my suitcase clacking down the steps behind me.

I stepped through the rotating doors and finally made my way to the street, where a sparse line of taxis awaited me.

"Can you drive any faster?" I asked, more than once along the way.

The Hispanic-looking driver finally spoke with an accent. "You in a hurry?"

"Yeah, is it that obvious?" I asked.

"Tell me about it," he said, undisturbed.

I eyed him suspiciously.

"I have a teenage daughter at home and she would never speak like that to a stranger unless something serious was going on. So I am sure this is the case with you, especially because you asked me to drive you to the hospital." He reached for the rear view mirror and adjusted it to see me better.

I sighed loudly. "My mom's in labor."

Despite the fact that we were on the highway surrounded by rush hour traffic, he turned all the way around to look at me. "Why didn't you say so?" He smiled and floored it. We reached the hospital in no time.

∞

I hurried through the sliding glass doors and ran right into the nurse with the skateboarding smock, the one who had led my dad and me to mom's room the last time she was here.

"I'm sorry, dear. You look like you're in a hurry." She took a step back and got a good look at me. "I remember you. You must be here to see your mom."

I nodded.

"Follow me." She smiled broadly and held out her elbow for me to hold, which I didn't hesitate to do, because it meant reaching my mom's room faster. "Your mom's just fine," she reassured me.

"She is?" I said. "She hasn't—"

"Had her baby yet?"

"Yeah." I looked down, afraid I'd missed the whole thing.

"No, not yet," she said. "But she's very close. You arrived just in the nick of time."

"Wait, you said baby. So she's not having twins?"

"Twins?" she laughed. "Not that I know of, but she's not my patient so I really don't know."

We arrived at the room, but just as I started to the open the door, the nurse reached out and pushed it shut. "Your mom's in a lot of pain."

The hope I'd been clinging to that everything was okay sank to the pit of my stomach.

The nurse cleared her throat and spoke again very quickly. "Any woman would be in this kind of pain when she is this close to giving birth."

"Oh," I said dragging out the word. I released a long sigh.

"You stay out here. I'll go find out if she's in any condition to see you."

I nodded, combed my fingers through my hair. I watched her disappear through the door. Moments later she returned wearing an oversized smile.

"Your mom would like to see you," she said, and then paused. "Now young lady, please remember that your mom is experiencing labor pains every few minutes, so you'll likely see one very quickly. Don't panic. It will frighten her. Try to remain as calm as possible. Can you do that?"

I nodded. My palms felt sweaty and nervous energy skittered through me like a fast-beating drum. I pulled in a long breath and pushed open the door. Mom looked over at me and smiled, waving me to come stand next to her bed. I didn't notice Dad at first, even though he was standing on the other side of her. I'd never seen him look so nervous. Sweat pooled on his forehead and he kept wringing his hands. He hurried over to me and hugged me awkwardly.

158

"Don't think we won't talk about how you managed to pay for a ticket to fly here, Kenza," he said once he'd returned to his place next to Mom on the other side of the bed.

"Adam, please," Mom said softly.

He knelt down next to her and reached for her hand. "I know, I know, my Stars. I'll let it go for now." He looked up at me. "I am glad you're here."

I smiled and bent over to hug Mom, but her face had turned a deep shade of red. She breathed in and out slowly, clasping her hand over her stomach. Then she grimaced and moaned. "I think it's coming," she called.

I looked up at Dad. "What do we do?"

"Go get the nurse," he ordered, pointing toward the door.

"Which one?"

"It doesn't matter. Just go find someone."

I ran to the door and didn't find the nurse who'd led me to the room, but I did see a male one, with straggly blond hair and a moustache, heading our way. I ran toward him and grabbed his arm.

"Who are you?"

"Please," I said. "My mom's having her baby."

Moments later, a tall brunette nurse, the male nurse I'd just found, and Mom's doctor all gathered around her. By then, Mom's labor pains were coming fast and furiously.

The female nurse approached my mom and leaned against the silver rail. "Jackie, you are so close to having this baby. I know you are in a lot of pain right now, but it will all be over soon and you'll be holding a little bundle of joy in your arms."

Mom grimaced and groaned, but nodded to acknowledge what the nurse just said.

"It's time for your guest to leave," the nurse added.

"What? No," I protested. "I just got here."

The nurse turned to me. "I'm sorry, dear. I'm just trying to help your mom."

Mom cried out, then breathed a few quick shallow breaths. "I'd like her to stay," she finally said in a strained voice.

"Are you sure?" the nurse asked.

Mom nodded vigorously.

I squealed, went up on my toes for a moment.

"Are you sure?" This time the nurse directed the question at my dad.

At first he didn't respond. He eyed me and then he looked down at my mom. "It's okay with me, too," he finally agreed.

The nurse pulled me aside and explained what was about to happen. She encouraged me not to hold Mom's hand because she'd squeeze so hard it might hurt me. She also explained that I could step away from the bed and sit down any time it got too intense, especially if I felt light headed. She assured me that Mom's pain would go away as soon as she held a baby in her arms, if not permanently, at least temporarily. She told me I was brave and she was proud of me, even though she'd never met me before.

The next several minutes crawled by more slowly than anything I remember. Mom's groans escalated to screams and her face remained a permanent shade of red. Her hair dripped with sweat and she was shaking uncontrollably. I looked up at Dad and he looked pale. I wondered if I did, too. He caught me glancing at him and I tried to smile, but I was sure it came out more like a crooked frown.

The doctor, who was now sitting on a stool on wheels, held his hands out like catcher's mitts ready for the baby. "Jackie, it's time for you to push."

Mom squeezed her eyes shut and grunted, tears running down her cheeks.

"Again, push," the doctor ordered.

Mom belted out a grunt that sounded like a body builder lifting heavy weights. She pushed for as long as she could and then her head collapsed back onto the bed. I stood there staring at her, wanting to help,

160

but feeling completely helpless. I thought of the baby inside her and wondered if he or she would be safe from Mazin, or in danger like the rest of my family. Babies were so innocent, so incapable of defending themselves. I knew my life was about to spin out of control and would soon be filled with noise and chaos and dirty diapers. Before I knew Mazin had resurfaced—even before I knew my mom was pregnant, I didn't think I could handle one more ounce of stress. I was still recovering from the trauma of last summer. Somehow, now that I was smack dab in the middle of another emotional tornado, I knew—hoped—everything would be okay.

But everything wasn't going to be okay.

Suddenly I felt lightheaded. The energy inside of me drained from my head to my toes as if the battery inside of me depleted within seconds. Sweat pooled on my forehead and my palms felt clammy.

"Kenza?" Mom said.

I wrapped my hands around the railing as tightly as I could, but there was no use. I felt myself going down, the light fading to black. I was losing control. Was this the end? Had Mazin managed to find me and destroy me?

∞

I woke up moments later, lying flat on my back, looking up at tile ceiling, with fluorescent lights beaming down on me. The nurse with the skateboard smock who'd escorted me to Mom's room was sitting in a chair next to me.

"Where am I?"

"Everything's going to be okay," she said, smiling.

"Did Mom have her baby?" I sat up fast and felt dizzy, so I lay back down, realizing simultaneously that I was sprawled out on one of the couches in the waiting room. "How long have I been out?" I squinted up at the bright lights.

"About ten minutes," she said.

161

"That's impossible. It was only a few seconds." I attempted to sit up again, and this time I was successful. I swung my legs over so that I was sitting normal on the couch.

"It probably seemed like only a few seconds to you."

"So is she still in labor? Did she have her baby?"

The nurse shook her head. "No, but it will be very soon."

I stood quickly. "I'm going back in there."

She reached for my hand and pulled me back down to sit. "Hold on there, bulldog. It will be best for everyone if you take care of yourself and let the team of experts take care of your mom."

"Something's wrong, isn't it?" I said.

"Nothing they can't handle," she assured me. "They've taken your mom in for a C-Section."

I leapt to my feet. "What? No."

"It's very routine," she explained. "The risks are extremely low. It might take her a little longer to recover, and she'll have a permanent scar, but at her age I am sure a scar is the least of her concerns."

I suddenly felt nauseous and bent over, clutching my stomach.

"Ah." The nurse winked at me. "It's very normal to feel sick to your stomach after a fainting spell. It might seem counter intuitive, but it's best to get something into your stomach." She stood and reached into her pocket, pulling out two one-dollar bills. "Come on then." She held her elbow up for me to take it, which I did.

We walked together down the long corridor, past Mom's room to a series of vending machines at the end of the hallway. I kept turning back, wanting to go be with my mom, but every time I started in that direction, the nurse tugged me forward. Once we got to the vending machine, the nurse instructed me to sit down in a nearby chair, concerned I might still be unstable. She helped me pick out things that would give my blood sugar a boost: some cookies and a bag of peanuts to keep me going once the sugar rush wore off.

As soon as she handed them to me, I ripped open the bag of cookies. I hadn't eaten for hours. She sat down next to me and stared, concerned, at my over indulgence. She stared so long that I finally felt embarrassed and offered a cookie, even though there was only half of a broken one left. She reached for the bag, but then looked down at the small tablet clipped to her waist.

"I have to go," she said, standing quickly. She strode off without another word.

I ripped open the bag of peanuts and poured them all into my hand, shoveling as many into my mouth as I could handle. As soon as I finished the bag, I dusted off my salty hands and sank into a couch in the small waiting area next to the vending machine. I felt like a heavy weight was pressing on me and, knowing mom was in surgery, I sprawled out on the couch and drifted into sleep.

I awoke to a loud sound and glanced over to see a man bent over in front of a pop machine, reaching his hand into the bin to retrieve a bottle of Coke. The loud noise must have been the bottle falling into the bin.

I sat up and stretched, yawning loudly. I didn't know what time it was and, spotting no clock in the waiting room, I stood and headed toward Mom's room.

Seconds later, I heard my name being called. I knew no one really called it out loud—that I only heard it in my mind. "Kenza . . . " I heard it again, long and drawn out, and a chill raced up my spine. It seemed to be coming from behind the door on my left, which was closed. I reached for the door handle and slowly pushed it open. It creaked as it opened and I heard a familiar voice call, "Who's there?"

Chapter 23

"Kenza." The nurse with the skateboard smock came running down the hallway toward me and I released the door handle, backing away from it.

"What is it?" I asked.

The nurse smiled. "Come with me."

I followed her back to Mom's room. She pushed the door open and held out her arm for me to walk in. I obeyed and as soon as I did, I saw Mom lying in bed. She smiled the moment she saw me. "Kenza, come over here."

I walked over to her carefully, delicately, as if the floor below me might crack into a million pieces and swallow me up, sending me plunging into some unknown world below. I stood as close to her bed as I could, my stomach leaning against the rail. She held a bundled blanket and I saw the most beautiful angelic face looking up at her.

"How are you feeling?" I asked.

Mom reached out and squeezed my arm. "I'm a lot better than I was the last time you saw me." She laughed at the memory. "How are you, Kenza?"

I nodded a few times. "Better." I reached out for the blanket, careful not to touch the baby.

"It's a girl," Mom said. "Her name is Daniyah. We can call her Danny for short."

I caressed the dark hair on her forehead. "Where's the other one?"

Mom squinted. "What are you talking about?"

"I . . . you didn't have twins?"

"Of course, not Kenza. Who told you I was having twins?"

"Kenza, did you meet little Daniyah?" Dad said behind me.

164

I turned abruptly, half expecting him to be holding another baby, but instead he held a cup of coffee. "I did meet her," I said. "She's a little angel."

He smiled and I turned back to Mom. She looked at me severely, still expecting an answer to her question. I spoke quietly, "I guess I thought I overheard you and dad talking about it. I must have misunderstood."

"Kenza, you should have just asked."

I nodded and bent over to kiss her forehead.

"You should hold the baby," Dad said. He walked over to the other side of the bed and reached gently for her.

"Be careful, Dad," I ordered.

He looked up at me. "Kenza, you gave me lots and lots of opportunities to get good at this. Now why don't you go sit down in the chair and I will bring your little sister to you."

I nodded, and sank into the chair in the corner. Dad carried Daniyah to me and lowered her into my arms. "Make sure you support her head with your arm." He released her and walked back over to Mom. "Are you feeling better, my Stars?" he asked.

They started talking, but I tuned them out. Little Daniyah looked up at me. Actually, she just looked up. I doubted she could really make sense of me or anything else yet. I leaned down and kissed her forehead as gently as I could, and then got lost looking into her tiny face and eyes. I inhaled a slow breath, exhaled slowly, and then suddenly felt my eyes burn and a lump form in my throat. This little child, precious and new and innocent, was my little sister. She was an Atlas, and it was up to me to protect her from the grave danger that haunted me. I squeezed her tighter as a tear spilled over onto my cheek. I didn't want this moment to end, ever.

"Can I take her now?" Dad said.

I didn't want to let her go, but my arms were getting tired and she was starting to wind herself up into a cry. I finally handed her over and stood up.

"Kenza, where are you going?" Mom asked.

165

I glanced at the door. "Nowhere, I'm just going to stretch my legs."

I made my way to the hallway and found myself heading back down the long corridor toward the room with the familiar voice. It was familiar, but I couldn't place it. As I approached it, I heard my name being called again—not by a nurse, but by a soft mysterious echo that drew me in. I finally reached the door and eased it open, walking through.

"Who's there?" the familiar voice called.

As I made my way into the room, I recognized the owner of the voice immediately. She was alone in the room, lying in bed, holding a wrapped baby in her arms.

"Megan?"

"Kenza, how did you find out I was here?"

"I didn't know you were here. My mom just had her baby." I walked closer to Megan's bed. "I have a little sister. I'm now a big sister." I laughed nervously. "I mean . . . that's something you and I always had in common. We were only children, but that's all changed now."

The tension on Megan's face drained and she smiled widely. "Congratulations, Kenza. I'm so happy for you."

I looked at her quizzically. It wasn't like her to react in that way. I took another step toward the bed and realized the baby she was holding was wrapped in a blue blanket.

"Is that—" I started to ask, but couldn't find the rest of the words.

"This is West."

I walked over to him and peeked down at his sweet little face, swaddled in a blue blanket.

"Do you want to hold him?" Megan asked.

I shook my head a few times and finally said, "I don't want to break him." I smiled and reached out for his little hand. He wrapped it around my finger. "I didn't know." I finally added.

166

"No one did," Megan said. "For a while, I wasn't even sure if I could go through with it. But now that I see him, how could I have done anything different?"

"Right?" I said, then added, "He's beautiful."

"He is. Isn't he?"

I stood there in silence, in awe that this was really happening. I was standing there next to my mortal enemy, no idea that she'd been pregnant. Now she lay there, vulnerable and full of love, her guard completely down.

"Mrs. Montgomery knew, didn't she?" I said.

Megan nodded and was about to say something, but was interrupted when her dad came striding toward us.

"Kenza?" he said. He looked just like I remembered, dark shaggy hair and scruffy beard. Usually, he wore a very serious expression, but today he was beaming. His arms were full of bags, overflowing with flowers and stuffed animals, which he hurriedly set down.

"Hi Mr. Hawk."

"How did you know Megan had her baby?"

"Oh, I didn't." I pointed toward the door. "My mom just had her baby girl today and I accidentally stumbled upon Megan. I guess you could say it was pure luck."

He looked at me quizzically. "That's pretty unexpected. Your baby sister and our little West will be twins, born on the same day, in the same hospital."

I stared at him, shocked, unable to speak.

"Kenza, is everything okay?" Megan asked.

I turned sharply in her direction. "What? Oh, yeah. Of course, I just . . . " I looked up and laughed. "Talking about my little sister makes me want to head back to Mom's room. I don't want to be away from her for another second."

Megan released a sigh. "I know the feeling."

I gave her a quick pat and wrestled my finger from little West's grip, then turned quickly to head past Mr. Hawk, toward the door. "It was nice to see you again, and congratulations," I said as I passed.

As I reached for the door handle, he called out, "Wait, Kenza."

I turned, raising an eyebrow.

"I have something for you."

"For me?" I pointed at my chest.

He nodded and reached into one of the bags he'd carried in. He pulled out a small clear keychain with a picture of West. "For you."

∞

Mom and Dad stayed at the hospital for the next two nights, so the doctors could monitor Daniyah's and my mom's vitals. I was exhausted from the trip and the worry and, most importantly, from Mr. Hawk's staggering words: "It's like they're twins." I'd somehow convinced my parents to let me stay home alone, so I could sleep in my own bed and get a good night's rest. Dad even let me drive home, the first time I'd ever been behind the wheel without a parent in the car. The deal was that I'd return first thing in the morning to say my goodbye's, and then call a cab to pick me up at the hospital so I could leave for a morning flight back to Oregon.

Even though I was completely exhausted, I had business to tend to. I needed to explore the rest of the Moroccan heirlooms locked securely away in the mysterious camel-bone box in the attic. I knew my dad would never leave Mom's side, so I was safe to explore for as long as I needed—safe from my dad getting in my way, at least. I didn't know how safe I would be from Mazin, especially alone in our house. And, if Mazin didn't get me, mice, bats, or other creepy nocturnal creatures might.

To help ease my nerves, I switched on the Datadrix flashlight on my wrist, turned on all the lights in the hallway, and propped the door to the attic wide open. I climbed to the top of the stairs, pushed on the overhead door with my free hand, until it flopped up and over, landing with a thud, and then stepped through the opening, my heart pounding furiously fast.

I quickly scoured the area, light jittering in frantic jumps from corner to corner. I wasn't sure what I was looking for—what form Mazin would be manifesting—but I knew I'd recognize his energy when I saw it. But nothing was there—no dark shadows that spotlighted Mazin's spirit form, and no good jinns to help ease my nerves. There was nothing but silence, dust, and cold air.

I stepped through the clutter to the center of the attic and tugged on the string hanging from the ceiling to flick on the light. It switched on and, while not bright enough to illuminate the entire attic, it was definitely a step up from the spotty light of the Datadrix flashlight.

I scanned the area where I'd last seen the camel-bone box and finally spotted it. I didn't remember it being in that same exact spot, and I certainly didn't remember the pile of papers and bags lying on top of it. Dad must have been up here snooping around—at least that's what I hoped. I dreaded the thought that Mazin might have discovered it, hoping against all hope that all the original contents, whatever they might be, were still in the box. But how would I know any different, since I hadn't seen the full contents?

I knelt down to clear away the pile of papers and bags, and then reached for the box and cleared the layer of dust from its top, realizing too late that the missing dust would flag my dad that I'd been here. I quickly shrugged my mistake away, aware that removing any contents from the box—which I absolutely planned to do—would also give me away. In essence, I was busted no matter what I did.

I lifted the lid on the box, only this time no light emitted from it— the papyrus drawing of the Amulet of Omnia was already safely returned to the nook in my bedroom wall. Nothing . . . not one visible thing awaited my discovery. I reached in and felt around to make sure I wasn't missing anything and felt the bottom give on one side. Was I imagining it?

Forgetting for a moment that the attic was a scary place to linger, I sat down, crossed my legs, and lifted the box onto my lap. I reached in and felt around the bottom, shining the flashlight in it to get a better look.

It really did look like the bottom of the box, but I wanted so badly to discover some secret compartment. I pushed on every corner and—while a slight give on each corner confirmed that I was on to something, nothing would budge.

I flipped the box upside down and shook hard, hoping not to damage it. When I turned it back over, I saw one of the bottom corners lift slightly. I reached my hand in to pull it up, accidentally pushing it back down. After repeating this little dance several times, each time trying to free the loose corner with my finger, I finally succeeded. Once the fabric covered bottom lifted out, I discovered a dark wooden compartment beneath. I tried to open it, but it wouldn't budge.

I shone the flashlight over the compartment and noticed a slit that reminded me of the one in the Cave of Shadow forest, the one that fit the Amulet of Omnia—luckily hanging safely around my neck. I reached under my shirt and pulled it out, not bothering to try and unclasp it from my neck. I bent over as far as I could and jimmied it into the hole until I heard the faintest click.

The wooden compartment creaked open to expose a small, clear crystal object, shaped exactly like the rectangular picture frame Mr. Hawk had given me of baby West. I reached in and pulled it out. The moment it left the compartment, the wooden door automatically shut and locked. I quickly placed the fabric bottom back in the box and closed it, attempting to return the pile of papers and bags back onto the box as best I could.

Chapter 24

When I arrived back at to camp, after showing everyone pictures of my little sister and telling them about the unexpected encounter with Megan and her baby, I convinced Ian to return to the Cave of Shadow Forest with me. We decided to sneak out in the middle of the night, when we'd be less likely to be missed. Somehow, he spilled our plans to Keelam and Isabel . . . so there we were, the four of us, standing in a row, facing the purple, high-tech elevator door deep inside the cave.

Keelam reached his hand out to the door and pulled it back the moment he made contact, shaking it hard. "What the hell is that thing?" he asked.

"A door, Keelam. It's just a door," I replied sharply.

Isabel glared at me.

"Kenza, please," Ian said softly.

Keelam walked over and stood in front me, making him the only thing between me and the door. "Kenza, what's wrong? Is what we're doing dangerous?"

I paused for a moment, looked down at the stone beneath my feet. "I can't answer that," I said. "It may be. All I know is that I've been thinking about this damn door ever since I saw it last summer. I've been wondering how, or if I'd ever get a chance to find out what was behind it. Now's my chance and I don't want to wait another second." I pushed past him.

"Kenza, wait. Haven't you ever touched it?" Keelam grabbed my arm.

"Let me go, Keelam."

He shook his head, refused to relinquish his grip, so I placed my hand on the door, anyway. I felt the energy from it pulse through me, but I didn't resist it or feel any pain. Keelam, on the other hand, yelled in my ear and released his tight grip from my arm.

171

I heard a loud noise behind me. It was the only thing that could break my concentration and distract me from finding out what was behind the door. When I turned, I saw Keelam had fallen onto the stone floor, his hand resting on his forehead.

"Is he okay?" I asked.

Ian knelt down next to Keelam on the ground, and quickly surveyed him. "He'll be fine. Do what you need to do." He waved me on.

I turned back to the door, briefly remembered that I still didn't know how to open it, but this time, I had something new. This time I had the rectangular crystal frame I'd found in Dad's camel-bone box. I'd been gripping it tightly in the palm of my hand this whole time. I held it up to the writing on the door, where the words "Gift of Twins" were inscribed in Arabic. When I did, a rectangular slot below the inscription lit up.

I moved the frame away, to examine the slot, but it vanished. So I held up the crystal again to see the slot below the words. I marked it with my finger to remember where it was when I pulled the crystal away. I even attempted to slide the crystal into the slot, as if it were an ATM and I had the magic card. To my surprise, the slot opened and swallowed the crystal.

Then, just below it, another slot opened identical to the first. Because of the reference to twins, I had the foresight to bring the keychain that Mr. Hawk had gifted me with the picture of the adorable little West still in it. I pulled that out of my pocket and inserted it into the second slot. The door split vertically into two halves, opening like a real elevator door.

"No way." It was Keelam's voice behind me.

I turned to see him now standing.

"Look who's feeling better," I said, smiling. I turned back to step through the door, and drew a breath. "Follow me, if you dare," I offered, trying to at least sound playful.

Once everyone was inside the elevator, or whatever it was, the door closed and the crystal from Dad's camel-bone box ejected from a slot on the inside, followed by the keychain frame from Megan's dad. I grabbed them both and shoved them back into my back pockets.

"Now what?" Keelam asked.

"Now we wait," I said.

Nothing happened for a moment and a heavy sack of nerves twisted in my stomach, but soon the elevator bounced once and then dropped. When it stopped, a monotone female voice said, "Please hold on to the railing."

Each of us grabbed for a part of the metal railing that wrapped all the way around the elevator and it began to zip sideways. When it stopped, Isabel let go. She shouldn't have because the elevator then shot upward. My nerves sank to my toes and Isabel fell to the floor. After Ian and Keelam helped her up, she gripped the railing hard. I grabbed hold of her arm, too.

The elevator finally stopped, bounced hard, and then opened. Due to the high tech nature of the elevator, I expected to exit onto a tile floor, surrounded by slate walls and maybe even an array of technologically advanced computers. Instead, we stepped out onto a rocky platform, suspended over a waterfall, which towered over the center of an enormous underground dome, lit by what had to be an optical illusion of the sky. Sunlight beamed down from all directions. But how could it reflect daylight in the middle of the night, deep under a cave in Oregon?

Even over the sound of the waterfall just below us, we could hear an array of birds chirping, monkeys chattering, and the fresh air flooding our senses. I turned in a full circle and took it all in. We had transported to a jungle paradise and were now standing at the most beautiful three hundred sixty degree vantage point. I looked down at the naturally worn pathways below and found myself wanting to explore the little ponds and streams, to cross the natural bridges, and to climb the various hills and cliff caves that encircled the jungle.

The elevator emitted a humming noise, and I spun around to watch it lift slightly, then shoot back down in the direction it came, disappearing from sight.

"Wait," Isabel called. She turned abruptly to face me, pointing down to where it sank back into its shaft. "How are we going to get back?"

I started laughing, just a little at first, and then hysterically, to the point where I couldn't stop. Isabel's face turned bright red. "What's so funny?"

I shook my head, but kept laughing, secretly worrying I'd lost it.

"Kenza," Isabel insisted. "Answer me. Hurry. What if we get stuck down here? Up here? Whatever."

"Looks like we have some time," Ian said, with the hint of a smirk. "I don't see any way down."

"Lots of ways down."

"Who said that?" Keelam asked, bending his knees and thrusting his arms out karate-style, as if readying for an attack.

"Not who," the small voice answered. "What?"

"What?" Keelam repeated, laughing nervously.

"Yes, what," the voice repeated.

Right in the center of where we stood, a round hatch door that had blended in with the rock platform flipped open. It was clearly not as thick as the rock platform and appeared to be a lot lighter, perhaps made of a synthetic material, like plastic coated in a top layer that matched the rocky surface.

A creature popped its head through the opening, clearly not human. It was an animal—a small adorable otter. It scurried up and onto the platform, sat on its hind legs and looked up at us, cocking its head. We stood there for a moment gawking until he finally scurried back down into the hatch, and we followed him through the opening. Ian went first, I followed, and Keelam and Isabel headed up the rear.

The hatch led to a long dirt tunnel, so low we had to crouch as we walked, especially Keelam. I couldn't see very well, and apparently Isabel couldn't either. I felt her hands wrapped around my shoulders. For a moment, I wished it were Ian's hands. The tunnel was dim, but we could see a light up ahead. The otter scurried several steps ahead of us toward the light, a soft lamp inside a small library that looked nothing like what I would expect to find deep within a cave. It looked like an old-fashioned den, only it had cave walls instead of wooden ones. Books were stacked up and piled one on top of the other, all along the walls.

174

I recognized some of the authors: Descartes, Jules Verne, Ray Bradbury, even JK Rowling. There were still so many that I didn't recognize. Many of them looked different from most books I was used to—some had metallic covers, and some had painted covers, clearly not printed. Some of the writings were foreign—not Hebrew or Arabic or Chinese, but something more ancient—something I'd never seen before with pictographs etched gracefully into the metal.

Isabel was already standing in front of the books, reaching out for one. "What are these?" She couldn't seem to help herself. None of us could. When one of her fingers nearly came in contact with one of the metallic books, she snapped her hand back, stepping back a few steps. "Ouch!"

"Be careful, my dear." It was the voice we'd heard on top of the waterfall. I turned abruptly and saw a short, thin man with graying brown hair. He wore round glasses that sat too far down on the bridge of his nose. He leaned against a knotty wooden cane.

"Who are you?" I asked.

He hobbled over to the chair next to the desk and slowly sat down before answering. "I, my dear, am Otto."

Isabel let out a stifled laugh. He gave her a quizzical look and she said, "Otto? Really?"

"Mr. Otto, if you like, but just Otto is fine with me."

"Okay, Mr. Otto," Keelam said stepping in front of Isabel. "What the hell are you doing down here?"

The man pushed his glasses up on his nose and they immediately slid back down. "It's a bit rude to be so abrupt, young man. I would think it's obvious—I've been waiting for her." He pointed at me, his finger long and boney.

"Me?" I asked, pointing at my chest.

He nodded, patted the ottoman next to the desk, urging me to sit down. I motioned for the ottoman, but felt Ian's arm shoot out in front of me to block me.

"What are you doing?" I asked, glaring at him.

"We don't know if it's safe," Ian said, his teeth clenched.

175

I sighed impatiently. "Ian, you know what I've been through and it's far worse than any of this. Besides, this place is protected. It has to be. Don't you remember when Jinny Zzaman placed a protective spell and made it so that only one with the Amulet of Omnia and now the Gift of Twam could enter? The doors both closed behind us, so there's no way Mazin could get in here—not without both of those keys."

"She's right, Ian." We heard a familiar voice—the confident and loving voice of Jamila of Diab. I turned back toward the door to see her standing in the room, next to Jinny Zzaman.

Without permitting another thought to create quick sand in my mind, I ran to Jamila of Diab and hugged her. Surprisingly, when my skin made contact with hers, she didn't jitter or blink out like the holographic image I was used to seeing. She was real, standing before me just like Ian, Isabel, and Keelam were. Jinny was floating, like usual, but her awful stench did not accompany her.

"What the—" Keelam said, as his mouth dropped open. He walked over to face Jinny Zzaman and stared like a child who'd just seen a ghost.

"It's nice to meet you," Jinny Zzaman moved her lips and her words echoed through the room, not just the channels of my mind.

"How are you doing this?" I asked, directing the question to them both. Then I pointed to Jamila of Diab. "How are you real? And you, Jinny Zzaman, how are you talking?"

Jamila shot Jinny a worried look, but Jinny smiled at her warmly. "We are not in your usual dimension," Jinny explained. "You left that dimension behind when you stepped into the transporter. All of you did."

"So, we're not on Earth?" Ian asked.

"No, you're not on Earth," Mr. Otto said, jumping into the conversation. "You're not even in your universe, anymore."

"Is this . . . Nor?" I asked, unsure I was sufficiently prepared for the answer.

"No," Jinny said. "This is not Nor, but it is an access point to Nor, which is located within this dimension and is very near."

176

"You tell them too much," Mr. Otto said, his face growing red, him wheezing until he had to sit down.

"Careful now, Mr. Otto. You need your strength," Jinny warned.

Keelam started pacing in the small space and knocked over an ancient, hand-painted clay vase, shattering it into hundreds of pieces.

"Young man, do be careful." Mr. Otto's strength had returned and he stood abruptly as he said it.

"I'm sorry," Keelam said. "I hope it wasn't too valuable."

Mr. Otto crossed his arms and dropped them hard against his chest. "Not valuable. Humph," he said. "It only dates back to an era just before the pyramids in Egypt were built."

"The pyramids in—" Keelam's words were slow and his eyes wide. He dropped to his knees, cupping his hands around the area above the broken vase, as if imagining that his hands alone could gather and pull it back together, but also knowing full well it would be impossible. Ian placed his hand on Keelam's shoulder and Isabel knelt next to him.

Jamila of Diab walked over and stood in front of him on the other side of the broken vase. He looked up at her, sadness and desperation in his eyes. "Let me," she said.

He stayed put, as she knelt down, just like him and Isabel. The whole time, I'd been eying the mess feeling responsible for bringing extra people down here. Ian glanced up at me and must have registered my concern. He smiled warmly and walked next to me, lacing his fingers in mine.

Jamila glanced up at us. "Not to worry," she said, as if reading my thoughts. "You have chosen your friends wisely. They clearly do not walk away from responsibility, as your Keelam who remains squatted here before this broken vase demonstrates. What's more, it's obvious they support each other in a crisis."

She glanced back down at the vase and gently pushed Keelam's hands away. She held out her own, as if squeezing an invisible ball between them. She started swirling her hands around in half circles and in a matter of moments the pieces of the vase lifted into the air and began swirling with the current of her hands. Soon, they started piecing

177

themselves together from the bottom of the vase, up to the middle, until the very last tiny piece landed in its place with precision.

Jamila held out her hands, palms up, so the vase could land gently into them. Ian squeezed my hand and we exchanged glances. Jamila held the vase out to Keelam, who held up his hands, waving her away. "Take it," she said, her voice offering a mother's comfort, even though she had never lived long enough to have children—she'd died while still a teenager, likely younger than we were, after she and her soul mate Amal were torn apart. "Fear not," she whispered.

Keelam took the vase from her hands, stood as carefully as he could, and set it back down on the pedestal where it had originally sat. He took a few big steps, backing away from the vase, and then thanked her profusely until she was able to convince him that he had sufficiently done so.

"Let me get you some refreshments," Mr. Otto said, clasping his hands together. "Your kind guides, Jamila of Diab and Jinny Zzaman, have much to tell you. Sit down, please."

I looked around, but saw no other chairs besides the desk chair and the ottoman next to it. Mr. Otto blinked hard and suddenly a couch shaped like a semi-circle appeared in the middle of the room, along with a small matching chair. He smiled, waved his hand, and then disappeared through an opening in the wall that hadn't been there before and closed behind him after he left.

We all sat down, including Jamila of Diab, but Jinny Zzaman didn't appear to be able to sit so continued to float. "Jamila," she said, her midnight blue dress casting shimmers of light all around the enclave, "Will you please begin?"

Jamila nodded, crossed her legs near her ankles and tucked them to the side of her chair, like a lady of the 1500s would be expected to do. "Where to begin?" she said, pulling in a full breath. She looked around at each of us, eagerly sitting forward in our chairs listening with rapt attention. "You will spend a lengthy stretch of time here— I must tell you."

"What do you mean by 'a lengthy stretch of time'?'" Isabel asked. "We have obligations back at Zenith Hill. Commitments that must be met."

"She means Mrs. Bartolli," Keelam said, laughing.

"Ah, your dear Mrs. Bartolli," Jamila repeated. "We have found her an interesting entity." She sighed, looked down for a moment, as if searching for words. "How can I explain . . . ? You will be down here for a long while, but you will miss no commitments or obligations."

We shot each other confused glances.

"Oh, I get it," Ian said, snapping his fingers. "We're in another dimension, so time above ground stays still."

Jamila smiled. "Yes, Ian. This dimension is not restricted by your earthly timeline, or your laws of physics, for that matter."

"Not tied to our timeline?" Isabel asked.

"Not even by the tiniest grain of couscous in an hour glass," Jamila said. "You will stay here long enough for us to prepare you—"

"Prepare us to do what?" I asked, fearful thoughts began streaming into my mind, and I couldn't wait another second.

"Do not fear, dear ones," Jamila said, smiling. She lifted her eyes to Jinny. "Do you wish to tell them?" she asked.

Jinny pressed her palms together, as if in prayer, but held our gaze. "You are each about to learn a new, highly evolved skill that you can use upon your return to your dimension. This will help you with any challenges that Mazin creates, as well as with your other earthly challenges."

"Each of us? I mean all of us, or just Kenza . . . and maybe Ian?" Isabel asked.

"All," Jinny said, nodding to confirm.

"Not just Kenza and Ian?" Keelam clarified.

Jinny Zzaman gently shook her head. "Isabel and Keelam, in joining Ian and Kenza on this journey, you are now a part of what will come. All must learn, all must progress."

Keelam stood abruptly and Isabel followed, holding out her arm in a gesture to calm him down. "Why us?"

"Keelam," Jinny said, her voice firm, "you are in service to them, to us. We may not survive without you."

Keelam raised his eyebrows, pointed at his chest as if to say, "Me?"

Jinny and Jamila nodded in unison.

Keelam sank back into his chair and leaned back, straightening his spine in the process.

Before anyone could say more, the door in the wall slid open and for a split second, I thought I saw the otter, but Mr. Otto emerged. Instinctively, I rubbed my eyes. He carried a tray of drinks and familiar snacks: crackers, cheese, apple slices, and yogurt.

"Where's your cane?" Keelam asked.

"I only need the cane when I need it. When I am carrying a tray, I do not need it." Mr. Otto blinked again and a table appeared between us, where he set down his tray.

Keelam rubbed his hands together and said, "A guy could get used to this."

We ate in silence, and I didn't realize until now how hungry I was, but it made sense after the long walk in the woods, our adrenaline, and the shock of experiencing a new reality in another dimension. At some point, I looked up and realized Jinny and Jamila were no longer in the room, but I had no idea how long they'd been gone.

Mr. Otto cleared away our plates and the tray of food, and then said, "Are you ready?"

"Are we ready for what?" Isabel asked.

"Are you ready to rest?"

We exchanged glances.

"We've been in this den for some time and the sun just set here," Mr. Otto explained. "You'll need your rest. Your training begins first thing tomorrow."

We followed him back into the tunnel that had led us to the den, down several long corridors and around a few bends, until we reached a rope ladder leading straight up through a hole in the roof of the tunnel.

He held out his hand, inviting us to precede him. I led the way, climbing up the ladder into what appeared to be a pitch-black tube. The only light was up ahead at the top. I kept climbing until my head poked through up above.

"Whoa. You guys have got to see this," I said, peering back down into the tunnel.

"We're coming. We're coming," Ian called from at least twenty feet down the ladder.

I hoisted myself up onto the ground and raced over to the clear glass wall overlooking the jungle we'd seen from above the waterfall. I could see the platform we'd stood on above, shimmering under the light of what appeared to be two moons. I gazed out over the moonlit jungle, and saw lots of exotic trees, roots, vines, animals, birds, and even bats. Aside from the two moons overhead, it didn't look that different from what I was used to. In fact, I felt like I was back at home in Omaha, walking through the Lied Jungle at the Henry Doorly Zoo.

I turned to see Ian and Isabel by my side, staring in awe as I had done only moments ago. When I looked back at the tunnel, Keelam was just climbing out and an otter followed him up through the hole. It took one look at me, before scurrying back down. I hurried to the hole to follow its trail, but when I reached the opening, I only saw Mr. Otto, panting hard. "A little help?" he asked.

I offered my hand and helped him out. "Where'd the otter go?" I said.

"Hmm?" he looked at me, perplexed. Then he hurried over to a thick curtain of vines and pulled them back with his hand. Behind the vines, cots for each of us had been lined up. They were designed to look like giant leaves but cozy enough, with plenty of blankets and pillows. The entire room consisted of glass walls, floors, and ceiling. The glass sheltered us from the elements, but allowed the amazing views of a walking trail spotted with overgrowth from the plants and trees, the birds, monkeys and unusual creatures unique to this dimension that inhabited them, and the distant stars overhead that reminded me of Jinny Zzaman's dress.

"How are we ever going to be able to fall asleep after seeing all this amazing scenery?" Isabel asked.

181

"The mist will help," Mr. Otto said.

We all looked at him but didn't have a chance to ask, as he was already halfway through the opening headed back toward his library of books.

Keelam rushed over to the opening and bent down to peer into it. "What the hell was he talking about?" he said.

Isabel walked over and rubbed his back. "I guess we'll find out, won't we?"

Keelam stood abruptly. He held his arms out wide. "Why are we here? What the hell is going to happen tomorrow? This isn't safe. This is crazy."

"Keelam, calm down," Isabel said.

Ian and I eyed each other nervously.

"Don't tell me to calm down," Keelam said. He kicked at the wall, which seemed to push him over the edge. He lost control, pacing at full speed in a circle all around the room. He looked like a caged animal. He walked directly to the wall facing the jungle and pounded his fist against the glass.

"Ian, do something," Isabel shouted.

Ian and I both rushed up behind Keelam and we each grabbed an arm, pulling it behind his back. Keelam squirmed and twisted, but Isabel starting talking in a very soothing voice. "Keelam, I know you're nervous, and it's right to be. I'm nervous, too. I don't know what's going to happen. None of us do. But if you think about it, we're probably safer down here than we would be back at camp. We're with the good guys."

The tension in Keelam's arms went slack. He motioned to face Isabel, so Ian and I released him. Isabel flashed him a huge smile. "Besides," she continued, "look at this place. We're in paradise. And we're in it together."

Keelam walked over and sat on one of the cots. "I don't know what got into me," he said. "You must think I lost it."

"It's okay, man," Ian said. "It could have been any one of us."

"He's right, Keelam," I said. "In fact, it has been me already. I hate that feeling—you know, when you lose it. It's the worst."

He looked down at his hands and released a short laugh. Isabel walked over and sat so close to him. "They're right, you know."

He kissed her forehead softly. "Thanks for talking me down off the cliff. So do you think both of us can fit in this cot?"

"We won't know until we try," Isabel said.

They both kicked off their shoes and crawled under the blankets together.

"Just no funny business over there," Ian said, pointing at them. "I mean it."

"Ian, you read my mind," I said softly.

"Did you also read my mind that I want you to lie next to me."

In moments, I was stretched out next to him, with my head on his shoulder. Before I could think another thought, a very light mist sprayed down on us like a light rain. Then everything went black.

Chapter 25

"Who would like to go first?" Mr. Otto asked. We were sitting in an oversized room, with stadium seating that reminded me of a university lecture hall I'd seen with my dad. There was a platform in the front, where Mr. Otto paced back and forth using his index finger to push his glasses up every few steps.

Just for fun, and so the room wouldn't seem so huge, we had interspersed ourselves on different levels. I sat about halfway up. Isabel was off to my right and up a few rows, and Ian was almost directly behind me, as if he was determined to watch my back. Keelam, of course, claimed the front row.

"Go first for what?" Ian asked.

Mr. Otto paused in the center of the platform and gazed out over his small audience. "This is no ordinary room," he explained. "This is a place where the limits of what you think is possible are removed, and you will be able to do things you normally could not do. This is where your training begins. You will each learn a new skill that most, in your culture, would call supernatural."

"Why would we need—or want—a supernatural skill?" Isabel asked.

"Why wouldn't you?" Mr. Otto said. He looked down, paced left, and then right, bobbing slightly up onto his toes and back down again. "To be more specific, you will need these skills for the challenges ahead."

"You mean Mazin," I said, employing a matter-of-fact tone. Supernatural powers could be fun, but I was constantly aware that my friends—my love—were only here because I dragged them into this. I felt massively responsible, and afraid for their safety.

Mr. Otto smiled. "Mazin, yes." Then he added, "Mazin and all of his supporters, expected and unexpected. Now, who would like to go first?"

Keelam raised his hand and then jumped to his feet.

Mr. Otto's silhouette blinked out and then blinked back in. Before I had time to process what just happened, he blinked out again and I saw the otter that greeted us at the cave entrance. He—the otter—was wearing Mr. Otto's glasses. "Yes," he said, in Mr. Otto's voice. "What you just saw really happened. I am Mr. Otto. And I am also Ashram, the otter standing before you."

I exchanged glances with Ian, Isabel, and Keelam.

"That's right. You heard right," Ashram said. "In our dimension, each human takes two forms: one as a human, and the other as a creature."

"You mean a civilized animal, right?" Ian asked.

I turned to smile at him. Ian would want to be civilized.

"Usually an animal," Ashram said, rubbing his front paws together. "But not always. Some of us take the form of a plant, a tree, or other natural element. In any case, we take on two forms, so we always remember to consider different perspectives."

Keelam was still standing, scratching his curly head, looking completely confused. "So, what? Are you going to turn me into a monkey or something?"

"Not a monkey, no." Ashram shook his head. "A bat. Actually, we're not going to turn you into a bat exactly, but rather we're going to pair you with a bat trainer who will teach you to fly."

"No friggin' way," Keelam said.

"Well, are you ready or not?" Ashram asked.

Keelam jumped up onto the stage. "I am ready to fly." He zoomed his arms out to the sides and dipped his body down and up again. If he weren't so curious, he would have likely zoomed all around the stage.

"Good." The word came from a deep voice. The man who spoke it emerged from a corner and walked out onto the stage. He was tall, dark-skinned, broad-shouldered, and dressed in a black tuxedo and black wing-tipped shoes. His hair was slicked back, which made him look either high up in the mob or like Dracula's cousin. "Let me introduce myself. My name is Asouke. When I channel my bat form, others refer to

185

me as the Asouke King." He approached Keelam until they were standing face-to-face. He was the first person I'd seen who was taller than Keelam, though only by a few inches. His image blinked in and out a few times, then transmorphed into a bat, flapping his wings. "Lift your feet off the ground, Keelam," Asouke commanded. "Believe that you can."

Keelam stepped back a few feet. "I've never been this close to a bat before," he said, looking more freaked than I'd ever seen him.

"Does it frighten you?" the Asouke King asked.

Keelam nodded and the bat flew at him. Keelam ducked and swatted his arms, letting out a shrill scream.

The Asouke King morphed back into his ominous looking human form and laughed a deep guttural laugh.

"All right, all right," Keelam said. "If you stop laughing at me, I'll try."

Asouke silenced himself and nodded his encouragement.

Keelam shuffled from foot to foot. "I can't lift my feet off the ground just like that."

"You can and you will," Asouke said. He hovered in front of Keelam, but nothing seemed to happen. Keelam stood there for several long awkward moments. Asouke reverted to his bat form and flapped his wings to gain height. "All right," he said, "come with me, on your legs, if you must."

Keelam followed his teacher, stomping out the side door. Isabel went next. Her trainer's human stood nearly as tall as Asouke—but Denise was blonde and blue-eyed, with high cheek bones and angular lines. Denise walked with elegance and, with little effort, stole the attention of everyone in the room, especially Ian. A twinge of jealousy slithered through my heart, but I tried to shake it off. Still, if we hadn't been told that her name was Denise, I would have referred to her as Barbie.

She soon morphed into a tall yellow orchid with long elegant arms and legs, wide hips, and an enchanting, vibrantly colored face. "Hello my dear Isabel," the flower curled a limb of leaves around in a

186

gracious circle. "I am Dendrobium Tetragonum at your service." She bowed deeply and gracefully. "But please call me Tetras."

"You've got to be kidding me." Isabel flung both arms out to her sides. "Everyone else gets a talking animal and I get stuck with a bowing plant? I don't believe it."

The plant's flower turned from pure white to a fiery pulsing red. Tetras crossed her leafy arms and pouted, then turned in a huff and marched back to a terracotta flower pot off to the side. She climbed in, faced away from us, then turned and issued one more dirty look in Isabel's direction before planting herself securely into the pot. The red drained out restoring her to her pure white beauty once again.

"Great," Ashram threw both of his front paws up and slapped them down hard against the sides of his hind legs. "Now look what you did."

"What?" Isabel said, crossing her arms defensively.

I shot her a sharp glare.

"Not you too, Kenza?" she said.

I frowned.

"Come on," Isabel said. "You know how I am with plants. I kill them."

Tetras suddenly came back to life, shaking her flowers and leaves. She hopped out of her terracotta vase with ease. "Okay," she said, almost begrudgingly, "you definitely need some training."

"What are you talking about?" Isabel asked, her expression blank.

"What I am talking about, Isabel, is your skill. I have been assigned to teach you how to seduce anyone you come into contact with." With that, Tetras bowed again.

"Gross," Isabel replied, remaining defiant.

"No, no, silly child," Tetras said, laughing so hard she shook from flower to stem. "I'm not talking about physical seduction. I'm talking about something far more powerful. In your world, humans have created a multi-billion-dollar industry called advertising, but even that falls short. What you will learn from me is far more powerful. You'll learn how to snake your way into people's minds and control their thoughts—how to influence them to see things the way you want them to see them."

Tetras morphed back into the tall and lengthy girl who referred to herself as Denise and walked across the stage toward the door, her heels clicking loudly against the wooden floor. She turned gracefully, one hand resting on the doorframe. "I was hoping you'd be able to convince me you had at least a minute level of mind control powers and would instinctively use them to calm me down, but you failed miserably. So, Isabel, I need you to follow me." She turned around and strode gracefully into the hallway, confident that Isabel would follow, which she did.

Moments later, Ian's human tottered into the room covered from head to toe in tattoos, but when I got a better look I discovered it was his veins showing through the surface of his translucent skin. I saw no visible hair on his body—not his arms, his face, or above his eyes. His head had been clean-shaven, hence the name Buzz—and he quickly assumed the form of a bee he called Stripes.

"I will teach you, Ian," he announced.

"What, to seek out honey?" Ian said, laughing. I could tell he was nervous under the laughter, but a bee, really? I would have pictured Ian as a horse because he always stood tall, yet cared so much about others.

Stripes buzzed closer to Ian's head and then swept down to the stage and morphed back into Buzz. "Bees have the ability to sneak up on humans—and other species—and get so close that they can hear their thoughts.

"So, I'll be a mind reader?"

This made my ears perk up. If Ian could read my thoughts without my knowing, that could prove dangerous—but maybe only in a good way. At least he'd know how much I loved him and wanted to express my love. I wouldn't want him to know, however, how afraid I was and how much I tended to doubt myself. He might think I was lame if he knew the crazy things that shot through my mind occasionally.

While I got lost in my thought, Ian followed Stripes out of the room, and I was left alone with Ashram, wondering if he was my trainer or if I'd even get to learn a new skill. Soon thereafter, my trainer joined us. She was tall and thin, like Isabel's trainer Denise, but rather than blond hair, hers was a rich dark purple that hung down to the middle of her back. At first glance, she reminded me of Morticia from the Addams Family. Like Morticia, she wore a long tight black dress and thick black eye liner.

"My name is Varuta," she said, her voice elegant and mysterious. "I am here to teach you about protection."

I was thrilled to hear this; there was nothing I needed to learn more than protection, but my excitement shriveled the movement Varuta shrunk down into a leggy hairy tarantula. I stood stock still, watching her every move and let my eyes follow her toward the door. She turned to face me, "Aren't you coming?"

"Why can't we do it here?" I said, not wanting to budge from my spot. For whatever reason, I trusted Otto more than Varuta, and I didn't know where my friends had gone. Besides, what if this dark-looking character was a part of Mazin's army? Worse, what if she was Mazin in disguise, yet again?

She scurried back toward me, moving much faster than I expected. She crawled all the way up to the top of the podium and began speaking once she was perched on top, facing me with her beady little black eyes. "My dear Kenza, I don't expect you to feel comfortable with me."

I looked down at my feet, embarrassed.

Varuta went on. "I have information that is essential to your survival, and what's more, to the survival of your family and friends. Would you really let your discomfort get in the way of you being able to learn something that might save your little sister?"

I stood taller, shifted my weight. "No way." I shook my head, but felt my stomach tighten.

"Then this time, please follow me," she said. "And bring your full attention with you."

I chewed nervously on the inside of my cheek. Varuta crawled to the edge of the podium and morphed back into her human form. "I'll remain in this form until you have a chance to learn to trust me," she said.

189

I followed Varuta out the door and down a long winding trail, deep into the jungle, until we reached a fallen tree, next to a warn trail. She sat down on the tree trunk and crossed her legs. "So now we're here, now what?" I asked.

"Sit down."

"Where, with you on the tree trunk?" I asked.

"Sit yourself down on the trail," she said. "It will allow you to relax that wandering, scare-mongering mind of yours, while also feeling connected to the earth."

"Wait, the Earth?" I said. "I thought we had left the Earth yesterday and were on another planet, in a different dimension."

"It's merely a manner of speaking about the ground," she explained. "When I said earth, I meant dirt. Earth sounded better. Now, you are not going to continue questioning my orders, or pretending to resist, are you? Jinny warned me that you'd be stubborn, but perhaps I foolishly welcomed the challenge."

"Jinny Zzaman?" I asked.

"Yes, of course. Who else?" She laughed. "Oh, I see. You presumed I was not worthy of access to such a powerful being. You thought she was your special jinn. You have a lot to learn, Kenza, as most young girls do. Things are not what they seem. No, they are not."

I sighed deeply, but didn't know what else to say. Still, at hearing mention of Jinny Zzaman, some of the tension in my shoulders drained away.

"Good," Varuta said. "Silence is our next step. You must sit quietly on that dirt trail and free your mind from all distractions. Let it wander until you no longer remember that you are in a body, or even have a body. Use the silence to connect your chattering mind to your inner essence."

"So you want me to meditate?" I asked, feeling even more annoyed.

"Yes, how do you know about meditation?" she asked, sounding optimistic that perhaps I'd already aced the technique.

"They taught us how to do it at school. We meditated every other day for two weeks, as part of our yoga lessons."

"Mmm . . . hmm." She shrank into her creature form and scuttled back and forth across the tree trunk several times, looking like a spider frantically seeking the tiniest morsel of a bug, as if her life depended on her doing so.

I jumped to my feet; my readiness for trying meditation instantly halted.

"Oh not this again." She released a sigh and morphed back into her human form. "I'd already forgotten how afraid you are of me in that form," she said. "I will remain in this form until you've had a chance to meditate, but don't expect me to remain like this all day. As you can imagine, this form is extremely uncomfortable here in the jungle compared to when I am an arachnid."

I sat in silence for what felt like hours. Every so often, I stood to shake out my legs and flopped over "rag-doll" style to unkink and straighten my back. I also let my eyes draw me into the jungle at least several yards in every direction, so I could mark our location and find it again, if the need arose. After the painstakingly torturesome assignment of sitting very still, doing absolutely nothing, and clearing my mind of all thoughts for hours on end, Ashram called us back to his library. From what I could tell, everyone experienced the same exact training as I had: sit very still and clear your mind.

As soon as lunch was over, we returned to the training room and—creatures of habit that we were—reclaimed the seats we'd chosen that morning. Keelam volunteered to demonstrate how he'd progressed since his training began that morning and bounded onstage next to Asouke.

"Keelam, try to forget that we are in this room, with others watching," the Asouke King instructed. "Better yet, focus on what we practiced during our meditation earlier. Imagine that you are completely free, that nothing is holding you back, that nothing can possibly hold you down." Keelam nodded and smiled nervously. He seemed excited, but not really sure what to do.

191

After a few moments, the Asouke King spoke, "You cannot fail. It is impossible. The force of Nor is too strong. Just trust it and let it do what it is meant to do."

A chill skittered through me at his words. "The force of Nor" must have been closer than I thought.

While my mind wandered, Keelam closed his eyes, inhaled a few slow breaths. When he opened his eyes, the training room walls transformed into the color of a sky dotted with clouds.

Keelam's feet still hugged the floor, but when he slowly drew in another deep breath and closed his eyes to concentrate, his feet slowly lifted off. He smiled and opened his eyes, still hovering a foot off the floor. He gave a triumphant laugh and glanced at Isabel first, then Ian, and last me. We stood and cheered, but it apparently had no effect on his concentration, or his ability to climb to higher and higher altitudes.

When Keelam began to let his limbs move more freely, he reminded me of a frog paddling through water. The Asouke King hovered in the front of the room, watching Keelam circle above us, not just in the front, but all the way to the back where Ian had claimed a seat. Then the Asouke King joined Keelam in flight. They darted and swayed, dodged and dipped in a delicate dance. Keelam appeared to be in a pure state of joy, which radiated out to everyone in the room, energizing and inspiring us to be successful at demonstrating our new gifts.

The Asouke King flew to center stage and hovered, facing the audience. "May I please have a volunteer approach?"

"I'll do it," Isabel said. She jumped up eagerly and ran down to the stage.

"Thank you, my dear," said the Asouke King, flapping his long, black wings to hold his position.

"What do I do?" Isabel asked meekly.

"Nothing," the Asouke King said calmly. "Just stand where you are and don't move." He flew closer to her and landed on her shoulder. She squirmed nervously. "Please try to stay still," he said.

"I'm trying," she reassured him, struggling to be as respectful as she knew how. "But what are you doing?"

"Oh not much," he answered, snickering. The Asouke King suddenly shape-shifted back into his human form, standing right behind Isabel. "I'm just going to suck your blood."

Isabel screamed and Keelam instantly appeared by her side.

"I'm kidding, just kidding," Asouke morphed back into his bat form, let out a high-pitched cackle, and folded his wings over his little bat gut. No one else laughed.

"You're crazy, man." Keelam's voice boomed, echoing off the walls.

"I'm not the one talking to a bat," the Asouke King replied.

"He does have a point," Isabel said, and hunched over laughing. She was almost in hysterics, which was probably just her letting her adrenaline levels drop.

"Are you okay?" Keelam asked, stroking Isabel's back.

Isabel did her best to squelch the rest of her laughter, but a few uncontrolled giggles escaped. "Yes, I . . . I think I am now," she reassured him.

"Ready?"

She nodded. Keelam stood behind her and reached under her arms. He began concentrating so hard he gritted his teeth. After a few moments of intense focus, they lifted off the ground, but only by a few inches. Without warning, they fell to the ground, Keelam landing on top of Isabel.

"Ow," she cried.

Keelam sprang to his feet. His face flushed bright pink, and I realized I'd never seen him embarrassed. He reached for Isabel's hand to help her to her feet.

"Try it again," the Asouke King ordered, "but don't try to so hard. Concentrate, see yourself as a flying bat."

"Don't try so hard?" Keelam shrugged and walked over to stand behind Isabel.

"No." The Asouke King tsked and shook his head. "Just place your hand on her shoulder."

193

"But how can I—"

"Just do it," he ordered.

Keelam did as instructed and within seconds, he and Isabel lifted into the air. They were several feet off the ground when Isabel looked down and screeched. They instantly lowered by a foot, but Keelam kept his hand on Isabel, not risking her safety for even a second. They lifted back up and toured the training room from corner to corner, and then returned to the stage, where Keelam eased Isabel down until her feet gently touched the floor.

"Very nice," the Asouke King said. He instantly morphed back into his tall human form and started clapping. We all followed his lead.

"All right," Ashram said. "Who's next?"

Isabel went next, demonstrating the abilities she'd learned from Tetras by controlling Keelam's mind. It was easy for her to do, since he was already crazy about her, and far more relaxed and trusting than I'd ever be—or so I worried. Ian demonstrated his ability to read my mind, and I knew he'd done it successfully when he blushed. I had to stop thinking about his lips softly caressing mine, his hands on my breast . . . concentrate, Atlas, I commanded, and Ian laughed. I went last, managing to place a two-foot bubble of protection around myself that Varuta could not get through to reach me in her spider form. Somehow, seeing her scurry toward me allowed me to use my instincts to activate the bubble and keep her away.

After our intense day of training, we devoured our dinners and then slept hard, repeating our schedule of meditation the next morning, followed by practice in front of the group in the afternoon. We continued the same routine for a full week, with no contact whatsoever with the outside world. Every time I found a moment to catch my bearings, I thought of little Daniyah. Before I left the hospital, my parents informed me that her name means someone you hold close to your heart. And I did—in fact, it burned a hole in my heart to be so far away. She'd never know that I spent the second day of her new life stretched over a week in a different dimension, near a portal to Nor.

And I did it all for her, to make sure she'd never have to face evil jinns and tricksters like Mazin. Whatever it took, I was determined to keep those I loved safe. I carried that determination back with me when

194

the day finally came to leave this mysterious dimension, returning through the high-tech elevator and back to the Cave of Shadow Forest to re-emerge into the campgrounds at Zenith Hill.

Chapter 26

Back at our apartment at Zenith Hill, Isabel lay sprawled out on the loveseat scratching Jazz's furry head. She was wearing shorts, and giggled each time Jazz's tail wagged back and forth over her legs. I could hear Jazz purring all the way from the couch, where I lay fully stretched out, my head supported by a decorative pillow, staring up at the ceiling.

Suddenly, the front door flew open and I flung myself up into a sitting position. The door banged against the wall and rebounded back to close on itself. Jazz jumped off Isabel's lap, scratching her bare legs on the way up. The door flew open again, and we saw Ryan grasping the handle so the door couldn't rebound. He burst through, with Ian right behind him. Isabel was already in the kitchen, fishing around for Band-Aids.

"Ryan, I told you to wait," Ian admonished, panting.

Ryan had already plopped down on the loveseat—where Isabel had been lying only seconds before—arms stretched out on both sides along the back, looking like he owned the place.

Isabel walked from the kitchen back into the living room, waving a Band-Aid. "Found it!"

Only Isabel could be cheery when she'd just been rudely interrupted and scratched to the point of bleeding. I was not so cheerful. In fact, Ryan's intrusion annoyed the snot out of me, and the only thing that appeased my frustration was the fact that Ian had trailed him. Ryan had not been himself lately. He seemed arrogant, which was nothing like the Ryan I'd known the previous summer. Ian had warned me several times that, with all the time we spent with Isabel and Keelam, Ryan felt left out. He must have been trying to somehow compensate by acting like he was worthy of being worshipped.

"So what do you want?" I asked, crossing my arms firmly in front of my chest.

"Come on, Kenza. Why can't you be more like Isabel?" Ryan crossed his leg, resting his foot on his knee. He proceeded to bounce it vigorously.

"Oh, that'll make me more likable if I pretend to be someone I'm not." I rolled my eyes, pushed myself off the couch, and headed toward my bedroom.

Ryan jumped up and grabbed my arm. "Kenza, wait. I'm sorry."

I jerked free and shot him a dirty look.

"Kenza," Ryan said it so oddly he got my attention. "Stay, please." He tilted his head and looked at me with those ridiculous puppy dog eyes of his.

"All right," I said, huffing. I couldn't resist seeing him look vulnerable. It was not familiar, but it fit him nicely.

"Cool." His smile stretched out and he turned and wandered over to the fridge. With his butt sticking out and his head as far as it could fit, he said, "Where's the grub?"

"Ryan," Isabel called out in a sing-song voice, "the fridge is full, silly."

"Yeah." He pulled his head back out and closed the refrigerator door. "But that's not food. It's all healthy junk. Who eats bean sprouts and hummus?" He shook his body convulsively, making us all laugh. And then he stood there, looking like he wanted to say something, but wasn't sure where to start.

"So what is it, Ryan?" As soon as the words came out of my mouth, I knew I'd regret them. Ian glared at me, warning me to tread lightly.

"You noticed?" Ryan looked like I'd just invited him to a party. He was more sensitive than I thought—than Ian thought.

He rushed over and plopped onto the couch, arms stretched out wide. "I want to be a part of it."

I knew exactly what he was talking about, but I was shocked that he was being so direct about it.

197

"You are Ryan. I told you," Ian said, clearly trying to shut this down.

"You know what I mean, Kenza." He looked at me, not Ian.

Isabel jumped in. "Ryan, we love you. You know that. We do everything together."

"Not true!" he bellowed.

I looked over at Jazz who had come prowling back from her retreat in my bedroom and jumped up on the table. "Isabel, what's Jazz after?" I asked, giving Isabel a hint to shift Ryan's thoughts to something safer for us to discuss. None of us wanted to draw anyone else into our new reality. We loved Ryan, and Naomi, but wasn't it enough that the four of us were living under the threat of danger?

Jazz darted to the top of the counter next to the windowsill, and then onto the windowsill. She began meowing and swatting the lovely plant, the one souvenir that Isabel snuck back with her from the underground. Jazz wasn't declawed, so I knew Tetras wouldn't put up with it for very long.

"Isabel, do something," I said, trying to modulate my voice to indicate urgency without drawing Ryan's attention.

"I haven't practiced enough," Isabel responded, looking undone.

"What are you guys talking about?" The lines on Ryan's forehead wrinkled as he looked from person to person, narrowing his eyes. "Now you've got some kind of secret code?"

I was halfway across the room when Tetras' lovely white flower shifted to bright red. She spread her petals out wide and shook hard. Jazz leapt back but didn't bolt.

Ryan leaned forward, his eyes wide, shaking his head. "Did you see that?"

"See what?" Ian asked. Isabel and I acted like we didn't know what he was talking about either.

Ryan jumped up. "Come on, guys."

I ran across the room, trying to get Jazz out of there, but she meowed and clawed me as she wriggled away, leaving streaks of blood running down my arms.

Tetras responded by shaking her flower and all of her leaves hard. Then, she jumped right out of her clay pot and ran—her roots moving her like legs—to the refrigerator, where she leapt from the counter to the side of the refrigerator and climbed her way up, looking like a miniature Tarzan swinging from magnet to magnet.

Ryan stood halfway between the couch and the fridge, his head craned forward, both hands clasped over his mouth. He turned to face Ian, "Dude, you're right. Maybe I don't want to be a part of this." Just as Ryan bolted for the door, Ian beat him to it and spread his arms out across it, blocking his ability to leave.

"Let me out," Ryan ordered.

"I can't do that . . . yet," Ian said, "Sorry, buddy." He even shook his head with conviction. Then he called, "Isabel," his voice rising with the last syllable.

"Isabel," I echoed, "we need you to focus. There's no way out of this, unless you convince Ryan that he didn't see what he just saw."

"I can't. I can't," she repeated. "I haven't practiced enough in the real world, and his memory will be too strong if we drag him all the way to the other dimension where I know I can do it."

I grabbed both of her hands, held her gaze. "Please listen to me. You have to try. This is why Jinny and Jamila gave you this particular gift." I laughed, shrugged. "Besides, it's just Ryan. How hard can it be?"

Isabel let out a short laugh. "You're right. How hard can it be?"

She walked over to Ian and Ryan, who were still bickering by the door.

"Fine," Ryan said. "If you're not going to let me out, then at least tell me what the hell just happened." He pointed toward the windowsill.

Isabel reached out for Ian's arm. "Let me," she said.

He nodded, but held his position in front of the door.

199

"Hey Ryan, how's it going?" Isabel said, cheerfully. A wide smile stretched across her lips.

Ryan blinked a few times and drew his head back, looking dazed. "Isabel, where have you been?"

"I've been here the whole time, silly. Don't you remember?"

"Remember," he repeated softly, appeared to be thinking. "Wait, the plant. I saw it leap out of its pot and—"

"And what, Ryan?" Isabel laughed. "Are you talking about that plant over there?" She pointed at the empty pot on the windowsill. "The one that is just sitting there, soaking up the rays?"

I locked eyes with Ian, who looked as concerned as I felt.

Ryan looked toward the windowsill and squinted, then cocked his head and walked toward the window. As he was walking, Isabel hurried to me and grabbed my arm. "As soon as he sees that non-existent plant in the pot, you have to get him out of here. I can't hold this much longer."

I didn't say anything. I was still stunned at what I'd just witnessed.

"Kenza, I'm serious. Do you hear me?"

I nodded.

"Wait, where did it go?" Ryan asked.

Isabel shot me one final warning and then rushed over to stand next to Ryan.

"Where did what go?" she asked.

"What?" He looked at her. "Nothing. I was talking about . . . nothing." He reached out and rubbed his fingers together over empty air, but the look on his face and precision of his movements assured me that he saw something the rest of us did not: an unanimated Dendrobium Tetragonan Orchid planted securely in the empty pot in the windowsill.

"Hey Ryan," I said, drudging up all the energy I could find. "I'm leaving for Jizzammee Dibs to start my shift. Want to walk me over there? I could use some help getting set up."

"Naw," he said flatly. "Why can't Isabel or Ian go with you?"

"Nope," Isabel said firmly. "We can't. We're both heading to work, too."

Ian shot her a confused look.

"Weren't we Ian," she said.

"What? Oh yeah, yeah. We both have to leave for work," he said.

"Besides," I added, "no one helps me with set up like you do. No one except Dexter that is."

"Who?" he asked.

"You've met him once before. But come on," I said. "I'll tell you about it on our way over."

Chapter 27

I'd just completed a ten-hour shift on my feet at Jizzammee Dibs and headed straight for the Africa fitness facility. I was in no condition to work out, but I wasn't going there to exercise. As I'd hoped, Keelam walked through the double doors and out onto the sidewalk. He didn't seem to notice me and kept his head down and his pace quick.

I ran to catch up with him, until he turned abruptly and let out a gasp, and only relaxed when he saw it was me. It's not that I was stalking him, but I had done my homework to find out the next time he'd be alone, so I could approach him in a way that wouldn't create any suspicion.

"Where were you going in such a hurry?"

"Dinner. I'm starving." He was still moving—someone who always had to be on the go.

I laughed. "I'm kind of hungry, too. Mind if I join you?"

"Sure, walk with me. But I'm getting a 'To Go' meal. I have some things I need to do."

I nodded. We chitchatted the whole way, and just as he opened the door to let me pass through the UN cafe entrance, my tone turned serious. "Keelam, we need to talk. I don't mind grabbing a 'To Go' dinner, but please don't just run off. Let me walk with you wherever you're going and I'll explain." I was growing desperate and didn't know where else to turn. I would have mentioned something about it to Isabel, but she would have thought I was being paranoid. I needed someone to believe me—and Keelam seemed like my best option.

He nodded, but didn't say anything other than, "Meet me back here by the door and we'll walk together."

I grabbed a turkey sandwich, a bag of chips, and water, and then headed for the door. It was getting late so there wasn't much of a line.

Within minutes, we were both back outside, in front of the UN, clutching brown paper bags.

Before I could say anything, Keelam beat me to it. "It's Ian, isn't it?"

I wondered how he knew, but simply said, "Yes."

Keelam started zigzagging his steps, expending much more energy than the straight line I was walking. At last he stopped several feet in front of me and turned to face me. "I knew it. I want you to tell me everything."

"I—"

"Wait, forget it." He took two long strides to reach me and held out his dinner sack. "Take this."

I grabbed his sack, not sure what he wanted. He maneuvered his way behind me and then slid both arms under my armpits. My feet lifted into the air. I squeezed my eyes shut, pretending like my feet were planted firmly on the ground and not hovering above. I looked down and immediately felt queasy. Keelam was now flying us at least twenty feet in the air. Several campers were walking along a trail below and one of them looked up. Keelam rushed us behind a tree. I relaxed a little when, peering through the branches behind the tree, I saw the camper scratching his head, as if questioning his sanity. I was glad his friends hadn't seen us up here, too, or it would have been more difficult for the witness to dismiss what he saw as his imagination playing tricks on him.

"Do you know how bad you're shaking?" Keelam whispered. "Is it from seeing them or from being up here?"

I didn't answer at first, but then my logical mind kicked in. "Both. So where are you taking me?"

"Uh-huh, that's what I'm talking about. I knew you'd like it up here."

"It's not bad," I said, through gritted teeth.

"Relax, it's amazing if you let yourself enjoy it."

That was easy for him to say; now that he could fly like a bat, he wasn't likely to fall from the top of a tree and break every bone in his body, maybe even die. Still, I somehow felt secure in his arms. I would have expected the pressure of his grip that kept me afloat to be immense by now, but it wasn't—not even a little. It amazed me that Keelam's powers, like Isabel's ability to convince Ryan he saw something he didn't, could be extended to others besides him. It was like he'd sprinkled fairy dust on me, but I wasn't naive enough to believe I could fly without his touch, at least not yet. I held tight to his hands, now wrapped around my stomach, while holding tight to our lunch bags.

"Keelam," I said softly. "Please tell me you're going to take me back to earth soon."

Keelam laughed loudly, and the whole group accompanying the recent witness looked up toward the tree we hovered behind, puzzled. He abruptly stopped making so much noise and whispered, "I could do this forever. Tell me you don't love it."

"I don't," I whispered back. "I'm feeling a little sick, actually."

"All right, all right," he said. "It's not far away."

He flew us further back away from the witnesses below, and we soon approached a cliff that jetted out over the ocean. "Keelam, I can't take this anymore." My stomach was doing flip flops. "Put me down!"

"Oh really? Are you sure about that?" He shifted his grip.

"Not here, not now, not from up here," I said, stifling a scream.

"But you said—" In true Keelam fashion, he was not going to let it rest without giving me a hard time first.

"Forget it all right," I said, anger replacing fear.

As we flew, the wind kissed my cheeks and the ground below us rushed by in blurred streams of color. Every so often I looked straight ahead to pacify the storm brewing in my stomach.

Once we reached the ocean, its salt water smell perked up my senses, relieving the butterflies in my stomach. We sped over the ocean and soon reached a small island far enough from shore that we wouldn't likely be seen. Keelam slowed and then hovered in place.

"This is it," he said, lowering us toward the top of the tallest island cliff. I squeezed my eyes shut, unable to bear the sight of ground barreling toward us. After a few long seconds, I found the courage to open my eyes, but regretted it immediately.

As soon as he released me, the light feeling I had been enjoying instantly turned to lead and my knees buckled as my body adjusted to gravity. It reminded me of the countless times I'd taken my skates off at Skate City, after circling the rink at least a hundred times. Keelam landed much more gracefully, and I could tell that either he'd practiced many times, or he was a natural bat.

"Feels heavy at first," he said, noticing my wobbly knees.

I walked a short distance, shaking my legs to reawaken them. There were only a few feet of room on either side of the long, narrow strip where we'd landed. When I leaned over the edge and saw the sharp jagged cliff below, my nausea returned, so I quickly straightened back up and forced fear out of my thoughts.

Keelam tromped up next to me. "Don't worry. Just like I said earlier, I've got you."

"You're not even touching me."

"I mean I've got your back if you f—"

"Fall? Keelam, don't even think that . . . besides, I'm fine . . . or I'll be fine." I tried to boost my confidence so he wouldn't worry about me and walked as close as I could to the edge. "This is actually pretty amazing. What a vantage point."

"I know," he agreed. "I come here when I need a break—when I need to think."

He stood next to me, our arms lightly touching as we gazed out over the setting sun. The fiery orange sphere of light inched its way toward the water, creating a rippling glow of light that grew in circumference as it approached us. As inappropriate as it might have seemed in that moment, I let out a sheepish laugh.

"What?" Keelam asked, looking puzzled.

"Oh nothing. It's just . . . it's really romantic here." I let out another awkward, sort of squeaky laugh.

"I know. Isn't it?" He turned to look into my eyes. "Just so we're clear, I didn't bring you here to edge my bro Ian out."

"Sheesh, I know," I said quickly. Guys could be so dim sometimes. If you even talked to them, they'd think you wanted to be with them. "You and I are just friends, Keelam. That's what makes it so funny. It's totally cool to be up here and not have it be romantic ."

We neither one said anything for a few moments. He draped his arm over my shoulder. "I haven't brought anyone else here yet."

"Not even Isabel?"

He shook his head. "Negatory."

"Why not? You should. It's one of the most beautiful places I've ever seen."

"I'm planning on it. The first time I came I thought it was so cool and I wanted to share it with her . . . but I just haven't got around to it yet. I want to and all. It's just . . . hell, I can't explain it."

"Sort of like I can't explain about Ian," I said.

"Try me."

I looked at Keelam and smiled. I felt so safe with him, like nothing I could say would throw him off. I could have divulged anything and somehow I knew he would never judge me. Kind of like how I used to feel about Ian.

"It's just . . . it's like he's not himself. I mean of course he's himself, he's Ian. But something doesn't feel right." Where were my words? I was operating purely on gut instinct and it didn't translate well to logic and reason. I wondered if our experience in the underground changed the way Ian felt about me, about constantly having to wear a target on his back for me?

"I've seen it too." Keelam said, nodding in agreement.

I suddenly didn't feel so alone. "You have?"

He looked at me, nodded again but didn't say anything.

"Sometimes he acts just like the Ian I know and love, and one who's been my soul mate for 500 years." I looked up at Keelam, cringing. He acted like I never said the big "L word," much less soul mate, so I kept rambling. "And sometimes he ranges from distant to possessive, and feels like he's someone else."

"What do you mean by someone else?" Finally, Keelam reacted— by staring hard at me, looking alarmed.

206

"Sometimes he's aggressive and really focused, to the point of feeling like he wants to control everything. His eyes start to look cold and sometimes blank, like no one's home. It freaks me out."

"Kenza, he's going through a lot. He's working on mastering his new powers. Maybe that's thrown him off."

"Keelam, we all have new powers."

"Yeah, but not like him. Think about it. He doesn't just have to deal with his own new powers; he's listening in on our minds, probably being barraged by our thoughts, fears, you know, everything."

"But he doesn't have to tune us in," I said, stating what I thought was obvious.

"It's not that easy," Keelam replied. He stood and I watched his feet lift off the ground. "Ian probably didn't tell you this, but after a few somewhat disastrous efforts, he did try to stop tuning in, but it kept happening anyway. Now he hears people constantly. It's like he's cursed."

"Believe me," I said. "I know what it's like to be cursed."

"He has to concentrate really hard, just to tune people out, and it's been giving him a headache when he does. Except for you. He has an even harder time tuning you out, even if he tries. And believe me, he wants to."

"All this time I thought he was trying to eavesdrop on me," I mumbled, more to myself than to Keelam.

"He knows that," Keelam said.

"Then why didn't he just tell me what was really going on? How come you know this, and I don't?"

"He didn't think you'd understand."

I shook my head. "He should have told me." I stood, kicked the huge boulder I'd been sitting on, kicking it over and over. Each time I did, I could feel myself losing control of my emotions. For a moment, I lost track of where I was and started pacing frantically. Suddenly, I felt my foothold slip and I was tumbling over the cliff, toward the water far below.

A flash of something whizzed by me and suddenly I was in Keelam's arms. Our bodies sank a few feet on impact and I even heard his feet splash in the water below, but he recovered quickly and lifted us back up to the highest point of the island. Once he set me back down, I crossed my legs and placed my hands in a prayerful pose, secretly thankful that I hadn't fallen to my death. I waved my hand over the grass on either side of me, happy to feel each blade.

"Thanks to you, my shoes are all wet," Keelam said. He took them off and shook them rapidly, water flying everywhere.

"Yeah, well you didn't have to save me."

"You little twerp. If I'd let you fall into the water, you'd be the one with wet shoes."

"You wouldn't have done that." I let a smile spread across my lips.

"Well I won't save you twice. I'll tell you that."

"I bet you would." I jumped to my feet and edged dangerously close to the side.

Keelam's face tensed. "I'll push you myself this time."

He lunged toward me and we both flew off the cliff and into the air, saved by his ability to fly. I started laughing and so did he, and then neither one of us could stop, even though we were not quite in flight and not falling, sort of dangling in mid-air over the cliff. When Keelam began laughing so hard his whole body was shaking, my fear returned.

"Watch it, Keelam. Please. Maybe you should just put me down."

"What, here?" he asked playfully.

I released a frustrated sigh and he finally rose above the cliff and then eased me back onto the ground.

I dropped to my knees, bowed down, and started kissing the ground, then rolled back up on the back of my heels and said, "Sorry if I freaked out. It was fun—until I flashed back to last summer, when Mazin almost pushed me over the edge of our tree house. I just relived that sensation, feeling like I wasn't going to survive."

"Didn't you actually fall a few feet last summer?" Keelam asked, leaning against the boulder next to me.

"Yeah." I released an airy laugh. "More like twenty feet."

"That would have totally freaked me out, before I was able to fly I mean. Now it wouldn't affect me."

"You used to be afraid of heights?"

"Everyone's afraid of heights to some extent," he said, shrugging. Then he knelt down until we were eye-to-eye and his eyes narrowed. "So what are you going to do about Ian?"

"I don't know."

"He's going to know that you know how much he's struggling," Keelam said. "He'll know that I told you. He'll even know that we came here together—that we watched the sunset and that you almost fell into the ocean, um, twice."

"So?" I said, affecting a tone meant to sound rude or at least over-confident, but it was just an act. I'd already thought about how Ian might react once he had a chance to read my thoughts.

"So he'll be mad that I said something," Keelam said.

"Then, why did you tell me?"

"Because I thought you should know, Kenza. Ian and I aren't really close, you know, not like you and I are. We're not friends, at least not natural ones, but we're like brothers. I watch out for him and vice-versa. He's a good guy, Kenza."

My smile stretched out more widely than I wanted it to, giving away my happiness. But it didn't matter, anyway. It was Keelam, so there was no need to hide—no need to pretend.

"Thanks Keelam," I finally managed to say. I leaned back against the boulder and when I did, a light shone up from the face of the rock etching a warning into the stone:

Intruders Beware: Private Getaway or Perfect Trap.

Either way, be ready to cave.

"What does that even mean?" I groaned.

Keelam shrugged. "It's weird," he said. "I've never seen that before and I come here a lot."

"And I was just thinking that we should bring everyone here for a party. I mean, if you were okay with it."

"Actually, I was thinking the same thing," he said. "I've been monitoring the island and there's a land bridge visible during low tide. We'd just have to time our trip so we cross it before it is covered in water."

"Couldn't you just fly everyone over?" I asked.

"I mean I could," he said with hesitation in his voice. "But it would really wear me out. I'd have to go back and forth to retrieve everyone, since I can only carry two people at a time."

"It doesn't matter anyway. It's really not an option anymore," I whined.

"Why not, Kenza?"

I couldn't find any words. All I could do was point toward Zenith Hill. "Because that's the protected zone, the one Ayam created. This, where we are right now, leaves us completely exposed to Mazin."

"We have to live, Kenza."

I gave Keelam a playful shove. "You worry too much," I said.

He laughed. "Oh, yeah. That's right. I'm the worrier in this group. Not you."

I rolled my eyes at him, knowing full well what he was insinuating: I was the queen of worrying.

Suddenly, a fierce wind swept through, howling a warning so haunting that I could feel it at the core of my being. Keelam jumped to his feet and turned to reach for me, but a gust of wind sent him flying back over the cliff. He righted himself quickly, hovering in front of me over the cliff's edge.

"Do you think—"

"It's Mazin?" I finished his sentence. "Yeah, I do."

The wind howled again and ripped toward us, blowing Keelam a few feet back. I knelt down and gripped the boulder I'd been sitting on, my head down until the gust passed. When it finally died down, I glanced up at Keelam, ready to request that he fly me back to camp. His eyes flashed with a red curtain over them, and I hid behind the boulder.

"What do you want?" I said, trying to buy time.

"I want you." The words came from Keelam's voice, but I knew they originated from Mazin. He took a few steps toward me. I stepped back from the boulder. "I want you to suffer like you made me suffer."

I felt like a caged animal, with nowhere to go but over the jagged cliff's edge and down a huge drop into the waves crashing against the rocks below. My only hope was to use my new power from the underground: my power to protect. With the Amulet of Omnia around my neck, I knew its power would be magnified. I wrapped my fingers around it, which made my grip around the boulder less secure. With one hard push, Keelam sent me falling backwards and I grabbed on to a tree root, my feet dangling over the cliff's edge much like they did last year.

I reached up and yanked on Keelam's arm, while simultaneously wishing for his safety. He lurched forward and summer salted over me, heading straight for the jagged rocks below where the waves crashed the highest. I squeezed my eyes shut, but only for a split second. Curiosity forced me to watch him career into the rocks. I didn't hear the crashing sound of the stones pulverizing his bones and I didn't see Keelam's blood spray in every directions, not like I expected. Instead I watched Keelam bounce, as if surrounded by an invisible shield, and splash into the water.

I hung there, my whole body dangling over the cliff, my hands aching from the sting of gripping the roots, and watched for Keelam to resurface. Several long seconds passed and the pattern of waves below remained uninterrupted. Certain I'd be unable to clear the jagged rocks below, I wished for protection around myself and then released my grip. Just like Keelam, I bounced off the rocks as if inside an invisible shield and landed with a splash in the water.

After quickly checking to make sure I had no injuries, I inhaled loudly and submerged under the crashing waves. I kept my eyes open, but could barely see through the waves and the silt. I resurfaced and, while replenishing the air in my lungs, I activated the magnifying projection on my Datadrix—a feature I never thought I'd have to use. I pulled in another full breath and dove back into the water. Through the magnifier, my line of sight expanded tremendously and in moments I spotted Keelam resting on the bottom a few feet away.

I knew I didn't have the air left to rescue him without first coming up for a breath. As soon as I did, I dove straight for him and pulled him to the surface. He began sputtering and coughing the moment his head bobbed above the waves. Despite his struggle, I wrapped my arm around his neck and swam toward the rocky shore.

Once we were both on solid ground and his coughing finally subsided, I stole a long look at his eyes. They were back to normal.

"You okay?" I said.

He shook his head, seeming to try to make sense of what just happened. "How did I get here? The last thing I remember, I was standing on the top of the cliff. The next thing I knew, I was surfacing above the waves next to you. Did Mazin knock us off the cliff?"

I shook my head. "You did."

He squinted his eyes. "What? No. That can't be."

"Let me clarify," I said. "It wasn't you exactly. Mazin overtook you again."

"So he . . . what . . . flung me over the edge in an attempt to kill me?"

I cleared my throat. I felt my cheeks burning. "He tried to push me over, so I retaliated and sent him—you—into the rocks below."

"That can't be," Keelam said, feeling his head. "I'm not bleeding. Nothing hurts."

"I placed a protective barrier around you and literally saw you bounce off the jagged rocks into the water. It must have been too much for Mazin to handle."

"How long was I under?" Keelam asked.

"Too long," I said. "But I didn't even have to perform CPR on you when you surfaced. That protective barrier must have been powerful enough to—"

"Stop me from drowning, too," Keelam said. He reached out and pulled me into a bear hug.

"We need to get out of here," I said, stepping back. "Do you think you have the wherewithal to fly us both back?"

Keelam nodded and we were soon flying toward camp, the cold wind whipping at our dripping bodies.

Chapter 28

For the next week, Ryan didn't say anything more about Tetras, but he behaved suspiciously. He even mumbled some mumbo jumbo about seeing Keelam and me flying above the tree line, which I made sure to dismiss as complete hogwash. I'd spotted him following me a few times, and so did Isabel, Ian, and Keelam. He was asking us all kinds of questions: Why did we remain so secretive? And how did Ian suddenly know everything he was thinking before he said it? We each reassured Ryan that he was being completely ridiculous, but he remained skeptical. Naomi even tried to convince him that he was off his rocker, and that only made a small dent in his conviction.

Despite Ryan's growing suspicion, Ashram—Mr. Otto that is—ordered us to practice our new skills in the real world, as often as possible, so practice we did. He also invited us to return as often as we could to the other dimension beneath the Cave of Shadow Forest. Even though time stopped for us down there, we needed time in the real world to wrap our minds around our new gifts and how they'd save us when the time came, how using mine already saved Keelam and me.

So there we stood, once again, in front of the purple, high-tech elevator door: Ian, Isabel, Keelam, and me. I inserted the clear, credit card-shaped crystal key into the slot and the door swallowed it and then opened the second slot, into which I inserted little West's picture.

"What the hell?" I heard Ryan's voice behind me and spun around to see Naomi standing next to him, her big mouth gaping.

"What the hell is right, man," Ian said. "What are you two doing here?"

"Oh come on," Ryan sputtered, starting to pace back and forth, much like Mrs. Bartolli often did, only more frenzied and desperate.

"Ryan," Naomi said, her voice calm and firm, "let's hear what they have to say."

"No way." Ryan jerked away. "I'm getting the hell out of here right now, and you're coming with me." He pushed past her, and spun quickly to grab her arm forcefully.

"Ryan," she said.

He shook his head and pulled harder.

"Ryan," she said louder.

He still ignored her.

"Ryan!" Naomi finally yelled and he seemed to snap out of it.

"What? I'm sorry. What?" he said.

"Listen," she said softly.

He nodded. "Yeah, okay. I'll listen."

I stepped forward. "Look, Ryan, I get why you're way more freaked out than Naomi. You've seen a lot of things that don't click, that don't fit with your understanding of reality—and, to protect you and Naomi, we tried to convince you that you were crazy . . . but you're not crazy, Ryan. You're not crazy, but what's been happening . . . even us being here is crazy."

"Why didn't you just tell me what you were doing?" he asked, glancing around at each of us. "Didn't you trust me?"

"It's not that we didn't trust you, Ryan." I said.

"Then what, Kenza? What is it?"

"It's bad enough that Ian, Keelam, and Isabel were drawn into my really crazy world. I . . . we were trying to protect you. Once you get involved, you're involved, and there's no getting out of it. It's dangerous, or could be very soon."

Naomi puffed out her chest and took a step forward. "What are you? The leader of this little freak show, or something?"

I didn't respond.

"Actually, she is," Ian said, taking a step forward.

Naomi shot him a doubtful glance and looked to Keelam and Isabel for a different answer.

"She really is at the center of it all," Keelam said.

"And now we are," Isabel said, sighing.

Naomi still scoffed. "So, now we're here and we've caught you stealing away in the spooky cave, so what is it that we're not getting out of?"

Ian, Isabel, Keelam, and I exchanged nervous glances.

Naomi turned and grabbed Ryan's hand. "Come on, Ryan. Let's go back."

Ian stepped in front of her, blocking the way back. "You heard Kenza. You both let curiosity get the better of you and you followed us here, so, like it or not, you are now part of this. There is no turning back."

Naomi shoved Ian and tried to get past him, but the rest of us swarmed around her and shoved her into the purple elevator. Ryan followed us, not saying a word. As soon as we were all inside, the doors closed and the cabin began its descent. After several long seconds, it jolted to a stop and then sped sideways, just like the other times we rode it. When it finally changed course and shot upwards, Naomi busied herself by gnawing on her fingernails, while Ryan tightly gripped the metal rail.

When we reached the top and the elevator doors opened, Naomi and Ryan had very similar reactions to what we had when we first saw the amazing waterfall surrounded by a vast jungle. Their mouths gaped and their eyes widened as they stepped out onto the rocky platform with the 360-degree-view of paradise. The sound of birds chirping and water falling momentarily erased all my worries. For a few moments, I even forgot that I was in another dimension, one where human/animal hybrids taught us how to acquire superpowers, so we could fight evil spirits and save the human race, or at least save ourselves.

Naomi's words snapped me out of my reverie. "So now what?"

"I don't know," I said. "Last time the otter showed us the way."

"The otter?" Ryan asked. "A real otter?"

"Yeah, it . . . oh, never mind," I said. I walked to the spot that had opened to a tunnel and knelt down to wipe the dirt out of the way.

"Found it," I called. "Now, can someone help me figure out how to open this thing?"

"Let me try," Ryan offered. He knelt down next to the cover and moved his hand over it, examining the edges. Then he stood and walked around it a few times, before throwing his hands up. "This thing isn't opening for anything."

Just then, a mechanical noise came from under the lid. Everyone, who now stood in a circle around the covered opening, took a step back. The lid lifted and moved to the side. Mr. Otto climbed up through the opening. "There you are," he said. "We've been waiting for you." He pushed his glasses up and glanced at Naomi and Ryan. "All of you." He walked over to the edge of the waterfall and looked out over the jungle, pulling in a long slow breath. "I can never get enough of this place." He turned and clasped his hands together. "Are we ready, then?"

"So who is this . . . person?" Ryan asked.

"Oh, I'm terribly sorry. I should have introduced myself." Mr. Otto walked over to Ryan and extended his hand, but Ryan didn't reciprocate. "I'm Otto—Ashram Otto."

"I thought you said an otter opened the lid, not a man named Mr. Otto," Naomi said.

"Well, that's a long story, now, isn't it?" Mr. Otto quipped. He reached his hand out to Naomi and they shook hands. "An odd practice, isn't it?"

"What?" Naomi asked.

"Shaking hands. It's not something we do here in this dimension."

"In this dimension?" Naomi repeated, looking worried.

"Oh dear. I've said too much." Mr. Otto shook his head, made a tsking noise. "Not to worry. It will all be explained soon enough. Follow me, follow me."

He walked to the opening and climbed down into the tunnel. We all followed, Naomi and Ryan trailing us.

217

Once we traversed the long climb down the tunnel and the even longer stretch to Ashram's office, he brought us some food. This food was different from what he brought last time—no yogurt or crackers or anything we recognized. The tray he brought to us today had fruits as sweet as honey, with colors more vibrant than I'd ever seen. He brought a creamy soup and bread that melted in our mouths.

Just like the last time we'd come, Mr. Otto did not serve meat. When I thought about why, it made sense. If the people in this dimension could transform into animals—if animals made up half of their existence, how could they be carnivores? It was impossible. We ate every last bite, every last crumb.

When we finished, we were led to a stadium-sized room with high ceilings that we hadn't yet seen. It looked more like a cave than the other rooms, with rock ceilings, walls, and floors. The only evidence of technology in this room was four knee-high, metal-shaped objects that, if connected, would form a 20-by-20 foot square in the middle of the room. The objects looked much like torches sticking up out of the ground.

"Welcome to Nor," Mr. Otto said, waving his arm as if to spotlight something amazing in the middle of the room.

While I didn't see anything worthy of his excitement, his words struck a chord. "Nor?" I asked. "Are you sure?"

"Oh yes, I'm one hundred percent sure," he said. "And even though not all the keys to activate it have been found, this is the location of the portal."

"Wait, keys you say?" Ian asked, stepping forward.

"Yes, that's right," Ashram said. "I believe Kenza has three of them on her now."

This cryptic conversation seemed to be wearing on our new guests' nerves. "What the hell are you talking about?" Ryan blurted.

"The Amulet of Omnia—" Mr. Otto said, pointing at my neck.

I nodded, clasping the chain and pulling the amulet out from under my shirt. "It's right here."

He nodded and went on, glancing at Naomi and Ryan, "That amulet is a powerful wishing stone, as are the two rectangular keys Kenza used to gain entry into this dimension: the crystal and the frame bearing an image of the infant known as West."

"Bring the amulet over here and I'll show you." Mr. Otto pointed toward one of the metal stands.

As I walked over to it, I unclasped the chain.

"Good, now insert it into the base of this stand."

I did as he suggested and its base emitted a humming noise. We all took a huge step back. After a few seconds, a triangle shaped image projected up from the base, like a holographic screen. At first, the image was just snow, but seconds later, images and short video clips flashed on the screen.

The images and video clips revealed the story of my father's history and the bedtime stories he used to tell me when I was a child, including how Mom and I refused to believe them. The images also replayed the rainy night when Jinny Zzaman first visited me in my room, over a year ago. They sped like Cliff Notes through my trip back in time to Morocco, how I'd met Jamila of Diab, the love of her life Amal, and his evil twin Mazin. They even captured the scene where Jamila of Diab wiped out the entire army, but just like my own sight that night, the visual scene went black, leaving only the sounds of clinking weapons, groans, and falling bodies.

The entire story from the events that occurred that night, all the way up until the present time, played out, including Mazin nearly sending me to my death—first over the bridge in the Cave of Shadow Forest and then over the cliff of the Owens's tree house, and last over the cliff of the island with Keelam. It also showed me swimming in the aquarium under Atlantic Ocean Lake with the shark pursuing me, and the new abilities Ian, Isabel, Keelam, and I now possessed.

When the images came to an end and the projected light sank back into the metallic base, no one spoke for a long time. After a while, I couldn't stand the silence any more so I walked over and removed the Amulet of Omnia from the base, clasping it once again around my neck. I then spun around to face my friends and tossed up my hands. "Well, that's my crazy life. Now you know more about me than my own

219

parents. Now that you know everything, I can understand if you want to turn and run."

No one said anything; they just stared. I looked awkwardly from one to another. When I got to Naomi, she hurried over to give me a big hug. "I knew there was something about you that kicked butt," she said. "I just couldn't put my finger on it. I'll support any girl who's willing to go toe-to-toe with an evil spirit, and it's a bonus that your friends get to acquire superpowers. Speaking of which, do I get one?"

"Of course you do," Mr. Otto, now morphed into his otter form as Ashram, chimed in.

"Ryan and Naomi get abilities, too?" I said.

"Why do you think Jinny Zzaman has been haunting Ryan in his sleep every night?" Ashram paused to let his words sink in. "She wanted Ryan to follow you here, and she knew Naomi would follow him and, honestly, you need all of them. You cannot defeat Mazin without them."

"Well, like you said Kenza, we're a part of this now," Ryan said.

He reached out and gave me a huge hug. Then Keelam ran over and hugged us both, followed by Naomi, Isabel, and Ian. The last to join us was Mr. Otto, who'd morphed momentarily back into his human form to join in. When we finally released one another, Mr. Otto morphed back into his otter form as Ashram, shook his head and said, "Humans."

We spent several days in the underground with our new partners in crime. Ian, Isabel, Keelam, and I practiced honing our abilities while Naomi and Ryan learned what theirs were. As soon as we had a chance to eat lunch, we followed Ashram to his lecture hall to watch Ryan and Naomi get assigned their new abilities.

Even Keelam, with his gift of flight, was jealous of Ryan's ability. His trainer was an elderly Asian man dressed in a red robe and sandals who meditated constantly while in his human form, and turned into a sloth in his animal form. Through the sloth, he learned to manipulate time, fast-forwarding, pausing, and rewinding it on demand. According to his trainer, this ability was what made the sloth look like he was always moving so slowly when, in fact, to him it felt like normal speed.

Naomi learned from a short, squat woman who wore red glasses that complemented her medium-length blond hair, which she'd pulled back in a loose ponytail. She wore a hot pink skirt, with a red cardigan sweater, over a light pink shirt. She looked a bit sloppy, or rushed. Her shirt was only partially tucked in and she'd buttoned her cardigan wrong, leaving it off-kilter, with the top and bottom buttons dangling.

"What's your name?" Naomi asked, when they first met in Ashram's supernatural study hall.

"You may call me Vivian," her trainer replied.

"So what's your ability?" Naomi said. "Dressing like a nerd?"

"Watch yourself," Vivian said, a flicker of anger flashing in her eyes. She didn't blink in when she formed into her animal form, like the others, but instead faded before my eyes until she blended into the background. I could no longer see her, but I could still hear her high-pitched, whiny voice when she spoke. "Follow me, Naomi," she ordered. "We're going to practice your new skill."

"Why can't we do it here?" Naomi said, not budging from her spot.

"This is not the right place for your proper training," Vivian explained. "We must study along the stream that circles the jungle. There you will see me in my animal form: a brightly colored fish."

"So you're a Cuttlefish?" Naomi said, her eyes brightening. "I watched a documentary about them on the Discovery Channel. They're able to camouflage themselves against the backdrop of their environment."

Vivian's voice now projected from somewhere near the door. "Now you are getting it," she said. "Now please follow my voice."

Once they'd both left the lecture hall, Ian, Keelam, Isabel, and I each spent time with our trainers. I learned to practice projecting more protection at greater and greater distances. Ian learned to decipher and tune into meaningful thoughts versus random nonsensical ones. Isabel learned to influence more than one person at a time, by getting to practice on all of us. And Keelam learned to comfortably fly more than one person, something he'd already clumsily attempted in the real world. When it was finally time to leave, we welcomed a return to normalcy—to a camp full of teenagers, a refrigerator full of food we were used to, and to mind-numbing TV.

∞

Back in the real world, I swiveled in my chair, letting my eyes follow the shark swimming overhead in the aquarium under Atlantic Ocean Lake at Zenith Hill. A sea turtle followed close behind. I empathized with that sea turtle, trailing danger yet thinking its shell would protect it from harm.

I still couldn't believe that Naomi and Ryan had joined our supernatural group. Ryan constantly wanted to practice his new skill: the ability to rewind, stop, and speed up time. In fact, by popular demand, he'd stopped time for us that day, so we could all hang out in the aquarium under the lake and not have to worry about being late for our various jobs. Naomi's gift surprised us all: the ability to become invisible. Ever since I first met Naomi last summer, I never would have guessed she was capable of such a thing. All she seemed good at was making her presence known.

The aquarium water shimmered beautifully, light dancing off the exotic colors of the Pollock fish swimming in their silvery schools—safety in numbers. It was a moment I never would have asked for or even dreamed of before coming to camp. More importantly, it was a rare moment when Ian and I were alone. The others had gone to another room in the aquarium and promised not to return for a long, long time.

"Yes," Ian said, even though I hadn't asked him a question. "I asked Keelam to distract the others so we could spend some time alone together."

I finally pulled my eyes away from the steady predictability of the aquarium ballet and swiveled in my red chair to face him. My knees were only a few inches from touching his chair. He was staring at the water, not paying me any attention so I stared hard at him for a while. A smile swept over me as I pictured him standing with me on top of the cliff at the island Keelam flew me to. I imagined Ian reaching out, cupping his hand over my ear and hair, leaning in for a kiss.

222

Still fixated on the water and the fish swimming past, Ian started smiling and glanced over at me, a look of recognition on his face. It only took a second for me to realize how idiotic it was of me to forget that he could read my mind and I kicked myself for letting my guard down. He wrinkled his nose at discovering my sudden awareness of his eavesdropping, his eyes opening wide. He looked just as surprised that I figured out what he had done as I was when I realized he'd been listening to my thoughts.

"Kenza, please don't be embarrassed." He reached his hand out and rested it on my knee.

"Don't touch me," I said. I squeezed my eyes shut and concentrated hard, trying to exercise my ability to protect my feelings. After a few tries, Ian's chair wheeled back a few feet without either of us touching it, my ability to protect myself forcing it back.

"Please, Kenza," he pleaded as he scooted his chair, returning it to its original spot near me.

I burst out laughing. He reached his hand out for my knee again.

"I haven't forgiven you yet," I said as I managed to control my ability more carefully, sending him wheeling back even further.

"Come on, Kenza. Will you please let me come back. I want to be near you. I want to be close enough to look into your beautiful eyes."

"What if I don't want to?" My voice softened.

"I think you'll want to," he said, his voice warm. "Let's dance. That way, you won't be able to send me racing around on that rolling chair anymore."

I felt myself sit a little taller in my chair. "You have my attention," I said.

"Wait right here." He held out his hand, signaling me to remain in my seat.

I curled my legs up and hugged them to my chest as I waited for Ian to return. In moments, I heard one of my favorite slow songs playing; Ian knew its lyrics reminded me of him. He trotted back in a slow run, as if not wanting to look too eager. He reached for my hand and slowly pulled me to my feet, wrapped his arms around me and pulled me close.

He kissed my forehead and looked into my eyes. "Kenza, it's my fault. I couldn't resist reading your thoughts. To feel what you're feeling . . . it's something so profound I can't describe it with words."

Unable to find anything to say that could come close to matching the beauty of his words, I simply gazed into his cinnamon-colored eyes and smiled.

He tucked his chin over my shoulder and we turned slowly, barely moving. I focused on the warmth of his stomach pressed against mine, the musky smell of his cologne, the gentle rising and falling of his breath. When he moaned softly, I squeezed my eyes shut, wanting to record this moment permanently—vividly—in my memory. Ian lifted his hand to my hair and drew away from his perch on my shoulder. He started kissing me along the side of my neck, very gently. I tilted my head back as shivers danced up my spine.

His lips found mine and he kissed me slowly, deeply, his hands crawling up and down my back. I laced my fingers in his hair, and felt grateful for the sparse furniture. If there had been a couch or a bed, I was sure we would have ended up in it—unable to stop ourselves. And as much as I loved Ian, I still wasn't sure we were ready for that level of physical intimacy.

After a long embrace, he pulled away, stood back, held his hands in mine, and looked straight at me, as if he couldn't tear his eyes away from me. For a moment, it made me smile, but I began to feel self-conscious and turned my head toward the water.

And then I saw it—a lifeless carcass. Shark jaws—mostly teeth and jawbone, but some flesh dripping with blood—hung in the water like a deathly ghost. I instinctively shrieked, and thrust my arms around Ian's neck.

"Ian, do you know what's happening?" I'd leaned back, but gripped his arm, digging my nails in.

He stared back at me. His silence pained me.

"I know you know something, Ian. What is it? You have to tell me."

"I don't know, Kenza." He looked down, started shaking his head, puzzled. "I don't know," he repeated anxiously, more to himself than to me. "But it's bad. They're coming."

"Who's coming?" I asked. My heart was thundering and I could barely breathe.

He shook his head. "I can't say. I keep hearing words looping over and over in a chorus of menacing voices: We're coming . . . we're coming . . . we're coming."

Chapter 29

As soon as we knew danger was imminent, we scurried back to the underground for a week of intensive training. By the time, we resurfaced, no time in the real world had passed, but we'd returned hungry.

As we did everywhere these days, Isabel, Ian, Keelam, Ryan, Naomi, and I walked in a cluster to the UN cafe. After a week of eating Mr. Otto's healthy food, we all longed for a juicy burger. On our return from the other dimension, no one said much of anything. We were exhausted and starving, but I didn't think I could eat another banana, even if it was the last bit of food on Earth.

Before we reached the UN cafe, a loud annoying alarm beeped and bright lights flashed with intensity. A steady male voice began to loop the following phrases: "There is an emergency in the United Nations building. Please proceed to the nearest exit. If you are outside the building, please exit the area and do not approach."

"Is this for real?" Isabel asked.

"It can't be. What could happen here?" Keelam said.

"Yeah, right?" Isabel nodded. She must have forgotten that, just last summer, Keelam had been pushed into the lake and nearly drowned. Things could happen anywhere—bad things, especially around me.

"It's probably just another one of their stupid tests," Ryan said.

I believed him for a split second—until I heard a series of popping sounds. Moments later, the loudspeaker changed its message. "There is an active shooter in the United Nations building. If you are in the building, hide, take cover, barricade your door, or exit the building if you can. If you are outside the building, please steer clear and do not approach. The police are on the way."

Suddenly everything erupted, people outside either ducked for cover or ran away as fast as they could, and those inside burst through

226

the cafeteria doors. The placid scene, with birds chirping and the gentle breeze blowing through the trees that existed only moments ago, now offered random screaming and people running for their lives. I'd never seen panic in so many people's eyes at one time. The beautiful sunlit sky and fresh air seemed out of place in relation to the fear that suddenly burned through me.

We, too, ran for our lives. Keelam led the way with his lengthy stride, and the rest of us followed in a sprint. I heard a few more popping sounds, but not all at once. The sounds were spread out, as if the shooter delighted in making sure anyone shot saw it coming and experienced feeling paralyzed by fear before losing their life.

I started to call out to anyone I saw as we ran—anyone who might be able to fill us in on what was going on, but no one paid me any attention. They just kept running. I tried again and again, but not a soul stopped. My panic morphed from fear for my life to dread that Mazin was somehow behind this attack. If Mazin was behind it, then that meant I was ultimately behind it—and that made me feel hugely responsible, like I would vomit if there was anything in my system to vomit.

Mrs. Bartolli came running around the corner and practically crashed into me. "What are you guys still doing here?" She spit out the words as if they were little bundles of fire burning her tongue. "Run!"

We followed her around the UN toward the North America building, where the staff offices were located. As soon as we reached the North America building, Ian grabbed her by the arm.

"What the hell is going on?" he asked.

She gulped hard, tried to catch her breath. "I don't know," she said, huffing, "but I need to get back in there." She huffed another breath. "I'm glad you're all okay, but I have to go."

"Wait," Ian said. "Maybe we can help."

Our fearless leader stopped and looked up for a moment. She looked as if she were about to cry. I recoiled at the sight of her looking so vulnerable.

"Okay, but this isn't going to be pretty, especially for you, Isabel."

Isabel opened her eyes wide, placing a hand on her chest to confirm that Mrs. Bartolli was addressing her. Then a realization washed over her. "Oh my god, it's my dad, isn't it?"

Mrs. Bartolli nodded and we all stared at Isabel, our mouths hanging open. Isabel nodded, swallowed. "How bad?" she asked.

I'd never heard two small words twist my stomach as much as those did.

"A few of the campers were wounded; some are in serious condition."

"Who?" Naomi asked.

We swarmed around Mrs. Bartolli, worry lining each of our faces—none more than Isabel's.

"Someone has been killed. I can feel it," I said.

Mrs. Bartolli looked into my eyes. "It's Dr. Hendrix," she said. "He's gone."

"Gone?" I said. "You mean—"

"Yes, Kenza, dead . . . I saw it happen. I was with him when he took his last breath." With that, she shook Ian loose and readied herself to run.

Ian glanced at each one of us. "Guys, come on. We might be able to save him."

"Save him?" Mrs. Bartolli said, turning her head. "You can't save someone who's already dead."

"There's something you don't know about us," Ian said.

"Ian," I warned, my voice firm. I wasn't ready for my insane world to consume yet another victim.

Ryan turned to Ian, and then eyed the rest of us. "Are you so selfish that you won't do whatever it takes . . . to save a life?"

"Two lives," Mrs. Bartolli said softly.

"Two?" Keelam confirmed.

"I shot Isabel's father. I had to . . . I—"

228

Isabel collapsed to the ground and burst into tears. Keelam knelt next to her, wrapping his arm around her back, hugging her close.

"Then, we can save both of them," Ian suggested, looking more determined than ever.

"I'm in," Naomi said, "I'll do whatever it takes to help."

"I don't have time for nonsense," Mrs. Bartolli said.

"Naomi, show her," Ian said, nudging his head toward Mrs. Bartolli to encourage her.

"Naomi, no!" I said, practically shouting.

I heard the tiniest voice—Isabel's voice, "Please, Kenza."

A cascade of resistance to bringing yet another person into the fold of my chaotic life flipped through my mind, like video clips on speed. It was so risky, so wrong on so many levels. Mrs. Bartolli could turn us in. If she did, what would the authorities do? Lock us up for being crazy?

"Don't worry, Kenza," Ryan said. "If I reverse time Mrs. Bartolli won't remember, anyway."

He was right. We could reverse time and stop this whole nightmare from happening in the first place—and she'd never know what happened, no one would.

Naomi didn't give me another chance to protest, anyway. She faded into nothing before Mrs. Bartolli's eyes.

Mrs. Bartolli gasped. "What in the world?"

"We have powers," I said.

Mrs. Bartolli's eyes bugged out.

"Ryan can fast forward and reverse time. He can pause it, too, and Ian can read people's minds," I explained.

"Oh really?" Mrs. Bartolli asked. "What am I thinking then?"

"You're mad that the government never prepared you for this."

Mrs. Bartolli looked stunned. "All right, all right. You guys can do stuff. So why are you telling me?"

229

"Ian's right. We need you," I explained. "You know how to strategize raids. You know how to use the tools, the people, and the circumstances that are available to you. We have powers, but we don't know how to use them to fix this."

She stared at Ryan. "How far back can you rewind, Ryan?"

"Thirty minutes."

"Can you go forty? Your life may depend on it," she said bluntly.

"I can do forty."

"What about Keelam? What can he do?"

Keelam lifted himself off the ground.

"Can you do that holding someone?" Mrs. Bartolli asked.

"Yeah,"

"Good." Mrs. Bartolli nodded. "What about you, Kenza?"

"I can protect people . . . one person . . . or a group."

Mrs. Bartolli nodded. "Impressive."

"Didn't you forget someone?" Isabel asked. Her face was blotched with patches of red.

"Who?" Mrs. Bartolli said.

"I can brainwash people," Isabel explained.

"Of course you can." Mrs. Bartolli nodded. "Everyone, follow me. We have ten minutes before Ryan has to rewind time. We need to think and act fast."

We ran into the North America building and ducked into a conference room. She grabbed a marker and drew a crude map of where she first saw Isabel's dad and Dr. Hendrix walking together toward the UN.

"Wait," Isabel said. "How did you know he's my dad?"

"Dr. Hendrix introduced us," Mrs. Bartolli replied. "Dr. Hendrix seemed agitated and he was telling your dad that you have amazing friends who can work wonders—" She cocked her head. "Does Dr. Hendrix know about these powers?"

We all shook our heads.

"We don't have time to worry about that," I interjected.

"Right, let's focus. Ryan, rewind time back to forty minutes ago. Everyone else, as soon as you arrive, position yourselves behind this storage shed and when you see Isabel's dad coming, do whatever it takes to stop him. Where were you thirty-five minutes ago?"

"We were just getting back from Shadow Forest," Isabel said.

Mrs. Bartolli shook her head.

"Keelam, can fly us from the forest to the shed," I offered. "Naomi can make him invisible."

"Wait, how am I going to know I need to do this?" Keelam asked.

"How will any of us know?" I asked. I turned to Ryan. "Will you remember all of this?"

He nodded. "Yeah, I will, but no one else will."

"Then, you'll have to remember exactly what to do," I said.

"Okay, we're ready—"

Everything faded to black.

Chapter 30

We walked in a cluster toward the UN cafe: Isabel, Ian, Keelam, Ryan, Naomi and me. We were starved because we'd just gotten back from spending a week of suspended-time in the other dimension. I didn't think I could eat another fruit or vegetable unless forced, and we were all longing for a juicy burger. On our return from the other dimension, no one said much of anything. We were exhausted and starving, but I didn't think I could eat another banana, even if it was the last bit of food on Earth.

Just as we stepped out of Shadow Forest and into camp, Ryan, who had been walking a few paces in front of us—his back to us, spun around to face us. His eyes were wide and he looked like he was on the verge of wetting himself. "Something tragic has happened and we all have to use our superpowers now."

"Is it Mazin?" I asked, stepping forward.

Ryan shook his head. "I don't know and it doesn't matter. Listen to me, Kenza. Trust me, please."

I nodded. "What do you need us to do?"

"Keelam, we need you to fly us as fast as you can to the shed behind the UN," Ryan said. "Kenza, I need you to go first. Naomi will go along to cloak you so no one sees you flying over Zenith Hill."

"I haven't flown two people outside of the other dimension," Keelam said. "Not successfully, anyway."

"Then you're just going to have do it now," I urged.

"Kenza, the moment you land, you're going to need to place a protective shield around yourself and any staff members you see. Keelam and Naomi will fly back for the rest of us, so protect us once we arrive, too."

"Protect only the people you mentioned?" I asked. "No one else?"

"I can't say that no one else will need protection," Ryan said. "But since our abilities are all new, we have to prioritize their use for the most important tasks. So I wouldn't."

"What about Ian?" I pointed at him.

"I'll fill him in while you're gone so he's ready when Keelam and Naomi return to retrieve him," Ryan explained. "But he's going to have to read minds from far away." Ryan signaled for us to get moving.

Naomi stepped forward and wrapped invisibility around Keelam and me just as I felt my feet lift off the ground. For a few seconds, we could still hear Ryan's conversation with Ian.

"Be careful," Ian called in our direction. Then he turned back to Ryan. "How far do I need to read minds? I've never tried more than a block or so."

"Look, we talked about this," Ryan said.

Ian looked annoyed.

"Oh right," Ryan said. "You guys don't remember any of this—"

I couldn't understand the rest of their conversation, but I did hear Ryan say Dr. Hendrix's name. Keelam flew low, just over the grass, in case we fell. As we approached the shed between the UN cafe and the North American building, Keelam lowered me to the ground, but hung on tightly to Naomi. Keelam then shot up higher and flew a lot faster, as they jetted back for Ian. I stood there frantic, not sure what danger lurked, or who might be at risk, so I decided to duck behind a tree. All I could do was wait. I clutched the amulet tightly in my grip. As soon as Ian appeared, I waved him over to the tree. He quickly filled me in on the situation.

"Isabel's dad is here and he's carrying a gun."

"I have to protect Isabel," I said, my voice urgent.

"Yes, Kenza," Ian said. "You have to protect all of us, but especially Dr. Hendrix."

"Dr. Hendrix?" I asked.

"Trust me," Ian said.

When Keelam at last returned with Ryan, and finally Isabel, Ian had filled me in on everything Ryan told him. I'd already wrapped a layer of protection around each of them, the moment their feet touched down and they stepped outside of Naomi's invisibility. I wasn't yet skilled at splitting the protection into different individual bubbles for each person, so I hoped that Isabel's dad would not wander into it with us or I'd be protecting him, too.

Once the protection was securely in place, I demanded that Ryan explain what was happening in his words. He shared everything he knew, and Isabel stood there staring off into space like she'd been turned into a zombie, but she didn't resist the news like I expected so I knew Ryan must have filled her in already. As for me, I flinched when he revealed that he told Mrs. Bartolli about our superpowers—something Ian conveniently left out, but I was relieved when he explained that her memory of our abilities had been wiped clean when he rewound time.

"So that's why we don't remember any of this, either," I said.

"Right," Ryan nodded. "We needed her, Kenza. She helped us come up with this rescue plan. And trust me, you two were in on it." He pointed at Ian and me. "With her help, we are going to save Dr. Hendrix, and perhaps Isabel's dad, but Mrs. Bartolli warned us to be extremely cautious. If we're not careful, we could sacrifice more lives—maybe even one of ours."

"So what now?" Ian jumped in. "What's the plan?"

"Do you know where Isabel's dad and Dr. Hendrix are?" Ryan asked.

Ian closed his eyes and breathed deeply. After several long seconds, he raised his eyebrows. "They're in Dr. Hendrix's office. He's pointing a gun at Dr. Hendrix."

"We have to help him," I said and turned toward the North America building, ready to run.

"Stop!" Ryan shouted.

I froze and turned around, instantly realizing I might have just done something stupid. I saw Mrs. Bartolli in the distance, just leaving the Central America building.

"I see her, too," Ian said, turning to Ryan. "Is it a problem if Mrs. Bartolli is headed this way?"

"Shit," Ryan cursed. "Kenza, you need to persuade Isabel to brainwash Mrs. Bartolli into thinking she's seeing normal things when we use our superpowers, and stand ready to wipe her memory if she sees anything she shouldn't, and Dr. Hendrix, too."

"Sure, I'll do it." I spotted Isabel fast, but noticed something out of place. "Wait, where's Naomi?" I asked.

"Naomi's somewhere in the building, near Dr. Hendrix's office," Ian reported. "She's going to turn him invisible if she needs to so it throws Isabel's dad off."

I made sure the layer of protection around Isabel and me remained strong and together we followed Mrs. Bartolli in a fast clip, careful not to be seen. Immediately, we saw Dr. Hendrix walk through the door with Isabel's dad.

"Oh my god," Isabel said.

I put my finger to my mouth to shush her, but I knew they didn't see us. Dr. Hendrix and Isabel's dad were headed toward the United Nations building, so we had to intersect their path—fast. Mrs. Bartolli wasn't far behind them. She may not yet have known how serious things were about to get, but obviously knew something was up because she ran from tree to tree, ducking behind each one to avoid being seen.

"What are we waiting for," Naomi suddenly appeared from out of nowhere and I realized she must have folded Isabel and me into her bubble of invisibility. Instinctively, I hugged her when I saw her.

Together, we trailed Mrs. Bartolli, less concerned about being seen now that we were invisible, but still trying to be quiet. As we walked, I spoke softly to Isabel, as if she were a little kid, fragile and innocent—but she alone was capable of the task at hand, and we desperately needed her to use the powers she'd been given. "If Dr. Hendrix or Mrs. Bartolli sees any of us using our superpowers, you need to brainwash them, okay? At the very least, distract them so they forget what's going on around them. We don't want them to get too involved, and we don't want to arouse suspicion when this is all over. You may need to wipe their memory slates clean."

"That's not permanent. Their memories may return, but I might be able to trick them into thinking they saw something they didn't. That is more lasting," Isabel said in a voice much more mature than I would have expected for someone who just learned that her own father would kill Dr. Hendrix—and harm a lot of other people—if we couldn't stop him in time.

"You have to try, Isabel," I said.

"What about my dad?" she said.

"Not necessary." I shook my head. "When the police get here, if he tells them or anyone else that he saw one of us fly, or make ourselves invisible, no one will believe him. They'll just think he's crazy."

"Kenza, he is crazy." Her voice was a loud whisper. "When he came to our house a few months ago, I thought he was going to kill my mom and me. And before Ryan rewound time, he did kill someone. He killed the nicest person I know." Suddenly her eyes lit up with an idea. "Maybe I can use my powers to convince my dad to want something different, to not want to hurt anyone." Her eyes were pleading.

"No," I said. "It's too dangerous. You're too emotionally attached."

Just then, Isabel's dad turned toward us. "Did you hear that?" he asked.

"I didn't hear anything, young man," Dr. Hendrix replied.

"Don't call me that. And you didn't hear my Isabel?"

I turned to look for Mrs. Bartolli, but she was nowhere in sight. Naomi, however, was standing next to me. She had her hands extended forward, moving around in slow circles, as if she were doing Tai Chi and I was afraid she was losing her concentration and was trying to recover it. When I turned back, Isabel's dad already had his gun trained on Dr. Hendrix. Even worse, his eyes looked blank, and I literally saw a red curtain pass over them.

"Oh God, Mazin got to him," I said, gripping Isabel's arm.

Just then, Ryan froze time, but not for all us, just for Isabel's dad.

"Isabel, hurry, work your magic on Dr. Hendrix and Mrs. Bartolli."

She leaned in, her face reflecting intense concentration.

I ran toward Isabel's dad and Mrs. Bartolli ran for him, too. As I ran, I dropped the protection around everyone else and concentrated it directly around Dr. Hendrix, leaving the rest of us exposed. It was the only way to protect him from Isabel's dad.

"Kenza," Naomi called, but it was too late. I must have just slipped out of her layer of invisibility. Mrs. Bartolli looked at me suddenly appearing and acted as if she'd just seen a ghost.

"Can you disarm him?" I asked her, not giving her a chance to react to seeing me appear out of nowhere. "I don't want to touch the gun."

Mrs. Bartolli looked dazed. I didn't know if it was from seeing me suddenly appear, seeing Isabel's dad frozen in time, or if Isabel was feeding her a fictional reality. Regardless of what she really saw, Mrs. Bartolli did as I requested. Dr. Hendrix stood back and crossed his arms in front of him, and then smiled, looking much like a proud father.

Ryan and Ian came running from wherever they'd been hiding. "Isabel," Ian implored—even though none of us could see her or Naomi.

"I'm on it," she said. Mrs. Bartolli's expression instantly softened. Either Dr. Hendrix remained oblivious, or he was an amazing actor, capable of hiding what must have been equal shock and fascination.

"Did you get all the bullets?" I asked Mrs. Bartolli.

Our collaboration leader opened her hand to reveal five bullets in her palm. "That's all of them," she said.

"Good," Ian said. "Now put them in Isabel's dad's pocket and give him the gun back."

"But—" Mrs. Bartolli took an aggressive step forward.

Instinctively, I raised my arms, as if prepping for counterattack.

"It's okay, Kenza," Dr. Hendrix said. "I know what you are about to do." His words disarmed all of us. "Mrs. Bartolli, these kids have proven that we can and should trust them. I am quite impressed, in fact. They are about to trick us into not seeing what we see, and maybe even erase our memory of what just happened. When they do, you and I will think that Isabel's dad is armed. He won't know that the gun isn't

237

loaded, and he might even raise his gun to shoot. That's when you will realize that he should be arrested, and you will have witnesses."

"That's ridiculous." Mrs. Bartolli tried to protest.

"Ridiculous it may be," Dr. Hendrix said, "but it is brilliant. I wouldn't be surprised if you were somehow involved in this plan."

She looked confused.

"Was she?" he asked us.

Ryan nodded and I cringed.

Chapter 31

"I'm going to unfreeze him now," Ryan warned us.

Naomi must have let her feelings take over and she dropped the invisibility shield around herself and Isabel. I was relieved to see them standing out of view from Isabel's dad. The moment Ryan unfroze time for him, he pointed his gun at Dr. Hendrix and ordered everyone else to back off.

"You don't want to do this," Mrs. Bartolli cautioned.

Just then, a group of campers rounded the corner and, when they saw the gun, they ran for cover but peered around bushes and trees to watch the scene unfold. Moments later, the police appeared from behind the United Nations cafe, some taking cover behind trees and bushes and others running onto the scene, guns pointed in our direction. "Police . . . down on the ground . . . now!" One of them called it so loudly that Isabel jumped and then dropped to the ground.

The rest of us followed her lead, except Mrs. Bartolli, Dr. Hendrix and Isabel's dad, who glanced frantically from the approaching to police to Dr. Hendrix. He squeezed his eyes shut and pulled the trigger. When it didn't fire, he eyed his gun with suspicion and disappointment. Isabel burst into tears stealing her dad's attention. While a genuine display of emotion, it served as the perfect distraction for Mrs. Bartolli to sneak around her dad and pin him down. Until now, the terrified witnesses had been crouching behind anything they could use for cover, but they now walked hesitantly out into the open, taking pictures of the police cuffing Isabel's dad with their Datadrixes. The rest of us pushed ourselves up from lying on the ground.

After the police hauled Isabel's dad away, several detectives and officers stayed behind to investigate and obtain what they thought was the full story. Mrs. Bartolli whispered something in Ryan's ear and he nodded, I assumed something about manipulating time or she would have talked to me. The officers and all the witnesses—except Mrs.

Bartolli, Dr. Hendrix, and those of us with superpowers—froze in time. Mrs. Bartolli proceeded to school us on how to answer the authorities' questions so that nothing would look or sound suspicious. She even coached Dr. Hendrix, and made each of us practice, by asking us very confusing and redundant questions. When we felt ready, Ryan unfroze everyone, and we told the Police what we wanted them to hear.

When the whole fiasco was over and the police hauled Isabel's dad away, Isabel sank to the ground and wept. I tried to comfort her, but my guilt about Mazin being responsible for overtaking Isabel's dad weighed me down under a mountain of guilt. "I'm so sorry," I whispered. I wrapped my arm around her and she rested her head on my shoulder. I wanted to console her, but I had an ulterior motive. I had to convince her to wipe Dr. Hendrix and Mrs. Bartolli's memories of our supernatural abilities.

"No way, Kenza," she said, her sadness twisting into anger. "I'm not doing it. Didn't you see how willing they were to help us? We might need them on our side one day."

"But—"

"Enough, Kenza," she said, pushing herself up. "I couldn't even do it in this state if I tried." She started walking away.

"Wait, Isabel," I called. I didn't expect her to turn, so when she did—despite the disgusted look on her face—her willingness to hear me out told me that some part of her forgave me.

"What are we going to do about Mazin?" I asked.

"We're going to destroy him," she said.

∞

Later, hours after the whole ordeal was over, we—excluding Mrs. Bartolli and Dr. Hendrix, of course—decided a major celebration was warranted. The next day, we headed for the beach. Walking single file, we trounced across the land bridge at low tide, eager to claim the remote island Keelam and I had visited less than a mile off shore—each of us hoping we might get some solace after what happened yesterday.

As we crossed, I was thinking about my future moments alone with Ian, careful to balance my weight over the narrow strip of land under our feet. I imagined a quaint little cottage hugging the shore that faced the vast ocean. It would have one bedroom, just big enough for the two of us, and a kitchen with wide French doors that opened to the most amazing view.

Before I was able to get completely carried away with my daydream, Ian—who was holding my hand, pulling me along protectively—turned and shot me a quick smile. Once again, I'd let my guard down for long enough to allow him to break into my fantasy. I smiled sheepishly, more motivated than ever to find a way to block him. From that step forward, I concentrated on not letting my thoughts run wild again. It became particularly challenging to stop myself from basking in the warmth of his hand and where I might want it to wander. Instead, I tried to focus on the narrow path below me, and the waves that rolled quickly and gently against it.

"That's it?" Ian stopped and turned, his obvious disappointment erasing his smile.

"What do you mean?" I asked, pretending to play dumb.

"Sometimes I wish you could know what I'm thinking." He let his gaze admire my curves, to the point I felt my cheeks warm, probably reddening enough to signal my embarrassment.

"Sometimes I wish I could, too," I replied. "But with your powers switched on all the time, I don't get any privacy . . . ever."

"Kenza, I—" A splash up ahead extinguished our heated exchange.

The splash reached its full height and then shot back down, momentarily cloaking Keelam's bulleting body as he flew up out of the ocean and hovered above Ryan's head, leaving a foot of space between them.

Keelam then lowered himself just behind Ryan, who wasn't able to react fast enough, and snagged his arms, hoisting Ryan to unnecessary heights. Then, just as suddenly, Keelam let go and cackled loudly. I

241

snapped my head around, wondering if he'd lost his mind—or if Mazin had gotten to him. During the merciless drop into the water, Ryan uttered a guttural "ahh" sound, as he flailed his arms and legs, running in vain from his inevitable connection with the ocean.

He landed with a slap that resonated louder than the belly flops my round cousin Eddy, on my mom's side of the family, would make smacking into a pool. When the water swallowed Ryan, Keelam punched his fist triumphantly into the air, hooting and hollering. It all happened so fast—too fast. It wasn't until Keelam circled around in a victory flight above our heads that I registered the risk we were taking.

Anyone could have seen him from a distance—maybe even at the Castle on the Hill—and there was no way we could explain away two flying teenagers.

Ian yelled the words I struggled to find. "Get down, Keelam. Get over here. Now!"

Keelam swooped down and landed squarely in front of us, still coughing up a laugh every few seconds.

"How can you be such an idiot?" Spit flew from Ian's lips as he spoke.

"What the—?" Keelam's feet now floated inches off the ground, as if he was itching to take flight again. "Ryan started it," Keelam said. "You saw him push me into the water." He pointed dramatically toward the ocean, where Ryan still hadn't resurfaced.

Naomi dove in head first to help him.

"He'll be fine," Keelam added.

"I know he'll be fine," Ian quipped, his voice still a shade too loud. "I'm not worried about you two having a little fun. I'm worried about what people will think if they see you twenty feet in the air, flying like birds."

"Oh that." Keelam's head drooped. "Sorry, man. You're right. How about I wait until we get to the island?"

Ian shook his head and pushed past Keelam over to the spot where Naomi and Ryan were dragging themselves out of the ocean.

"Come on, Keelam." I grabbed his arm and pulled, shaking my head, laughing. "I wouldn't worry about flying on the Island. It looks pretty isolated. If you can't see out, then they won't likely be able to see us."

Keelam shifted his gaze from my eyes up to the cliffs along the shore. "Oh man," he called, "look."

I craned my neck around and followed his pointing finger, spying a crowd of people, who suddenly knew that we were watching them watching us. There had to be at least a dozen of them. They quickly shifted further inland on the cliff's face, until we couldn't see them anymore.

I trounced angrily across the rest of the land bridge, hoping to release my anger about Keelam flying in plain sight each time I stomped. At least he stuck to the ground the rest of the way. Even if he looked dejected, I thought no one needed to be grounded more than him. He'd foolishly put us all at risk—our superpowers were not meant to be toys, and the last thing we needed was having more outsiders know about them.

Once we reached the island, the land bridge extended into a lightly worn path that crawled up an easy hill. We rounded the top of the hill and saw—off in the distance toward the center of the island—a welcoming cove of flat land tucked in and protected by the surrounding cliffs. It looked breathtaking. Trees swayed inside the cove and climbed the cliffs around its perimeter. It looked so private, so uninhabited—our own little paradise, the perfect place to escape from Zenith Hill, and all the drama we'd just endured.

The previous night, while the rest of us slept, Keelam had flown to the site, made us a fire pit, and brought coolers of food, drinks and blankets. My gratitude abolished all the negative thoughts I'd just had, forgiving Keelam his folly. We all switched to party mode, trouncing over to the goods and claiming our territory.

Now that he was forgiven, Keelam became his usual antsy self. Rather than sit on the boulders like everyone else, he lifted up into the air and dodged from place to place—reminiscent of Casper the Friendly Ghost. He must have found something he liked because he eventually shot out further from base camp. Ryan jumped up and ran after him calling, "Wait up, man."

They were gone for at least an hour, and we barely noticed their absence, but we definitely noticed their return. Keelam swooped in and landed in a tumble, tripping over his own feet and skidding on the dirt.

"It's Ryan," he shouted, panic-stricken. He pushed himself up and patted his hands together to shake the dirt and pebbles off.

"What about him?" Naomi's voice sounded very concerned.

"I don't know where he went."

Naomi glared at him.

"Should we go look for him?" Isabel asked.

"Everyone just relax," Ian said. "He's probably just checking the place out, or he's off somewhere plotting his revenge."

Naomi socked Keelam in the arm. "You're right, Ian. He'll be coming for Keelam any minute." She then laughed, which made us all laugh. "We're alone on this island and the land bridge has probably been washed away by the tide, so no one is getting in or out, unless they have Keelam's flying skills."

Ian and I locked eyes for a second, confirming that we should worry, that someone—or something—could very well have the ability to get to the island, land bridge or no land bridge.

"Don't worry about it," Ian said, capturing my eyes, shaking his head. "We're safe here."

"Yeah." I nodded. "Yeah, of course we are." I repeated it, partly to convince myself that I believed it.

Isabel was sitting across from me, so I watched as Keelam floated up behind her, his finger on his mouth, instructing us not to say a word. He smiled and waved for me to come, then disappeared quickly behind some trees.

I yawned, and then stood up, "I've got to pee," I said, as casually as possible.

"Have fun," Isabel retorted.

I was worried she might have wanted to escort me but she must have already relieved herself while wandering around earlier.

As soon as I walked far enough into the trees, I literally ran right into Keelam. "What are you up to?" I asked.

"I need Naomi," he said, sounding very mysterious.

"Isabel and Ryan are not going to like the sound of that," I said.

"Her powers. I need Naomi to make a cloak around me."

"Why?" I asked, my suspicion growing.

"Please go get her for me," he answered. "Just trust me."

What did I have to lose? I walked back into camp and asked Naomi to have my back while I peed. She hesitated, but came to help anyway and looked relieved to find out that all I really wanted her to do was drape a cloak of invisibility around Keelam, while I went and did my business privately. When I returned to camp, I found Ian and Isabel facing the tree, suspicion and curiosity written on their faces. Ryan was standing behind them.

"What's that sound?" I said.

Suddenly, an invisible bubble around Keelam and Naomi burst. They were standing in front of a tree that wasn't even there before. Something above their heads was etched into the wood.

"Ooh, isn't that sweet," Ryan said.

Isabel inched her way to the tree until she could see what Keelam had carved into the trunk: the letters "KS heart IP." Isabel's face reddened and she thrust her arms around Keelam to give him a big-old bear hug.

"Aww, it's the 'Love Tree,'" Ryan said, sounding like a cheesy nightclub DJ. He rushed over, grabbed the knife and started scratching at the wood along another side of the tree, carving: "Ryan & Naomi 4Ever." It was so fifth grade.

After Keelam and Ian tried unsuccessfully to start a campfire, Naomi dismissed them. "Let me do it," she proclaimed, announcing that she'd learned how to make a fire during survival training with her mom one summer. Naomi's mom could be obsessive compulsive, a trait she'd passed on to her daughter, but we were surprised to learn that, at some point, she thought that the world, as we knew it, would come to an end and that she and Naomi would need basic survival skills to stay alive. Just knowing she'd gone through that sort of fearful mindset, made me appreciate Naomi and how she'd survived a tense upbringing. Of course, if she knew about my dad's random bursts of anger, she'd probably appreciate me more, too.

In no time, Naomi got our fire going and we spent the next few hours roasting hot dogs and marshmallows. Keelam even had the foresight to bring the supplies for s'mores, which the camp store in the UN stocked. We talked about childhood memories, about singing songs (but decided not to do that because we were all terrible singers), and somehow the topic of middle names came up.

"What's yours, Kenza?" Ian asked.

"Me? Actually, I don't have a middle name. My little sister, Daniyah, doesn't either. I guess it's a Moroccan thing."

"Daniyah is such a pretty name," Naomi said.

"Yeah, it means someone you hold close to your heart. What's your middle name?" I asked Ian.

"Amal," he said.

"What?" I felt my eyes open wide.

"Just kidding." He laughed and bumped my arm. "It's Pierce."

"Ian Pierce Hampton," I said. "It sounds very sophisticated."

"As it should." He tugged at the fabric above his shoulders, affecting a self-important confidence.

"Mine's Walter," Keelam said.

Isabel cocked her head to the side as she eyed him. "That sounds way too plain for you, Keelam Walter Sky."

"What did you think it would be?" He raised an eyebrow.

"I don't know. I guess something even more unusual . . . you know unique, like the rest of your name—like you."

"You think I'm unique?" he said, his eyes lighting up.

"Yeah, I do." A smile swept across her lips.

"Well, how would you like to take a walk with your unique boyfriend?" he asked.

"I'd love that," she said, her voice softening. They got up and walked away, hand-in-hand.

"Oh hurl," Naomi said. "So what about you, Ryan? What's your middle name?"

"Who me?" he said. "You don't want to know."

"Yeah, we do, Ryan." Naomi cocked her head in my direction. "Don't we, Kenza?"

"Yeah, I'm game," I agreed.

"Fine," he whined. "It's Dexter."

"Ryan Dexter Amara." Naomi leaned back and looked up at the smoke rising above the crackling fire in the center.

"Wait, what?" I exclaimed. "Did you say Dexter?"

"Here we go." Ryan sighed. "You heard me right."

"That guy who helped me that one day when I was about to lose my mind at Jizzammee Dibs . . . he looked just like you—a younger version of you, that is—and his name was—"

"Dexter." Ryan nodded. "Yeah, that was actually me."

"No way." I jumped to my feet.

"Hey there, easy," Naomi said, jumping to her feet, too.

"No, I'm not mad, Naomi. I just don't get it."

"Oh come on, Kenza. Ryan can rewind time," Naomi reminded me. "If things went terribly wrong for us, you know he'd go out of his way to change history, right?"

"Wait, you knew about this?" I said, anger rising up inside me.

"Wait, whoa there," Ian said, standing and walking between us. "I think we should take a walk."

He reached for my hand and I let him take it. "I'm not mad," I clarified. "I just want to know what happened."

247

Now that the rest of us were standing, Ryan stood, too. "I didn't know it was me either, until I gained my ability to manipulate time. Once I had my gift, I suddenly also remembered an alternate reality. It was like both of them happened. One possibility was me conjuring up Dexter—a younger version of myself, that is—to help you; the other was you not having any help and getting so frustrated you launched a strawberry smoothie, splattering at least twenty people in the crowd, losing your customers and ultimately your business."

"That did not happen." I emphasized the words.

"It didn't happen in your reality," he said, "because I rewound myself back to a younger version of myself—young enough to trick, or at least confuse you—and even me. Then I rewound your time back to that day at Jizzammee Dibs when the line snaked into Tree House Lane."

I shook my head, looking down at my feet. "That's crazy."

"Crazier than the things we saw in the underground? Crazier than finding out that Isabel's dad killed Dr. Hendrix, who is now alive and well thanks to our machinations?"

"No, it's not crazier than that, I guess. It's just . . . things were so normal for so long, and I wanted them to stay that way." Unexpected tears burned my eyes and I tried to resist them. Ian squeezed my hand harder.

"Well, don't forget why we all gained our skills, Kenza," Naomi said, her voice stern. "There's a killer on the loose who's far more dangerous than Isabel's pathetic father. Hell, Mazin could be watching us right now, waiting for us to let our guards down so he can attack."

"Hey now," Ian said, patting the air downward with his hands as a sign to calm the conversation down. "I think it's time for us to take a break. Seriously. Besides, Kenza, I want to show you something."

I nodded, but turned to look at Ryan. "I'm calling you Dexter from now on, bud," I said.

Ian and I then wandered into the forest, through several patches of trees, until we stood facing one taller than the rest, with light from the moon illuminating its trunk. "Let's carve our own symbol of love," he said, "together."

248

We worked for a half hour. Every so often, Ian leaned in to kiss my cheek. When we were very close to finishing, he drew me to him and kissed me long and hard, leaving me feeling dazed for a few seconds. When we finally finished our carving, we took a step back, hand-in-hand, and gazed at our creation—a supersized heart, with "Kenza & Ian: Found by destiny, bound by love" carved inside it.

"Wait, it needs one more thing. Turn around," Ian said.

I obeyed and he took a few more minutes to scratch something into the tree.

When I turned around a few minutes later, he had carved an infinity symbol in the heart.

Chapter 32

We were standing, hand-in-hand, admiring our symbol of love carved into the tree when Ian stiffened, then pointed his nose upward, as if sniffing the air. I knew he sensed the presence of something that didn't belong. Suddenly, it felt like someone turned an industrial-sized fan on high. Tree branches began to sway and collide violently. Odd. I thought this part of the island would have been protected from such a strong wind by the island cliffs, but the open clearing—which was not at all protected—stood frozen in time, like a perfect photograph.

The trees rattled even harder and then straightened back up with a snap, coughing a chilling gust into base camp, swirling around us in a predatory threat, licking me first and then snapping at Ian. Then, just like the bullying wind, something else hit me. I could tell it hit Ian, too. It wasn't a physical hit, like a branch striking against our backs; it was more powerful—the kind of hit that started out as a tiny seed of realization, and then grew into a panicked warning to our nervous systems.

"What have we done?" I asked, shouting over the wind.

"Run!" Ian ordered. "Back to base camp, now."

As soon as we reached the campfire, the others had also returned, looking panic-stricken.

"What do we do?" Isabel said.

"We do what we've been trained to do." Ian's words masked what had to be gelatinous nerves.

Without a noise, Keelam slipped behind Ryan and swooped him up into the air, a clear sign they were getting along now. Facing a mutual enemy had a way of smoothing over disagreements.

"Hold them off," Keelam ordered. "We need to scope out our escape route, but we'll be back."

"Why are you rescuing him first?" Isabel asked, a look of panic on her face.

"Take us all with you." Naomi said, grabbing onto Keelam's legs, but he shook her off.

"What am I?" Keelam shouted, "Superman?"

"I think so," Isabel hollered. He shot up like a bullet, like a zip line directly connected to the cliff and disappeared from my line of sight in a few seconds.

"Great," Isabel said.

"Follow me," I commanded, leading Ian, Isabel, and Naomi in the direction of the cliff. "Naomi, can you cloak us in invisibility while we run?"

She'd already blended our skin and clothing to the forest around us, trying, at least, to buy us a little time. "Not yet, but I'll try," she said. We weren't very far up the hill when the cloak slipped off us and we had to duck behind a boulder, big enough to hide us and give Naomi a chance to rest.

Guilt and anger gnawed at every shred of my strength. We were all in this situation because of Mazin . . . because of me.

With no other option, we had no choice but to wait, silently thanking the boulder, praying it would be enough to keep us safe. How naïve.

Every few seconds one of us stole a quick glance in the direction of base camp. When it was my turn, I saw the most ominous sight I'd ever seen: a bluish-white, misty fog gathering steam, howling a trumpet call, announcing the onslaught of a bloody battle. It sounded like a woman's tortured voice crying through the wind.

Then the smell hit—worse than Jinny Zzaman's odor, worse than rotten eggs, much worse. It reeked of pure evil and felt vicious, bloody, and more powerful than I'd ever experienced. Desperate to regain my superpowers, I fell back behind the protection of the boulder. I could feel my powers giving way to panic, but I had to protect Ian and Isabel. I had to protect them or my life would have no meaning.

Mazin's evil energy affected me more violently than it did Ian and Isabel, but Ian hadn't shut off his ability to read minds and he soon doubled over in pain.

251

"Ian, shut it off," I ordered. "You have to turn it off."

"I can't," he said.

"You have to," I cried, my voice louder than I wanted it to be.

He gritted his teeth, clearly suffering pain. "I've forgotten how to shut it off."

"Shut up," Isabel hissed. "I think they heard you."

"How could they? You could barely hear—"

Then it hit me—they had powers, too. We'd been warned. Why hadn't we heeded the warning?

"They're getting close," Isabel said in a loud whisper.

The bluish white fog inched closer. It didn't come in the form of a wall, but rather long, thin fingers that spindled their way into our space. That's when I knew exactly what we were up against.

They moved fast and yet cautiously. The dozen or so people watching us across the land bridge had not been tourists or other campers, which in a very small way was a relief. At least normal people hadn't seen Keelam fly. No, there was no trace of normal in them. They approached in a run, but not a human run. They ran like animals, soft on their feet and fast as the wind.

When I stole another glance around the boulder, I had to blink hard a few times to make sure I wasn't seeing things because they looked like humans from the front, but wisps of light and shadows splaying out behind them created 3D-images of werewolves. Approaching us from an angle, they gave the illusion that humans were hunting us, but really they were a pack of werewolves—headed straight for us.

They were dressed in the same kind of white robes I remembered from my visit with Jinny and Jamila—long ago—to ancient Morocco, when I'd seen the Supreme Ruler of the Tribe of Diab sentence Ian's ancestor Amal to death. Had Mazin summoned these same forces, now tattered by the passing of time and death?

"Naomi, use your invisibility field. You have to," I said. "I'll place a layer of protection around us."

Naomi could keep us invisible. Isabel could use her charm to mesmerize and even brainwash her prey. I could use my shield to hide us, but all Ian could do was know what they were thinking. What good would that do? We already knew what they were solely focused on: attacking and killing us all. They apparently had the strength to convert the long dead into an army of lost souls.

"I'm going to distract them," Isabel called before we were ready, as she crouched down and blended into the tall grass, and slithered toward them.

"Isabel, no. I might not be able to protect you," I shouted, but it was too late. She did what she had to do, loyal as ever. Now it was my turn. I closed my eyes and concentrated hard. I shut out the nauseating smell as best I could and focused on protecting Ian and Naomi, which required every ounce of psychic energy I had. I was tired from feeling panicked and could feel fear coursing through me, interfering with my abilities.

Naomi donned a look of concentration. On her solar plexus, just under her rib cage, a fist-sized hole shone right through her. It grew outward—fast. Before anyone realized what she had done, the vacuum engulfed the boulder, making it look to our ghostly army like the boulder had suddenly disappeared. By the expression on their faces, they noticed, but didn't see us—yet. Ian and I stood frozen, but Isabel must have realized what was going on because she stood up, in plain view, to work her magic—risking her life, for us. She could die any second, and there was nothing either of us could do to help her. Nothing.

So we turned and ran, knowing it was what she'd wanted us to do. We ran and left Isabel behind, alone, surrounded by a pack of savage wolves. I glanced back to see the entire army, in a half circle around her. She seemed to be controlling them, though I had no idea how. We were invisible but still made enough noise for the wolves to follow in pursuit . . . but they didn't. Still, we ran as though we were running for our lives, but we weren't running for our lives. We were running for Isabel's life. We needed help. Pronto. We needed a rescue plan. We needed Keelam. We needed all of us—every last shred of power we could drum up.

We soon saw Keelam and Ryan rushing toward us, coming to help. They wouldn't have been so eager if they'd seen the werewolves and their ghostly army up close.

"Where is she?" Keelam spewed, desperation in his voice.

"She's—" A thick ball of guilt knotted up in my throat and tears filled my eyes. I crumpled to the ground.

Ian must have turned his mind-reading abilities back on and focused them on Keelam because he chose exactly the words that Keelam needed to hear to avoid coming after us, or worse, heading straight into the wolf pack alone and unarmed. All I heard, though, through the strain of my own emotion were the words: "A rescue plan."

I wiped away my tears and pulled in a full breath, filling myself up with whatever courage I could muster. I led my friends to the edge of the cliff. From there, Keelam flew us to a dry shelf that opened up to a cave, halfway down to the waves below. Once inside, I used my powers to cause an avalanche of rock and boulders, blocking the entrance of the cave. It was an unconventional use of my skills, but it served to protect us and I knew that's why it worked.

There was no way the Tribe of Diab could reach us. There was no way we were getting out either, but we found a way around that. We spent the next several minutes strategizing about what facts we needed to gather before acting, what our escape plan would be, and who would take on what responsibility. When the time came, Ryan would rewind us back as far as he could, certainly before the avalanche so we could return to base camp and rescue Isabel. Only Ryan would remember the full plan we devised while in the cave, and he would have to explain it in full detail when the time came.

"Are you guys, ready?" Ian asked when we finished ironing out every last detail of the plan.

"I've been ready," Keelam said, pacing in half circles around us.

"Remember," Ryan said, "this is just a reconnaissance mission. This time, we collect facts and we save Isabel, if we can, but if we can't get her out on this first round, I can probably rewind time one more time."

"Probably," Keelam said, shaking his head.

"It will work," I said, springing to my feet. I cared about Isabel just as much as Keelam. "It has to work."

"Let's go then," Ryan said. He looked like the weight of the world rested on his shoulders—in truth, the weight of Isabel's life did. It rested on all of us.

Keelam lifted us up off the dry shelf and as close to the Tribe of Diab that we could get, without giving away our position. We made it back in record time, enough to keep the element of surprise on our side. When all five of us were in position, Naomi threw the cloak of invisibility over all of us, creating a dome that we used to sneak back to our spot behind the large boulder, right outside of base camp. This time she was careful not to swallow the boulder in the shield. Once we were all crouched behind it, she dropped the shield so she could conserve energy.

Before anyone dared to peer around the boulder, I looked at Ian's distressed face and knew something hideous was happening. I wished Ryan could have rewound us further back, but we had to make the best of the situation. Ian's job was to get a read on the scene by piecing together thoughts of various tribe members. By the look on his face, he had a world of filtering to do to ignore the evil thoughts and memories of our pursuers and focus on what was happening to Isabel. Ian's face turned red and sweat formed on his forehead. He clenched his fists, then finally cried out, "No!"

The rest of us snapped our heads toward the direction of the Tribe of Diab, worried that he'd given away our position.

On the first day of camp last summer, when I met Naomi, I never would have believed that someday everyone I held dear at camp would put their lives in her hands, but here we were—counting on her for invisibility. I watched as she squeezed her eyes shut and appeared to concentrate hard. The wind suddenly picked up, swirling about fiercely, which luckily muffled the sound of our voices.

"I'm going out there," Keelam declared.

"No," I grabbed his arm. "Stick with the plan." Then I turned toward Ian, "Try to shut it off, Ian. You have to."

I stole a quick glance around the boulder and saw Isabel had been tied to a tree. It wasn't just any tree. It was the tree—the one with "KS

255

heart IP" carved in it. About a foot of space sat between it and the top of Isabel's head. The tree, so recently marked by love, was now marked by hatred, fear, and blood—Isabel's blood. Her arms were stretched as far back as they would go without breaking and her wrists and ankles were tied around the trunk of the tree.

One of Mazin's beasts stood before Isabel. He wasn't tall, but his bulky stature and the sick smile exposed how menacing he really was. Mazin stood right next to him, close enough to savor whatever this man was about to do to her, but acting too high and mighty to participate in the physical act of inflicting punishment.

Mazin and his beast both looked human from the front, but from the back, a smoky outline of a wolf trailed behind them. I shivered, wondering if the legend of the werewolf originated with the Tribe of Diab when it was under Mazin's deadly rule. I didn't recognize the man standing in front of Isabel—not until I heard him speak.

"I'm going to enjoy this," he said. I stiffened immediately, not upon hearing his disturbing words, but upon hearing his voice. It was the voice of Sidi Borj, a voice I would never forget. It was only a year ago that I witnessed him punch Ian's ancestor, Amal, square in the face, while he was chained to a cave wall in 1500's Morocco. I shivered again, imaging Sidi Borj do the same thing to Isabel. A hot claw of fear gripped my throat and my mind raced, desperately weighing our options.

Sidi Borj missiled his fist into Isabel's face, and then again into her stomach. He paused briefly before starting in on her again, this time relentlessly pummeling nearly every inch of her.

After a few punches, she barely reacted. Her cheeks were already stained from tears and blood. Her nose looked oddly crooked, like it could never be straight again. Her head slumped. Everything slumped, limply hanging over the ropes that kept her prisoner, just below the heart with her initials in it: "KS heart IP."

I felt myself slump, too. We all did. Keelam started pacing behind the boulder, which infuriated me. If we had any hope of helping Isabel, we had to remain as still as statues. Ian flinched and gritted his teeth. I could only imagine how painful it would be to feel the pain that she felt, multiplied by the helplessness that each of us—especially Keelam—felt as we waited for the prime opportunity. Normally, we would turn to

Isabel to pacify our fears. She would use her charm and calm us down. She probably wouldn't even need to invoke her powers, at least not with Keelam. She had natural powers over him.

Weirdly enough, those few seconds I turned to watch the restlessness of my cherished and powerful friends were a welcome distraction. It was a million times better than watching Sidi Borj pummel Isabel, with Mazin gloating—no salivating—next to him. What finally snapped my attention back to focusing my eyes on her was not my own will, but the sound of the worst noise I'd ever heard. As my head swiveled back and my eyes hurried to catch up, I saw it.

I saw it, right there before me. I saw it and I'd never ever forget it. Isabel's teeth, her spit, and her blood flew out from where they belonged—and she was dead. I doubled over and whatever food my high-alert metabolism left me with raced up my throat and sprayed violently out around me, polluting the air with a ghastly odor.

It had all happened so fast—too fast. A few hours ago, Isabel was cracking jokes and holding Keelam's hand. A few minutes ago, I first witnessed my best friend being beaten. A few seconds ago, she gave up whatever life was left in her. I stood back up and stole one final glance. I had to be sure, and I was sure. I was more certain about her death than anything else I'd ever known before. The body that slumped against the tree, held upright only by ropes, wasn't Isabel's anymore. It was nothing but a damaged, decaying body, with a caved in face, gushing dark blood.

Isabel was gone.

But that monster Sidi Borj kept hacking away at her with his fists, refusing to stop, even though he knew she was gone.

The agreement we had was to hang tight. Observe. Then regroup and strategize. I had known that, but it didn't matter anymore. I couldn't think about anyone else. I couldn't even think about myself. I had to stop this monster's attack. Even though I knew it was too late, I had to stop him. I ran out from behind the boulder, and Naomi followed me to keep me protected by invisibility. I placed my body in between Sidi Borj's hurling fist and Isabel's dead body. I wanted him to hurt me, not her. I wanted to hurt myself for dragging her into this mess . . . for not being able to protect her in time.

When his fist made contact with my invisible body, it surprised him. He stumbled back, crippled by the unexpected resistance. I flew into Isabel's body and wept like a grunting animal. I wept for the pain. I wept for the hopelessness. Most importantly, I wept for the suffering that Isabel—that no being—should ever have to endure. That was it. By placing myself between Sidi Borj and Isabel, I'd sounded the alarm and hoards of tribe members poured onto the scene just as Naomi lost concentration letting both of us slip perilously back into view.

"Do something." I vaguely heard Ian's voice, like he was shouting in slow motion through a distant tunnel in the back of my mind. Then I felt myself being pulled like elastic. I was not being pulled by rope or touch or anything visible. I was being raked back by the tug of time. And then everything went blank.

∞

I felt woozy and, after experiencing Ryan rewind time before, I knew we'd just experienced a rewind. It felt oddly false, like we had been mysteriously plucked from one spot and placed like paper dolls into an entirely different place and time. We were already headed to the cliff, where Keelam would fly us to a dry shelf halfway down to the waves.

"Ryan, man, what did you do?" Keelam asked, sounding angry. "We don't have time to mess around."

Ryan's face was whiter than usual, stripped of his usual cheery disposition.

"What happened?" Keelam demanded, focusing intently on Ryan. He leaned forward on his toes, as if prepared to spring into combat at a moment's command.

"Sit back, please," Ryan said. It looked like he was trying to gather his strength, not for a battle, but for a message we needed to hear.

I felt strangely sick to my stomach.

"You did it, didn't you? You rewound time," Ian said what we all knew, but needed to hear voiced out loud.

258

After a few seconds, Ryan nodded slowly, looking down, as if trying to erase some horrific memory.

"Tell us, Ryan. We can take it," I said.

Ryan let out a hiccupy desperate laugh.

"We can," I repeated, this time with pure conviction.

He shook his head back and forth rapidly.

Finally, he found his courage. "I rewound us back to the moment we first landed in this cave."

"What happened?" Keelam asked again.

I had the feeling he would ask a hundred times until he got the answers he wanted.

"We don't have much time." Ryan said, skillfully dodging the question for a third time.

I shivered.

"I need all of you to concentrate," Ryan said, his voice deadly serious. "Even more than the tragedy at the UN, we will need to stay calm. Stay calm, but act fast. But first I have to tell you the plan."

"God damn it, Ryan! Is Isabel okay or not?" Keelam cried.

"Yes," Ryan said forcedly. "She's okay now, but if I don't do this right, she won't be. Now, are you are ready to listen, or do you want to risk her precious life by mouthing off?"

Keelam was silenced.

Ryan looked around the circle, locking eyes with each of us in turn. "We are in very real danger. This is no joke. We will do as we agreed: use our individual powers. We need them now more than ever. Isabel will soon be tied to the Love Tree in base camp."

Keelam flew to a standing position and barely restrained himself.

"Listen," Ryan warned. He turned to Naomi. "Use your invisibility to get close to Isabel. You'll have to ignore whatever they're doing to her. Otherwise, we'll lose the advantage of surprise. Fight it. Resist letting it take your focus away. "

"Damn it, Ryan," Keelam said. "Why didn't you take us back further? Why didn't you take us back to the land bridge and stop us from coming?"

"I couldn't all right! This is as far back as I could go, and I don't know if I can do it again, so we have to make this time work."

Keelam used his gift of flight and was on top of him.

"Keelam, don't fight me," Ryan said, desperation in his voice. "I'm trying to help. We have to pool our powers so we can save Isabel's life."

Keelam flew off, stunned, and landed on his feet. We all jumped up to our feet. No one said a word.

"What are they're doing to her?" I asked, speaking the words Keelam had to be thinking.

"You have to trust me," Ryan said, pleading. "We don't have time to get into all that now."

I nodded. Everyone kept quiet.

"Naomi," Ryan continued. "When you get to the tree—and make sure you don't cloak it or you'll give your position away—untie her knots. I'll help you with the knots, too. Keelam, you stay out of that part. That's all I'm asking you to do."

Ian produced a knife. "For the ropes." Naomi nodded and took it from him.

Ryan turned to Keelam. "As soon as the knots are free, I'll freeze-frame everyone in the scene, except you, Isabel, and Naomi. You'll need to swoop in and fly Isabel out. You'll have to be gentle with her. She might be badly hurt. Then Naomi will cloak me so we can escape together on foot."

Keelam said nothing. Tears welled up in his eyes and he swatted at them, kicked at the cave wall, and then inhaled a long breath and gave one solid nod.

"Be gentle, but be quick. I used up most of my energy rewinding us back to this moment. I'm not sure how long I'll be able to freeze the enemy. Are we clear?" he added.

Nobody responded.

"Good," Ryan said, looking relieved. "Then we're ready."

"What about me?" Ian finally said.

"And me?" I asked, stepping forward.

"Ian, you've already done your part, so I'm begging you to stay here in this cave."

Ian looked puzzled.

Ryan continued, "You've already read their minds. You don't remember it because I rewound time, but we now know that they know about this cave. What we don't know is if they realize it will lead us to the other dimension, if we can make it. That's where you come in, Kenza."

"What do you mean?" I asked.

"They'll be fast on our trail. There's a chance we won't be able to get away."

"So I help make sure everyone gets to the cave?" I said.

"No, something even more important."

"More important than helping us escape?" I asked.

"You saw that the tide is rising. By the time we get back, the entire entrance will probably be buried in water."

"I need to be the one to allow you guys in with Isabel once she's rescued," I said.

"And block Mazin and the Tribe of Diab from following us deep into the cave," he added.

Ian and I locked eyes—me feeling relieved that I had such an important part to play and him looking helpless.

"Are we done, yet, Ryan?" Keelam said, frantic. "Don't you remember why we're here?" Ryan went silent. "Isabel, remember? She needs us. And from the way you look, I can tell her life depends on us. Now let's get the hell out of here."

I wanted to protest, concerned about the danger that faced them—that faced all of us, but how could I delay us a second longer after

261

what Keelam just said? Not another word was spoken. We all stood up on cue, as if ordered by an Army General. Ian and I watched as Keelam lifted Ryan and Naomi off the ground and flew them out the cave entrance. Ryan had been right about the high tide. A splash of water was already lapping over the cave floor. I prepared to use my powers of protection and work my magic on this rising tide while Ian watched me—unable to help.

Chapter 33

Despite Ian not thinking there was anything he could do to help, he suddenly had an idea. "Ryan said something about escaping through the back of the cave, right?"

I nodded.

"I'm going to go check it out . . . warn them we're coming." He darted toward the back of the cave and kept running until I couldn't see him anymore.

After what seemed like an eternity, Keelam returned to the cave with Isabel. He flew her right through the water and into the bubble of dry space that I'd managed to protect from the flooding that would have consumed us by now. Sidi Borj had inflicted some damage—probably a broken nose, gashes over her eye, lots of bleeding. According to Keelam, she was barely conscious by the time he, Ryan, and Naomi had arrived to save her, and she apparently passed out as soon as Keelam lifted off the ground with her in his arms.

Because of her condition, as Ryan predicted, Keelam had to leave him and Naomi to run for their lives. According to Keelam, they were probably still running, but how could they escape on foot from an army of werewolves and ghostly soldiers after them?

"You have to go back for them," I urged.

"I can't leave Isabel." Keelam was knelt down over her, now laying on the cave ground.

I heard footsteps pattering behind me. "Kenza's right, Keelam," Ian said, his voice firm even though he was out of breath. Keelam did not appear to hear him. "I mean it, Keelam. You have to go help Naomi and Ryan. If something happens to them, you'll never be able to forgive yourself."

"Besides," I piped in, hoping my words might force him to act. "On foot, they'll lead the Tribe of Diab directly to this cave. How will we

263

be able to rescue Isabel if we're fighting for our own lives? She'll be completely helpless."

He looked up, appearing to chew on my words. Then he abruptly stood and lifted immediately off the ground flying back out through the wall of water outside of the dry bubble of protection I'd formed.

In what seemed like only a few moments, Keelam returned through the wall of water blocking the cave entrance. He was holding onto Ryan who now gripped a limp Naomi in his arms. Blood gushed from her head.

"What the hell happened?" I said, standing up from my position next to Isabel and rushing to Naomi. "Is she—"

"Alive?" Ryan blurted. "Of course she is. How could you even ask that?"

"They're coming!" Ian shouted. "I can read their thoughts. The first one just dove into the water. Come on. Ashram is waiting for us."

I pointed firmly toward the back of the cave. "You guys need to go, now. Keelam, you take Isabel. Ryan, can you take Naomi, again?"

He nodded, but when he tried to pick her up his arms started shaking and he nearly dropped her.

"Ryan, I've got this," Ian said. He swooped down to pick her up. Ryan looked at him, his eyes pleading as if he wanted to be the one to save her, but knew he was too fatigued. "Besides, Kenza needs you with her in case they get too close."

"He's right, Ryan," I called. "Come walk next to me in case—" I couldn't bring myself to say in case Mazin breaks through my barrier and tries to kill us all.

Ryan nodded and let Ian carry Naomi down the long corridor, following Keelam who'd already gotten a head start and was several hundred feet down the corridor, with Isabel in his arms. As we followed them, Ryan and I walked backwards so we could keep our eyes glued in the direction of our pursuers. The half-animal half-human outline of one of them suddenly appeared outside the bubble. He tried to penetrate the protection, but bounced off. Then another appeared, and the same thing happened.

"You're doing it, Kenza," Ryan said eagerly.

"Yeah," I said, and regretted losing my concentration the moment I did because one of them broke through, into the dry space with us.

"Ryan, freeze him," I ordered. "Now!"

"On it," Ryan called as the wolfman froze in his spot.

I turned, looking away from our pursuers for a split second. "Keelam, Ian, run!" I turned to Ryan. "You too."

He shook his head.

"Now," I said. "You can still freeze them from further away, right?"

He nodded.

"Then go," I shouted. "Go!"

I turned back toward the entrance and saw two more frozen wolfmen. I stopped in my tracks, squeezed my eyes shut, and wrapped my hand around the amulet around my neck and wished for a forceful barrier of protection. I couldn't afford anymore Tribe of Diab attackers to break through. I turned and ran toward Ryan at the back of the cave. He'd already gained at least a two-hundred-foot lead; I could barely see him that far away in the light of my Datadrix.

"We made it," I heard Keelam call from the back of the cave. I hoped he would come back for me, but I didn't expect him to because I knew he wouldn't want to leave Isabel again. I ran harder, tasting a hint of victory on my tongue. Suddenly, I heard Ryan call, "Kenza, watch out!"

I turned to see Mazin lunging for me, but I jumped out of the way just in time. I didn't see anyone else with him, besides the three frozen wolfmen toward the cave entrance. I knew I had to get myself as close to the back of the cave as I could, or I'd never have a fighting chance, so I ran backwards keeping my eye on Mazin the whole time.

He started laughing at me. "You think you can get away from me that easily?" His overconfident voice grated on my last nerve.

Behind him, I saw a dozen wolfmen break through my protective barrier, realizing that Mazin had distracted me enough to weaken the protection. I kept running backwards, despite his laughter, and despite the army that now pursued me. I let my mind keep running, too—now my best defense for getting through this alive. Despite Mazin being my biggest threat, I decided to wipe out his army first. I closed my eyes for a split second, allowing my focus on the barrier to change. Essentially, I pulled the bubble of protection in and flooded more of the cave, the water knocking Mazin's intruding army off their feet one-by-one.

Mazin cried out in anger and pounced on me, leaping through the air like a wolf attacking its prey. I fell back hard, banging my head against the cave floor. He reached for the Amulet of Omnia and raked it from neck. He leapt to his feet and turned to run.

"Ryan, freeze him, now!" I yelled at the top of my lungs.

Mazin froze in his tracks, but I knew the hold wouldn't last long, not with the powerful amulet in Mazin's hands. I rushed to him and stole it back, turning to race as fast as my feet would carry me toward the door at the back of the cave. I ran hard, not stopping to think about whether Mazin was now able to move, not stopping to think about him likely closing in on me, or being feet from attacking me again. I just ran.

"Kenza, he's coming," I heard Ryan call.

I turned abruptly to see Mazin, still twenty-five feet away, leap into the air heading straight for me. I grasped the amulet in my hands, squeezed my eyes shut, and wished for a protection so great that it would destroy Mazin, at least for long enough to allow me to reach the door. I opened my eyes just in time to see his essence turn a dark smokey blue and shatter into a million pieces that scattered in every direction like a bomb exploding inside of a statue. I turned and ran the last one-hundred-feet to the door and slipped through, not stopping to look back.

When I stepped inside the safety of the other dimension, I saw Keelam with Isabel, Ian and Ryan with Naomi, and Ashram. I exhaled a long sigh of relief. Now that I knew everyone was safe, I realized the back of my head felt wet. I reached up to touch my hair in that spot and when I brought my hand down, it was covered in blood. The moment I saw it, the energy drained out of me and everything went black.

Chapter 34

I opened my eyes, relieved not to be holding back a wall of water, or worse, an army of evil spirits. I was lying on a cot. "Where am I?" I started to sit up, too impatient for the answer. My head throbbed so I lay back down, reaching up to feel a bandage wrapped around it.

"Kenza." Ian knelt by my side and reached for my hand. "We're back in the other dimension. We're safe now."

"My head," I mumbled.

"Shh . . . it's okay. This is a healing chamber."

"Mmm," was all I could muster, as if healing chambers were all the rage.

"Go back to sleep," Ian whispered. His hand waved over my eyes, closing them, just like they did on TV when someone died. Still, I obeyed without resisting.

My dreams were the most vivid I'd had in a long time. Most of the time, I dreamed of running by myself down a long dark tunnel. Once I heard Ian's voice. "Kenza, I'm right here." His voice was just around the next bend so I ran after him, my bare feet splashing on the damp slate floor. At one point, I caught a glimpse of him rounding another bend. It was a maze in there.

"Ian," I called. "Slow down."

"I'm just here. Right over here," he said.

I chased him around a few more bends. He turned, hugging the next one. His face looked strange, distorted. I ran harder, rounding the corner into a wide-open space with a big, crystal fountain in the center. Torches lit the perimeter of the cavern. I looked up and saw a mirage of water dancing in short swirling motions above my head. When I looked back down, Ian stood before me, but not as one person, as many. They all stood around the base of the fountain. One wore jeans with a sporty T-shirt and tennis shoes. A second one had tattered garments that dated him back several hundred years. Another stood opposite me, in between the others, and wore a long black robe. The rest each looked different: one representing the night Ian met me at the Italian restaurant and another looking like Mazin with the outline of a wolf trailing behind him.

"Kenza, I've been waiting so long for you." They started toward the fountain, as if they were going to walk across it. Then they all stood directly in front of me. They moved so fast, in the blink of an eye.

I gasped.

The one that looked like Ian the day of the Italian restaurant let out a cackling laugh that reminded me of Sidi Borj. Then he reached out to touch my face. I tried to jerk away, but suddenly I couldn't move. I expected sand paper across my face, but instead his touch was cottony soft and gentle. When he touched me, every kiss I'd ever shared with Amal and Ian flashed through my mind. I closed my eyes. When I opened them again, his were closed too.

When he finally opened his eyes and dropped his hand, the cinnamon hue of his eyes had turned to red. He breathed deeply and every version of him except the one he was today transformed into smoke and floated toward him, merging with him. He grew taller before my eyes, and I shrunk with fear from the red curtain that flashed over his eyes.

"Where's Ian?" Desperation cut through my words.

"Where's Ian? Where's Ian?" He laughed. "You should be asking where I've been."

I looked at Mazin, perplexed.

"I created Ian. I am Ian."

I awoke, gasping, and looked furtively around, finally remembering that I was back in the safety of the dimension under the Cave of Shadow Forest.

"What happened to Mazin?" I sat up like a bullet. My head no longer ached.

"Shh." This time Ashram knelt by my side. "He's gone. You destroyed him."

"He's never coming back?" I said.

"You know Mazin," Ashram said. "He's hard to get rid of permanently, but Jinny Zzaman and Jamila of Diab estimate it will take him months if not years to reform his physical body."

I spoke no words, just closed my eyes ready to drift back into a peaceful sleep. Then I saw an image of Isabel and Naomi, both injured.

My eyes blinked open wide. "What about Isabel and Naomi? Are they okay?"

"They're still sleeping. They'll take longer to heal."

I followed his gaze and saw Isabel and Naomi both lying on cots next to me. I started to cry and then my tears turned to sobs. At first, I wasn't sure why, but faint memories of Sidi Borj beating Isabel flooded into my memory. Even though Ryan had rewound time, some memories could not be completely erased. Some were too powerful—too painful—to erase. I cried for a few minutes, trying unsuccessfully to muffle the noise. It didn't matter, though. Isabel still lay lifeless on her cot.

"Are you sure Isabel's—" I hesitated. "Is she . . . still with us?" Tears pooled in my eyes.

"Of course she's with us," Ryan said. He squeezed in next to Ashram, placing a hand on his little furry shoulder. "Thanks to some fancy time travel."

I rose slowly and walked over to kneel next to Isabel. I reached out and softly stroked her hair. The bruising was fading and the cuts were healing. Her face looked almost normal, nothing like my faint flashes of memories in the alternate time of her shackled to that tree.

"What happened to me?" I asked, reaching to touch my now dry hair.

"Don't you remember?" Ian said walking toward us, reaching for my hand. "Mazin pounced and sent you falling backward. From what Ryan said, your head bounced like a basketball on the cave floor." Ian looked down and covered his face with his hands.

I gave him a minute, and so did everyone else leaving us to our privacy. He drew in a long breath, exhaled, and shook his head, like he was trying to shake off some sort of inner demon.

269

"Rough day, huh?" I whispered.

"Yeah," he choked. "I thought I might lose you today."

"Yeah, well, you didn't."

He leaned toward me and kissed my left temple, then my right. He stared into my eyes for several seconds and I nearly melted at seeing the love in his eyes. He then slowly, gently kissed my lips erasing any remnants of pain I'd been clinging to.

∞

When the last day of camp finally arrived, and our inner scars were healing just like our outer scars had healed in the other dimension, I was more ready to return home than I had been the first year we were here. I dreaded leaving Ian again, and all of my other friends, but I also looked forward to going home. I felt this incredible longing to hold Daniyah in my arms again.

"Have fun with your invisibility cloak," I said to Naomi, as we hugged a final time before parting ways.

"Already have been," Naomi reassured me. "And apparently, Mrs. Bartolli likes to dance to Madonna." We both glanced in Mrs. Bartolli's direction and busted up laughing. "And you, my dear Kenza, had better use your abilities to protect that little sister of yours. Do it for me, okay?"

I winked at her, then turned to hug Ryan next. "I'll miss you, Dexter," I said, flashing him an oversized smile.

"I'll miss you, too, my smoothie dropping, evil spirit exploding friend," he said.

On instinct, I socked him in the arm, apparently a little too hard by the looks of how much he winced.

I hugged Keelam next. "Thanks for showing me things from a perspective I've never seen before," I said.

He ruffled the top of my hair and I scolded him for it.

270

"Isabel," I said, turning to her, holding my arms open. "You take care of yourself, you little charmer."

"Who me? Nothing ever happens to me." She laughed and waved away my worries. "But I will have fun practicing my new mind control powers back home. They won't even see it coming."

"Hey now," I warned. "No abusing those powers. Be nice."

Even though Ian and I had just spent the equivalent of the last several days together in the other dimension, he stole me away to our favorite spot on the beach—where I dug up the Bottle Full of Wishes. We had a half hour to spend alone together, which didn't seem like nearly enough time.

"I'm not sure I'm ready to say goodbye," I said.

"If you were, I'd be worried," he whispered, as he wrapped his arms around me. "Honestly though Kenza, I sometimes wonder if I can keep doing this."

"Keep doing what?" I said, worry lining my words.

"I really thought you were going to die. I'd rather die than lose you."

"You're not going to lose me," I reassured him.

He leaned back, his arms still wrapped around me, and kissed my forehead. "I better not."

THE END

Wish loud and follow your dreams!

CPSIA information can be obtained
at www.ICGtesting.com
Printed in the USA
LVOW01s2223100516

487650LV00014B/207/P